THEFT

Also by N. S. Köenings

The Blue Taxi

THEFT

❦ *stories* ❦

N. S. KÖENINGS

BACK BAY BOOKS
Little, Brown and Company
NEW YORK   BOSTON   LONDON

Back Bay Books / Little, Brown and Company
Hachette Book Group USA
237 Park Avenue, New York, NY 10017
Visit our Web site at www.HachetteBookGroupUSA.com

First Edition: March 2008

The characters and events in this book are fictitious. Any similarity to real
persons, living or dead, is coincidental and not intended by the author.

Grateful acknowledgment is made to the publishers of earlier versions of
these stories: *StoryQuarterly* ("Pearls to Swine") and White Eagle Coffee Press
("Setting Up Shop").

Library of Congress Cataloging-in-Publication Data
Köenings, N. S.
    Theft : Stories / N. S. Köenings. — 1st ed.
        p. cm.
    ISBN-13: 978-0-316-00186-1
    ISBN-10: 0-316-00186-4
    I. Title.

PR9130.9.K64T47 2008
823'.92 — dc22   2007033062

10 9 8 7 6 5 4 3 2 1

RRD-IN

Printed in the United States of America

CONTENTS

THEFT

❁ Pearls to Swine

Western Europe, Summer 1980

A weaker person than myself might have been changed by so much rudeness. By what happened in the garden. But I am still the same. I will not frustrate a hungry child or snub a thirsty man. With proper guests, a visit would be smooth. Our home and grounds are gracious. I have not given up. I do still like the sound of silverware on dishes, and a good raspberry jam ferocious in a jar. A bedsheet turned down by the pillow, an ironed towel on a chair. But you know, vraiment on ne sais jamais. Think twice, I say. Be careful. Because once you've given them a washcloth and a bed, nothing can protect you. Not your sweetness, not your natural desire to involve an honored stranger in your life, and not even—here's the worst—not even your good taste.

And yet, how pleased I was at first. Before telling Gustave my idea, I went into the tower rooms one after the other and gazed onto the grounds. Just look at those big fields, the pine trees in the distance! See how pale and blue the town, the bathhouses, the spires, so small from our fine heights! And closer in, how promising the urns looked on the patio—filled with snow just then, but already I could fathom them abubble with petunias. And beyond the berry hedge, the real curiosity: the animals Gustave fashions from the bushes. Now, *that's* something to look at! A camel and a horse, an egret and a pony. Yes, we have a world unto ourselves. Filling my big eyes with grass, the pines, and sky, I practiced what I'd say when I went up to his office: Gustave, I'd say, in a bright, loud voice so he would have to pay attention, it's time we had some guests.

It isn't that we're lonely or have nothing to do. Gustave has many things to occupy his time. There's that big collection of clay potsherds and celadon, and nice beads made out of glass, which he has gotten through his work—for we have crossed the world on lecture tours and digs—and he has other hobbies. A person in Bulgaria, to whom Gustave pays large sums, mails butterflies and moths. Gustave frames the specimens and hangs them in the hallway. Those butterflies alone could give an afternoon of pleasure! And, as I've already mentioned, there's that very special zoo: the topiary, as Gustave likes to say.

Every other Tuesday in the summer, people come from town to see, though Gustave worries for the beasts. He fears the children will strew carbonated drinks and ice creams in the flowers. But I called l'hôtel de ville especially, to say that they could come. To date, which you would notice on your own if you were to come out on a tour, and as I've already said, Gustave has a horse, an egret, a camel, and a pony. He's begun a tortoise, too, but it is taking him a little longer to complete, which I for my part think, ha ha, is not a big surprise. And better twice a month when you expect it than at any time they please, I said. So the people come from town, though when they do, Gustave goes upstairs.

I myself am always busy. I could have my hands full, for example, with just the correspondence. Though we've not traveled in some time, I keep in touch with all the people we have met. Why, just three days before the first girl came I wrote another letter to Morocco's Minister of Culture, and I told him, as I always do, that I will never let myself forget how kind he was to us, how nice the ride on the Corniche so very long ago, and how much I did appreciate that very sweet mint tea. He'll reply in his own time, I'm sure. And of course, I cook, I pickle things. I read.

I make preserves for us when the berries come in summer. I like to tease Gustave and say that both of us excel at keeping things just so: You dig and prune, I say. I pickle and conserve. We're both proud of how we label things—Gustave says precision with a label separates the shoddy from the great. In fact he had just typed up a card for a new butterfly and was pinning the blue thing onto a heavy cotton sheet when I went to his office. I said, to see if he would soften up, that those gauzy little wings were the color of our winter sky, but he did not answer me. He said something about labels, and I had to interrupt. That may well be, I said, about the labels, but what we need here is guests. Some visitors, I said. All those foreigners we've met, they've been so generous with us. It's our turn now to push back into the world the kindness we've received.

Gustave was thinking of the bushes, if you please. "I don't want strangers tramping on the grounds," he said. He was mumbling, as usual, pin between his lips. I told him I would never ask into our home a person or any pair of persons who would be capable of tramping. *Tramping.* We ought to send some invitations for the summer, when everything is best, I said. We have so much to give.

"Do what you like, Celeste," he said, and because he couldn't open wide for fear the pin would fall, his voice came out a blur. I did do what I liked, of course, although I wish sometimes, looking back, that Gustave had put his foot down. Afterwards, he said it could have been predicted. That mixing comes about through hard, unpleasant business: if you find a Chinese plate with a plain old East Coast pot, you'll know there was a war. Never some sweet intercourse, or friendliness, or trade, as I thought might be likely. Gustave, whose place it is to know, insisted: war, each and every time. And as to pots, he even said, "It's fortunate for us their owners are long dead and we won't see the carnage for ourselves." Well, that may be fine reasoning or poor when it comes to beads and bones, though I reserve my judgment. What I do know is that he doesn't understand the world of living beings like I do, that we need company and gentle conversation. Gustave even said this morning, "At least they didn't hurt the bushes." The bushes!

So I sent out my invitations, one to my old friend Sylvie, who now lives in New York, U.S.A., and the other one to Liège, which although it is not very far from here you might think another country. I wrote to La Maison des Jeunes Femmes Abandonnées, which has a well-known program for the girls they like to help. From New York, Sylvie wrote to say it would be wonderful if Petra came to see us. The House in Liège was also very gracious. The nuns would send us an unmarried girl who had fallen into difficulty but would by then be on the mend, and to whom our kindness was surely going to do a proper world of good. I had brightly colored dreams in which the two became great friends. It was exciting to envision—one girl come from Liège, another from America, not a thing in common but their girlhood and the grounds.

We've been all over Europe and the best places in North Africa, but never to New York. I think it would be charming. I know some feel the U.S.A. is poor in taste, from the Rodeos to that big Statue and le foot Américain. Yvette said so herself when I told her where Petra would be coming from, and she was wrapping me a nice half kilo of pâté. She said, "Don't buy too much of this, then. Hamburgers, that's all they like to eat." Well, I took my regular half kilo and paid her no attention. I'm sure I don't agree. Where would we be now without Americans, I always like to say.

When I told Yvette the girl Thérèse would be coming from the House, she threw back her big head and gave a hard snort through her nose. "She'll steal the sheets from under you," she said. I thanked her very nicely and snuck a sample of salami while she was counting out the change. Her view of human nature is nothing to be proud of, but I can get along with people of all kinds. Don't I send my flowers to the abbey when the beds come into bloom? I was sure Thérèse would be well mannered, and that Sylvie's girl would bring me some nice gifts from big and busy, interesting New York.

Petra came three days before Thérèse. I had just washed the breakfast dishes, and was having a verveine by the window in the library upstairs, where Gustave has shelved my novels. Our place was blooming with the springtime! We had sparrows shaking in the trees, and the baby bees, though it hadn't quite got warm, were spying on the ivy. I was wearing blue. Gustave was standing by the window with a cup of Chinese tea, look-ing out at nothing as he sometimes does, and, nodding at the glass, he called out to me. "It must be Sylvie's girl," he said. I went to stand beside him, and as I pulled the curtain to the side I caught a whiff of his tobacco. I straightened up my slip beneath my skirt and set my toes right fast in the bottom of my shoes. I held my head high. Here we are, I thought, the hosts. And what a couple we still make. I stood beside my husband, and I looked down at the girl.

She had traveled from the station in a taxi. Her driver was a fat man, panting with the case he'd just extracted from the trunk of the Maria. He'd left the engine running. I could see the steam rise from the cab. And I could see the girl. Wild hair, thick and dark. A velvet purse was dangling from one long bony arm, and she was fumbling with her money. I thought Gustave must be wrong, that it had to be the other one, the unfortunate from Liège come a few days early. When she bent to gather up the coins she'd scattered in the stones, her spine showed through her dress. It can't be, I told him. That's got to be Thérèse. That cotton dress had seen far better days, and her white socks were bunched up at the ankles from a pair of buckled shoes. They must have got the days confused, I said, moving closer to my husband. Below us in the drive, the girl was nodding-bobbing at the driver as though he were a head of state, a king.

"No, don't you see?" he said. "She looks just like her fa-ther." All I could make out was that her dark-haired head was large and the rest of her was thin. The fat man raised an empty hand up to his temple and moved it in an arc out from his brow as if he were a gentleman tipping a good hat. The girl was easily amused, I saw. She giggled as he popped back into the cab.

I watched the taxi barrel down the drive, skidding on the gravel. Strange, I thought. Cars like his take people on fine trips now, and we don't think about it twice. Used to be a Black Maria meant the S.S. were out and coming to take stock. Well, the girl had no idea. As she said later, she feels like an American, doesn't know a thing about it, not Marias, not potato cakes, not hiding in a basement. And she's never heard of chicory.

Anyway she must have felt us looking at her, or perhaps a bird flew by, or there was a rustle in our ivy. Because she lifted up her chin and I saw exactly what she was. *My* goddaughter, what a sight. Gustave was right, she did look like her father—an Antwerp face with dusky, caterpillar eyebrows, like something in a cabaret. Though it was clear she was a girl, and it's true she was attractive in a serious sort of way, with a big and heavy head—a Hannah, or a Ruth, if you can get my meaning. Then I looked hard at her hemline and at those awful crumpled socks, and I caught sight of her knees. She did have stunning calves. That one time Sylvie came to Tunis with her husband, I remember thinking Hermann's shapely legs were wasted on a man.

She didn't have the sense to come knocking on the door. She just stood there, holding to the suitcase with both hands, that old purse drooping to the ground on its sorry knotted string. She stood biting at her lips, frowning at the ivy. A baby! Sylvie said she was sending a grown daughter and instead we got a baby. I thought, It's a good thing Gustave heard the car come in the first place, or she'd have stood there until lunch-time and we'd not have known a thing.

Downstairs, Gustave took her case away. She tried to shake his hand, but instead he put his arm around her shoulders and brought her in himself. I was quite surprised at him, although you will agree Gustave can be disarming when he remembers where he is. Arching her long neck like a farsighted person at a bug that's landed on their chest, Petra looked as if no man had ever put his hands on her before. What a cardigan! I thought. A thing the color of pea soup that slid all over her, and by the time she'd come into the foyer it had fallen off her shoulders and was bunched around her elbows. To convince myself again that this was the delinquent girl instead, I squinted. I opened my eyes wide. Let this not be mine. But it was not to be.

At that moment I was so distracted by her looks I couldn't think what her name was. Gustave—bless him, he always knows what things are called—must have sensed what I was thinking. "Petra," he said (to help *me,* I believe), "this is your godmother, Celeste." When she looked at me and smiled, she looked exactly like her mother and it took my breath away. Here is what was strange: she had her father's lips, full and wide from top to bottom, but quite short side to side, yes, Persian-like, you know, but when she smiled and brought out dimples, I could see old Sylvie laugh. What a combination. Dear God, I thought. Out loud I said, "That settles it. Petra. Goddaughter-of-mine." Gustave rolled his eyes, but I think he was amused. I kissed Petra on both cheeks and while I was leaning in she took my hands with hers and held them very tight. She kissed me back with her eyes closed. I smelled milk and eucalyptus on her. She's not a woman yet, I thought, no, she's just like a sick child.

I told Petra I'd have lunch for her quite soon, that she should bathe and change her clothes. She didn't speak, but she turned pink. Sylvie's smile and that dark hair. I never did get used to it. Gustave took her to the tower room, which I thought would be pleasant for her since you can see the chamomile and from the other window on clear days the bathhouses in Spa. I wanted her to understand how nice it is here, and to make sure Sylvie knew it, too.

She spent a very long time upstairs, I thought, and she used a lot of water. When she came down, her hair was even blacker. She'd tied it in a rag and changed into some trousers. I myself don't wear them, but women these days will, and she looked a little better than she first had in that dress. Brown trousers with a periwinkle blouse, and the pea-soup cardigan again. I thought she looked Polish. Or Italian. Petra.

For lunch we had salade frisée and eggs and some nice slices of roast beef I'd got in town from Chez Yvette. I asked Petra if she had ever eaten this before and Petra said that yes, her mother made it here and there, but the lettuce she was used to was not so nice as this. That bath must have done her good because she wasn't shy at lunch. She finished off the salad and asked for more meat twice. She clutched the fork in her right hand and barely used the knife, which I forgave her at the time, because they left when she was three.

Petra's French was not too bad. She didn't have an accent when she spoke, and although later I kept hoping that the girl would make mistakes, she didn't. But she thought hard about what words to choose, and sometimes she'd wait with her mouth open in an "o" until the right thing came to her. Son séjour améliorera peut-être son français, her mother'd written, hoping we could get the language streaming through her daughter's blood again. Elle n'a personne avec qui parler. Well, Petra had two people now to speak it with, and I impressed the fact upon her. We'll talk a lot together, you and me, I told her. I have a lot of novels. Petra nodded carefully across her empty plate. She was quiet for a moment. I wondered if she was imagining the two of us together on the terrace, as I was, companionable, sipping our cassis.

As it turned out, she spent very little time with me, even early on. Instead, she worked it up to say that she was very enthusiastic about walking by herself. She would like to see the grounds alone. Like a mental convalescent, I thought then (she did sometimes seem gloomy). "J'marche vite," she said. And I thought of telling her that I, too, in my time, could keep up a fine pace, but she smiled like Sylvie does, and to be truthful I felt warmly towards her, yes I did. I thought, She is a good child.

Gustave, who is not a hearty eater, was already drinking coffee. He said to Petra that if she was going to be looking at the topiary could she please not touch the animals, as he liked to be meticulous with the shaping and the binding of the boughs. I did feel he was harsh with her. He should put up a sign, I sometimes say—"Do Not Feed the Animals!"—and see what people think.

After lunch, Petra followed me right into the kitchen and I almost fell over with the shock of it when I turned and saw her with our three plates and silverware stacked up in her arms. The cardigan had slipped right off her back again. "Can I help you?" she asked me. I thought of telling her that it's not done to stroll into strange kitchens dropping dishes into other people's sinks—that's rude even in Morocco. But I didn't, no, I slapped those words right back down my throat, and said, Not today, dear. You sit down and start behaving like a guest. She was not stupid, no. I think she understood. She handed me the plates and then her mouth closed and she shuffled back without another word.

Gustave left the table, as he does, and while I was rinsing off the plates I heard him say to Petra that he was going to frame a something-*polyxena,* and how it's also called Cassandra, would she like to see it? She said thank you very much for now, perhaps some other time. When I came out again, Gustave had gone upstairs and she was standing by the window. She said she'd like to take a walk. Enjoy yourself, I said. She did not know how to please, it struck me then, but surely she did want to.

You know I'm always up at five to make the bread. For those first three days I made cramique, with raisins and lump sugar, which I save for special times, and I'd set the table fresh with cloths we got in Egypt. Damascene, they call it. And arrange the fruit jars in the center of the table: gooseberry, blackberry, and, my favorite, a clever marmalade I do with winter oranges from Spain. Then I'd pull the heavy curtains up so I could feel the light change. I love this place the best at dawn, when the sky gets keen with that strange blue that comes between the sunset and the night. I had an aunt who used to say that blue meant it was l'heure des loups, when wolves can see but people can't. Though my eyes are pretty sharp, I tell you.

I'd put coffee on the stove and sit down by the window in the dining room to wait. I myself like mon petit café at ten o'clock, with a novel on the patio, but coffee in the morning is a habit Gustave picked up in his travels, before he married me. And Petra liked her coffee, too, I found out on the first day. At first she got up early. And she did dress for breakfast, not like Americans we see in films who wear their bed clothes to the table. But she drank more coffee than Gustave ever does, three cups one after the other, like grenadine in August. From then on, I made sure there was enough for Gustave, too, when he came down at eight.

After breakfast Petra would go off by herself. She didn't think to ask me if I'd like to sit with her, or if I had a book that she could read. I suppose she didn't show much interest in us. But it seemed all right at first. She's just a child, I'd think, and she was raised abroad.

We'd have a lunch at noon, and then a nap for Petra and Gustave while I sorted out the dishes and planned the next day's meals. *Chicons* and veal on the first day, then quiche Lorraine, with mushrooms from the woods, which we still had for dinner on the third because I made enough to last. Reibekuchen with salami for our dinner on the second (because there was no need, I thought, for Petra to imagine we were fancy all the time), and on the third for lunch a filet de sole with asparagus besides, and for dessert a crème brûlée.

Just the day before, the nuns had called from Liège to say that everything was set for the poor girl and they would put her on the train at seven in the morning. We could expect her here by lunchtime if she caught the omnibus, and earlier if the train was an express. But we ate the sole and les asperges, the three of us, alone. Gustave very wisely said, "She'll get here when she gets here," and there was nothing to be done. Petra said that now, yes, she would like to see those butterflies if Gustave was going to be free. He raised his eyebrows very high, as though he couldn't see her well, and shut his mouth quite tightly, as though thinking. Then he held his elbow out so she would have something to hold, and they went up the stairs with Petra asking if he'd strolled the mountains with a net and caught them all himself. "No," he said, with quite a throaty voice, I thought. "My beauties come to me." She laughed. I stayed right there at the table with my crème brûlée. I do like a dessert.

Later I went out to the patio and sat down with my novel. A story by Françoise Sagan, it was, in which a young Parisian girl fools her student-suitor with his worldly sailor uncle. It's silly, but I even wondered, not seriously, you know, if Petra had a boy at home and now was upstairs eyeing Gustave and the butterflies as this girl in my book was doing with the uncle while the wife stitched napkins in the garden. It was a lovely afternoon with lemon-colored sunlight—cool enough to wear a wrap, and the geraniums in their pots were brilliant, shivering now and then, just giving up new flowers. I wondered where Thérèse was.

As it turned out, it was Petra who came across her on her walk, which she took after Gustave had shown her all his frames. She went inside without my seeing her and called me from the dining room, through the open window. Once the three of us were in the house and I was settling my mind around the look of the new girl, Petra told me how it was. She'd gone into the woods, she said, and she was heading for the abbey when she saw a stranger on the path, struggling with a suitcase. "I asked where she was going, and, imagine, she was coming here!" Petra looked—although I didn't like to think it—like a dog that's found an old shoe in the grass, very happy, and her color was quite high. Strands of her thick hair were loose and springing like fresh parsley. That French was really flowing in her veins again, and hotly too, to look at her.

"*N'est-ce pas merveilleux?* At first I thought she must be wrong." I don't know what is marvelous in meeting with a plump girl who is sweating through the woods and finding out that she is going where you've come from when you know that she's expected, but I will give Petra credit for at least being surprised that we would knowingly invite a girl like that to stay in our fine home, despite how it all ended. I'll just tell you now that Thérèse was not at all as I'd imagined.

What did I expect, you ask? Someone thinner, first of all. Worn by care, and shy, not well fed, but pure. Before she came I could already see myself scooping squares of butter from the loaf and slipping them into her soup while she looked the other way. Someone pale, whom I could fatten up. I'd thought she might be gaunt. The sisters wrote, back when I arranged the thing, that by the time she came to us she would have had the child and a good home be found for it already. They were particularly pleased about our place, the head sister had written, because "it will soothe Thérèse to recover in the country." The letter had made much about the fact that just beyond our woods there is an abbey. "She will be close to God," they said. Oh, it's silly, perhaps. We ourselves don't go to church, because Gustave won't allow it. But I expected someone just a little saintly, someone who'd been wronged. Someone I could look over and think, as Gustave does when he contemplates his potsherds and the dullest of the moths, Her kind will inherit the earth.

But there was not a saintly thing about her. Just as Petra did not look like her mother, Thérèse was nothing like I'd thought. She was like an abbot, not a saint, the kind of abbot in a Brueghel painting you can almost hear. A loud one, yelling about pigs, and belching in between. There was something oily, too, an unctuous glow about her nose and lips, a thickness to her. Her hair was dark and just as greasy, rather thin, and falling on her face so she was always peering through a fringe. Her eyes were very narrow, and blue like morning glories, which I do admit surprised me. She had heavy forearms and thick hands, with two rings on her big fingers, plastic, the kind with a false jewel glued on you find in bubbles at the newsstand.

Welcome to Spa, Thérèse, I said, anyhow. Her dress was the color of blood oranges, very raw and sunny. It was far too small for her. She was quite a fat girl, really, soft and loosened in the middle, and it was clear she didn't know at all how to make herself look smaller. Her waist was done up very tightly with a yellow plastic belt that was meant to match her dress. I thought, She looks like an actress in the vaudeville. But I remembered she had had a baby, and maybe that's why she was fat, and perhaps that dress would fit her in another month or so.

That's right, I told myself she was too poor to buy herself loose clothes. I even felt that when she knew me better I could reach out to her forehead with my hand and rearrange her hair, tuck it back behind her ears so I could see her better.

But then she spoke—with what a voice, I tell you, low and even like a man's. "Madame," she said. Nothing shy about her blue ones, sharp, they were, like mine. Petra was in the kitchen making tea, which she had never done before. Well, I sat down with Thérèse at the table and asked about her trip. We expected you at noon, I said. Honestly I didn't mean to chide her, but she did take it that way.

"Forgive me, I had things to do," she said. She began to pluck the brambles from the sleeves of her bright dress. I watched her press them to the table in a line, and I thought that even with her crumpled socks Petra looked more saintly. *This* girl wore high heels—dancer shoes that matched the belt, with ankle straps that bit into her feet. I thought, No wonder she was sweating in the woods.

Conversationally, I asked, "What things?" So she could see I'd be her friend, I scooted closer to her, leaning forward in my chair. I smiled, I did. "Things." She put her elbows on the table and started pulling at her cuffs. She crossed her legs and swung one heeled foot back and forth at me. What she said next to me with that low voice I still can't quite believe. "Private things, if you have to know." The look she gave me would have got a rise out of a man. I know I sat up tall. With those narrow eyes still on me, she scooped the brambles up into a pile, then brushed them all at once to scatter on the floor. Then she propped her chin up with her fist and gave me a thick smile. I knew then that she had tricked the sisters, and tricked me. She hadn't come here to recover, and she hadn't come to be near God. I didn't like to think what private things she meant, but I had some good ideas.

Petra came in with a tall pot of verveine and three good coffee cups, looking quite excited. I was too unsettled at the time to tell her that's not how it's done—there's a cupboard full of lovely china meant for tea in the next room. Thérèse dropped five cubes of sugar in her cup and stirred her tea quite noisily, I thought. Petra sat across from me and beamed. Petra was behaving as though this girl were a queen—doing all she could to please her, at least that's how it looked to me, right at the beginning. It wasn't really a warm day, but I felt peculiar, let me say.

Thérèse said in her deep voice, "The pony's nice, though. Who would take the time to make a pony out of bushes?" They had passed the topiary, of course, on their way up to the house. I was about to answer her, thinking, at least she's found something considerate to say, but I could see that she was saying it to Petra. Petra nodded smoothly—as though she'd lived with us for years—and said proudly, "That's Gustave who did it." She gave me that smile of hers and poured me out some tea. I was going to say something about the china. But I couldn't. You understand me, don't you? It would have been silly then to talk about the cups.

Here's what it was like in our house after the bawdy girl arrived: loud, dangerous, and strange. Gustave *liked* her! While I was telling myself all the time to feel good things about Petra, who couldn't help where she'd been raised or looking so much like her father, Gustave, when he paid attention, behaved as though Thérèse was a something-*polyxena*. It must have come from that digging in the earth he does, which I've always thought unhealthful. "For buried treasures, *ma jolie Celestine,*" he's often said to me, "you must put your hands in muck." Well, that may be fine for broken pots, that muck. But it's another thing for girls.

Her lipstick! I would say to him. She came down to meals with her mouth the kind of red that looks like accidents there is no pleasure in recalling, red like a balloon. Her paint would mark my things: the forks she used, my crystal glasses, the napkins that we bought in Egypt. And no matter what we're meant to think of napkins, that they're for making stains on you'd rather not see on your clothes, I know whoever thinks so hasn't washed white Damascene by hand. Once I asked her, not to make a fuss but I was curious, Do the sisters allow you girls to put on makeup out at the Maison? My voice was very cool, as though it weren't important. "Am I at the sisters' now, madame?" She looked right back at me and took such a bite of mashed potatoes I heard her teeth scrape on the spoon.

All Gustave could say, weakly, absentminded, as though I were asking about curtains, was "She's pretty, Celestine." He'd look up from the clay bits he had set out on his desk and put his cold hand on mine. "We've had nothing bright in this house for so long!" I thought then that I do have three different shades of pink I do put on my lips if I am going into town. But when Thérèse put her shiny mouth on everything, it hit me that maybe Gustave's never noticed. Not for a long time.

She's rude, I'd say. "No, no," he'd say, as though he'd spent any time with her to judge. "She's spirited, that's all. C'est la joie de vivre." Joy, is it? I would think.

At dinner that first night the girl asked me straight out how much I'd bought my blouse for—the ruffled silk one I had made in Liège, you've seen it, light blue with long sleeves and those sweet golden clasps. Then she said, Why spend more than two, three hundred francs on something you were just going to take off. The way she looked at Petra then, it made me wonder what she thought one did exactly after taking off a blouse. And Petra! Petra's sunken little cheeks looked so flushed to me just then, I nearly asked if my goddaughter, too, was taking up the face paint.

Next Thérèse turned to Gustave and asked how much he thought our old house could be worth. "Expensive keeping this house up," she ventured, talking with her mouth full. "You could make a great hotel here, really quelque chose, and bring some German tourists." *Germans!* Thankfully, Gustave didn't hear her right. He just looked at her over his glass of vin de table and let out a little "hmm." He looked at her so much you'd think he'd never seen a girl.

At breakfast she dropped jam across the tablecloth because she'd talk and shake her knife before the berries could get safely from the pot onto her toast. When she saw the coffee cups, she said, "Oh, moi j'bois du chocolat." I brought her cocoa in a cup and, looking through her oily hair, she said, "Celeste, you don't have any bowls?" It made me shiver, that, to hear her use my name.

To top it off, she *sang.* I'd hear her from downstairs some-

times, bellowing up there. Not nice songs, either. Not "Les
Cloches de la Vallée" or something like "La Vie en Rose,"
that I could sing along to, but ditties she must have learned
from sailors, or the father of that child the sisters said she'd had
and given up. And there'd be Petra laughing up there, too.
My goddaughter, chortling, learning the refrains. That was the
very worst of it, I think, that she had Petra eating from her
hand.

The last time I'd seen Petra she was no bigger than a bread
loaf and she was swaddled up in white. It was me who held her
while the priest splashed water on that powdered baby head.
I'll witness this new child come waking to the world, I said to
Hermann and Sylvie. I'll care for her if anything should happen.
I shudder now to think it. Long life to Hermann and to Sylvie,
I say each time I pour out a cassis, if I catch myself in time: À la
bonne votre, I say. *L'chaim!* Is that not what the Jews say? Though
I did try to be nice to her, I did. I offered to go with her to the
topiary several times. She'd only glimpsed the pony after all, at
least that's what I thought, and it does take some time to see how
fine, how delicate, those beasts are. I myself like on hot days to
take shade under the camel. We could walk among the beasts,
I said. But each time I asked Petra, she said, "Not yet, not yet,"
measuring her answer like salt into a spoon. "I want to wait until
I can't bear not to go." Whatever that could mean. I was hurt,
that's the truth. But I kept trying with her.

I never let her do the dishes, and I insisted that she leave
the tablecloth for me. I like to brush the crumbs together first,
then shake the cloth outside—for birds, you see—and Petra

wouldn't have, I know, thought of such a thing. But I did everything I could. I made sure that she had coffee, food enough to eat. I filled the cold box with roast beef for her and two kinds of Edam. I did more than my part, and it's a shame that Petra couldn't see it.

I barely saw them after breakfast. They would disappear upstairs, and I'd hear nothing from them until noon. Sometimes I'd see them walking through the kitchen, coming from outside, when I didn't know they'd gone. No, I'd spend whole mornings in the house, thinking they were in the library, finding things to read, or napping, only to discover they'd been playing in the woods. How did they get out? Unsettling, it was. Sometimes it made me wonder if I knew where I myself had been.

Well, I was feeling strange already, but it's the topiary did it, that first Friday morning. That's when I knew for certain the whole thing was a mistake. I had come in from the patio and picked up Gustave's demitasse and saucer from the table. The day was green, we had a dim and chalky sky, and it was definitely damp. I was standing at the sink, as I often do, looking out the window just above the taps. From the kitchen window I can see a nice expanse of chamomile, which, when it's pale outside, all looks very soft. When the wind blows it's got quite a smell, like a steeping cup of tea. Just beyond it I can see as far as Gustave's bushes.

The sweetest one is certainly the pony. Gustave read up on breeds before he did it, and this little bush is now a perfect Shetland, feasting on the grass. From the kitchen I could see it, and the egret, too, although it's smaller, and that big old bucking horse. Gustave is proud of that one, which took seven years to build. And, like the Shetland, it's a special breed. A Lipizzaner, if you want to know, with flaring hoofs and hairy ankles, up on its rear legs.

Well, at first I thought I'd seen a bird. We do get gulls out here, though we're far out from the sea. A flash of white, it was. But then it passed again and I thought it was a flag. But could that be? I put down the cup I had been washing—a fluted one, gold-rimmed, which I used for Petra's coffee—and took some steps outside and got out my wolf eyes.

The white thing was no kind of bird or flag at all, but Thérèse's very blouse afloat above her head. She was running back and forth between the Shetland and the horse, skipping now and then—just like a horse would, I dare say. Of course she didn't have the blouse on anymore, and she was bouncing, you know what I mean. I could hear her yelling, too, or laughing.

There's no cover among flowers. But a standing person is much more quickly seen than one who matches the horizon. When I got a little farther down the hill, I crouched down. I did then as soldiers do. I got out of my shoes and tucked my feet under my skirt. I rolled my sleeves back and got down on my elbows. It was a hot day, remember, despite how gray it was, and I felt very damp. I could feel some nettles on my legs—that itch!—but a person will put up with pain if there's something dreadful happening. Tell me, I thought, this time out loud—as though the flowers could have helped me—that she's out there alone.

In vain, it was. Next I saw Petra shooting out from underneath the horse, laughing just as loud. Her parsley hair was loose, and she waved her purple scarf around to match Thérèse's flag. Petra got down on all fours and pranced over to the pony and then she huddled underneath it. She had kept her blouse on, that was good, but it hurt to see her chuckling with that girl while I was by myself. I thought, They are playing hide-and-seek.

Thérèse was not a handsome girl, not really, and she had just had, supposedly, a child. So she had little business taking off her skirt, but that's exactly what she did. She was standing right in front of Petra and she let the brown thing drop and she stepped out of it, still hollering. Something like, "Oh! Cruel cavaliers!" or "Come here, cavaliers!" In her yellow panties! Even from where I was lying I could see how her reddened thighs, their plump insides, were wobbly just like my preserves are when they've come out clear and right.

Then she started leaping. On the *down,* she'd crouch and dig her fists into the grass and pull some up in clumps. On the *up,* she'd raise her hands into the air and let the grass clumps go, so the blades would scatter wildly. Up. Down. Up. Down. With my good eyesight I could see that loose grass sticking on her, although from where I was and with the greenish light the blades looked black, like tiny eels, pasted to her limbs. Petra turned her head away and then I saw her arms come up around the pony, from below, like the strap that holds a saddle to a horse. She was pretending to be scared, but she must still have been laughing.

Thérèse sang another song. I couldn't make all of it out, but I did hear Petra's name, "Petra, ma belle. Petra, ma jolie." My hair started to prickle then, from heat, and I felt water pooling in my eyes. I wanted them to stop, but—it's terrible to say, and here's what it can come to when you bring the wrong girls home—Thérèse made me feel shy. Laughter can really harm a person, don't you think? On my own land I was too frightened to go down there myself and order them to stop. I got up on my knees again. I took one look back near the kitchen and the last thing that I saw before I pulled myself onto the tiles and locked the door behind me was Thérèse, in a pair of yellow panties, raising up a leg in a very loose and ribald way as if to mount the pony's back. Petra had been ruined.

I knew I couldn't tell Gustave. He might have fainted, or had a heart attack, and I would have had to ask that big girl for help. And while, God forgive me, it would have done poetic justice if she caused her own host's death through all that foolishness of hers, of course I couldn't tell him. And perhaps they hadn't done the bushes any damage. But *I* was damaged, I can tell you that. The nettles were the least of it.

That night Gustave was in good spirits with a call that had come through for him from Egypt. It must have rung while I was shoeless in the field. I'm usually the one to fetch the phone, and I enjoy it, especially when it's a foreign scholar. North Africans, they are, professors. They're always so polite it makes my toes curl and my ears feel very damp. It made me even angrier with that big girl, that she'd made me miss my call.

A year ago it was a man calling from Khartoum, asking if Gustave would be their guest and give a talk, as they'd found something new out there. Of course we couldn't go, and

Gustave later said they hadn't any money, something about the Sudanese professors all being kicked out of their schools and how the man I'd talked to was a fraud. But still, that professor'd been so nice to me I felt I should remind him that I was someone's wife. In any case this call from Alexandria had Gustave very pleased, and he opened up a bottle of Sancerre, which I do like very much. Of course Petra drank it like she drinks her coffee, as if it were water, but Thérèse drank hers very slowly. She sat circling the mouth of her wide wineglass with a finger, which as you know will coax a humming sound. I thought, That's the way to make a crystal glass explode, but I couldn't bring myself to say so.

I can't shake the feeling, either, that that night after the scene among the bushes there was something new with us, sitting at the table. The two of them looked different. Petra didn't talk. She hadn't worn her cardigan. She'd put on a black blouse without sleeves that had a pointed collar and buttoned at the neck. Perhaps it was my headache, but it seemed to me her arms glowed, as though she'd rubbed them down with vinegar or lard. She was drinking like a fountain.

I made a point of asking her what she'd done all day, to see what she would say. She looked up very coyly and couldn't keep my gaze. Her eyelashes were so very wild and long, they looked like those tarantulas Gustave has a picture of. Gets those lashes from her father, I thought, or maybe that Liège girl had lent her some mascara. Petra couldn't keep her eyes on me, and she only nodded at Gustave, who was explaining how the two of us might take a trip in winter. "To Alexandria," he said, "where the world's best books once were." Petra said, "A trip is nice," and Thérèse gave out a smothered little laugh, as though she had in mind some journeys of her own.

But all in all, she was quiet, too. Now and then she made a show of listening to Gustave's every word, blinking her blue eyes at him like the wings on a still butterfly that's sucking at a flower. I chewed a bit of anchovy from the salad for a long and salty time, and then I took another. Though thinking about Alexandria did make me feel better. Not so dirty, and not so—oh, I hate to say it—old.

I asked Thérèse if she would do the dishes, please, and told them all that I was going to bed. She must have been accustomed at the sisters' to doing work around the place, because she said she didn't mind. She got up from the table and she strode into the kitchen before I had folded up my napkin. Perhaps she was relieved. Perhaps it was too much to ask her to behave like a person who belonged. I peeked into the kitchen then before going up the stairs, and it was true, Thérèse knew how to care for our domestic things: she was very careful with the plates, put spoons with spoons and knives with knives, she did not break a glass. My head hurt and once I got to bed I wished Gustave would hurry up and lie beside me. One likes a man's warmth, now and then.

I know they say if you are on the trail of evil, evil you will find. And when you've brought it home yourself, in some ways it's your fault. But the worst was yet to come. I've said already how I like to get up early, how the house is mine then, in the hour of the wolves. Well, I woke up extra early for the whole of that next week. I couldn't sleep past four.

The first morning I thought I should stay in bed a little longer and try to pull some warmth out of Gustave, who when he's sleeping deeply doesn't mind it if I curl myself around him. But my eyes were open wide, and you know it's wearing to be conscious by a man who's sleeping like the dead. So I made myself get up.

The sky was black, not blueing at the edges, and once up I felt good. I took to walking through the whole of our big house, corridor by corridor, up each and every hallway, as though I were on patrol. Our bedroom is au premier, which Petra found amusing. For her it was on "the second," and downstairs was "the first." Why the ground, which is most of all itself, ought to have no number she could never understand. Anyway, I'd walk first up to the second floor, where we've closed up the rooms. I'd take a candle with me and try not to think too hard about all the gathering dust. It was drafty, too, and even in my housecoat I was chilled. But the cold will do you good, I always say, cold will keep you sharp.

It made me feel just like a girl, wandering in that house with nothing on my feet, awake while everybody slept. I'd walk all the way past the central staircase and to the far one that goes up into the tower, and then down again, in stone. They were in the tower—that's where I had put them, one room across the landing from the other, Petra's looking out to Spa over the pines, and Thérèse's, come to think of it, with a nice view of the chamomile and of my husband's zoo. I'd put gardenias in their rooms the day each of them came, and I'd given them replacement flowers to take up on the Thursday just before that hideous, hideous show. I liked to tell myself that I could smell the petals in the stairwell—a cool smell, that, so white.

The first few times I made my rounds, the girls' doors were both closed. Shut very tight against me, that's what it felt like. I'd move to each in turn, and listen. I hoped that they were sleeping well, honestly I did. I wished each of them good dreams. The best ones come at dawn, they say, and that's what I think, too. One morning I tried to think of Petra as a baby, how she'd looked when I held her up to that old Brussels priest so he'd toss some water at her. When we walked out onto the Sablon she didn't make a sound, not even when we passed the antiques vendors, and you know how startling, how pushy, they can be.

Like I said, I'd make the rounds, and then go on as usual, as though I hadn't slept a little less than a person really should. I'd make the bread and coffee, set the jams out in a row, and put out four fresh napkins. I'd read in the dining room until Gustave had come for coffee and to tell me what he was tackling that day. Once Thérèse arrived, Petra stopped coming down so early. No, the girls came down so late I left them to it. It was as if we had no guests at all, just a presence, and even—when Thérèse took to washing up the breakfast dishes, too—as though we had a maid. But I tried to be forgiving. I thought, Well, all right.

With all of my patrolling, I'd get tired in the afternoons. And the truth is you can't keep watch with your eyes closed. I'd go out with my book onto the patio and in spite of all my fears I always fell asleep and when I woke up it was six. I'd wake up very cold and need to get a cardigan upstairs, then race into the kitchen to start cooking for the evening.

It's because I fell asleep that those girls got so free. If they'd told me they had dreams of going into town, I would have taken them, I would. I would have pointed out the extra bicycles we keep in the garage beside Gustave's MG. And I would have remembered how the sisters had advised me not to let Thérèse wander alone. That she needed supervision. But I think now that several times they looked as though they'd been doing things in secret—something hot about their hair, and the way they'd come down from the tower, sometimes holding hands.

When I discovered I was missing money, I can't say I was surprised. It must have been Thérèse. Because although Petra had a slight look of the cabaret about her, she was not born in the gutter. And if Petra knew of it, or if she had a hand, well, she would not have done it all alone. Sylvie may have gotten married to Hermann, but that does not mean she was dishonest. It was after dinner that I found my wallet short. After I'd made them all a quiche, with which I'd served a plate of carrot soup and sweet creamed radish greens. I'd had my purse out in the kitchen, because I thought I'd make a list of things to buy and slip it in the outer pocket so I'd know right where to find it. I didn't plan to count my money out right there, but something made me do it. And I have to tell you, though it pains me, that one thousand francs were gone. Gustave was in his study, and I couldn't go to him. He'd have told me to be more careful with my things, that precaution and precision are welded at the hip. As though my jams aren't labeled nicely with a date on every pot. As though I deserved it.

Well, it was one thing going to the tower rooms while the girls were fast asleep, but quite another to go up when I thought I'd find them wide awake. I waited. I'd go to them in the dawn. Maybe Thérèse would be dreaming thickly and so dead to our world that I could look through the girl's luggage and find my thousand francs.

It didn't turn out that way, in the end. I never got that far. The last day was a Monday, I remember, because as I was walking down the hallway in the dark I made a note to bring the mower out to straighten up the lawn. When the townsfolk come on Tuesdays, I've often got some tartelettes or bigger pies that I make the day before and leave out for the children, and I also thought that I could choose the apricots and pit a bucketful by noon.

I was just coming to the landing on the tower steps when I heard it the first time, and I blew the candle out. I set it down just near the door, and I noticed very sharply how the air was warm above the wick and the smoke around my ankles made the rest of me feel cold. It was a kind of shuffling, what I heard, the kind of noises thieves must make at night. It wasn't even four yet, so I thought, what could she be doing? I thought for sure it must be Thérèse, since she'd already stolen from my purse. It stood to reason she'd be up this time of night, doing things of which I could be afraid. But it wasn't. Or it wasn't only her.

Petra's door was open. I could tell because there was a moon. The light was shining through her window, and it would have glowed right through my dressing gown and shown me if I hadn't slipped myself very nimbly flat against the wall. At first I thought maybe Petra had a fever. She was making little sounds like children do when they're asleep and in the clutches of a cold. I thought I'd go to her and ask if she was well. I think I would have liked that: when you haven't any children of your own you think sometimes how nice it would be to help them when they're sick. I could bring a cool cloth for her forehead, sing a little song. But it was the moon that stopped me, how it glinted off a gold thing on the dresser before I looked closely at the bed. I'd got quite near now, had my fingers on the lintel. Like I said, I see quite well at night.

The gold thing was Thérèse's vinyl purse, unzipped at the mouth. And next to it—I saw, because I squinted both my eyes—was a pile of Petra's things, her *Illustrated Guide to Belgium, Liechtenstein and Luxembourg,* and a vial of L'Air du Temps. In the corner—which gave me quite a start—was Petra's purple case. Right beside it was Thérèse's yellow one, pointing straight out from the wall, like a pair of Gustave's shoes. On the chair there were some clothes, and it was another shock to see that old brown skirt tangled up with Petra's pea-soup cardigan, thrown one over the other. What's the use of making up two rooms if your guests are going to go behind your back and share a single one? I didn't like to think about the two of them so close, their things mixed up like that.

Of course it wasn't just the things that were pressed up together. Petra wasn't by herself. There was a lump beneath the blankets with her. Thérèse was a lot bigger than Petra, so I knew that lump was her. I heard that shuffling again, hands tight on the sheets, a sort of nighttime cooing, which sometimes Gustave makes. I must have made a sound, because they suddenly went still. All my breath went sailing out of me and into that warm room. I was like Lot's wife, I was, rooted to the ground.

I wondered how long they'd been together in one bed—if on the other days when both the doors were closed I was missing something all along. You can't know what goes on behind a door, not really, even if your sight could pierce the wood. My eyes were smarting in the dark, and it wasn't from the smoke. I looked over at the desk again to where that purse was gleaming, and I thought, That's where my thousand francs are. I wanted to walk right in and past the bed and take my money back, but my feet were stuck like leeches to the skin of the cold floor.

I did try to rally. So what if they know that I'm right here, I thought? They ought to be ashamed. The covers moved then, and that's what set my legs free, but I couldn't go inside. I reached out and shut the door, and then I ran downstairs so fast that I was panting in the kitchen. I went directly to the chambre froide, where we keep all the apricots and berries, and sat down against the door.

What would you have done? You understand I couldn't have the girls here any longer. Not like this, not mashed together in one room making plans against me. I'll tell you what I did. I didn't bake the bread that morning. I pulled out the ends from Sunday and had a cup of tea, which calmed me, made me think of England. They'd make the coffee on their own, I thought. I'd forget about the money if both of them would go.

In the end, Petra did it for me. She came down in that old dress of hers, long arms bare, her hair all wild and loose, and found me in the kitchen. "No coffee?" she asked me. And when I pointed to the Maragogype in the glass jar on the counter, she set to making it herself. I'd been crying, but I'm sure it didn't show. If it had, Petra would at least have kissed me on the cheek, or told me to sit down.

"Listen, *marraine*," she said, very friendly, as though nothing wrong had happened. In fact more talkative than she had ever been. "We'd like to go to Liège, to spend a few days there, is that all right with you?" She turned the gas on with the lighter, then walked into the dining room. "I thought, you know, that since this is my first summer *en Europe, on irait même à Knokke.* That's where the beach is, isn't it? Have you ever gone?" Well, I guess that "we" was Petra and Thérèse, though if she'd told me from the start, I could have gotten used to the idea and we would have gone together. I've been to Knokke once or twice. Blue sea, Italian ice in tiny cones, and a pretty little wind. I could have planned it for her if she'd told me. But it was clear she meant Thérèse. I told her she could do exactly as she liked. I didn't tell her that Thérèse was not allowed to go off by herself, or that I'd promised Sylvie I'd take good care of her daughter, make sure she was safe. I walked right past her to the bread box and got myself some jam. Gooseberry.

They must have agreed to act as though I hadn't seen them in the night, as if I didn't know that they had turned into a force. I couldn't bring it up to Petra. Not to Sylvie's little girl. She watched me chewing, and I had to put the bread down. I didn't like her eyes on me. I told her I was going to change my clothes. On the way, I got my courage up. If I couldn't tell my goddaughter exactly what I thought of her, I'd say something to the other girl. That's right, I thought. I'll talk to this Thérèse.

Petra's door was open, and Thérèse was in the room, which I guess she had come to think of as her own, and she was looking in the mirror. Mouth tight and open like a fish, she was putting on her lipstick. Still holding her mouth like that, which made her voice peculiar, she said, "Celeste," and my name sounded strange. With a tip of her big brow, she told me to come in.

I sat down on the bed. I saw her bags were packed, and I felt the wind go out of me again. It's crazy, isn't it? I'd gone up to tell the girl to go, that I'd be calling to the sisters to expect her, but when I saw she'd beaten me to everything, it almost made me sad. I hadn't thought that things would go so fast. You're leaving? I asked her. Today? I looked at my own hands along the crocheted bedspread for a moment, and though I didn't mean it, I was tatting at the blanket like a child. Thérèse put on her belt. She breathed in very hard to make her waist as small as it could be before fastening the buckle. Trussed up like a sausage, she let all the air out that she could, and then said, very softly, which was not her usual tone, *"Ah, non. Merde!"* I looked to see what she was doing. She was not speaking to me. She was frowning, looking down. My mouth went very dry. It's not pleasant to say, but the fact is that there was a stain on the girl's bodice. A leak, I mean. You know. She reached down to the bureau for a handkerchief, which she pressed against her breast and then tucked tight and rather easily into her brassiere.

When she looked into the glass again, more herself, or nearly, Thérèse smiled at me. You'll wonder what I did. I crossed my legs and leaned towards her. Serious. I had something to say. But my throat wouldn't open. When she spoke she sounded sorry. "C'est pas grave," she said. "It doesn't matter." I wasn't sure what didn't matter. She looked down at her chest. I nodded, I suppose. Then she put a hairpin in her mouth and started combing her brown hair. For a girl who cared so much about her looks, I thought, she isn't very lucky. Rather a lot of that thin hair came out into the teeth. She went on, "Petra wants to see the coast." Her hands moved very slowly. "A rest would do me good." She put the comb down, and she blinked. "All of that nice wind."

I was looking at her eyes. Very blue, they were. I looked into the mirror at myself to see if my own were that blue, too. I even wondered if her baby's eyes would turn out that same color. Then of course it came to me that Thérèse would likely never know, because she'd given it away. It didn't bother me just then that she was looking at me, or that we do get winds right here, and as I said, now and then some gulls. But it did make my jaws hurt, that they were leaving me before I could order them to go.

Then she made me jump. "It's not so bad, Celeste," she said, and winked at me. That wink felt like a slap, you know, the way you feel when you've held out a piece of cake to someone, and they keep talking and don't take it, though your hand is plain as day. The plump girl winked at me just like an actress would, as though we had a secret. And that wink helped me pull myself together. I do not balk at hardship. I smoothed the blanket down.

I said, You'll be out before lunch, then, and she looked a bit surprised, and I tell you I was pleased. I didn't feel like unwrapping any meat for them or cracking any eggs. I made myself get up from the bed and I went to see Gustave, who was in the study. He was clacking at the typewriter, and he didn't hear me when I pushed open the door.

The girls are leaving us, I said. And though sometimes I sneak up very close, and quietly sit down on the free arm of his big chair, I couldn't make myself go in. "That's strange," he said. "So sudden." And he kept clacking at the keys. "Both of them?" Clack-clack. Both of them, I said.

I waited in the tower staircase at the bottom, while the girls packed their last things. I made myself very small. I heard Petra going down one flight, but she did not come to me. She slipped across to Gustave's room to say good-bye, and I'll give her this much, she sounded awfully polite. Her French *had* gotten better. Then she came bouncing down in that pale dress, that cardigan pulled tight around her bony little waist. I asked if she wanted me to call a car for her, but she kissed me on the cheek and said they'd walk their luggage down the hill. "Don't worry about us," she said. "I'll write you." She giggled. "We'll send you a card!"

Did she think I'd gone to all the trouble of inviting her out here for the summer so she could run off to the beach with a cheap girl who'd given up a child? I guess she did. I guess that is exactly what she thought. I was wrong. I'd been wrong from the start. Here is what I thought about while she stood waiting in the hall. She never gave me presents from New York. She'd never smelled like eucalyptus or like milk. She was not well behaved.

Thérèse came down with her yellow case. She was far

more able with her suitcase than Petra was with hers, what with those broad arms. Thérèse stopped in front of me and I noticed that her posture was not bad. She looked right into my eyes. She'd put some hairpins in, and they looked very neat. I could look at her whole face. "Écoute," she said, "tu vas quand même pas leur dire?" She was asking me quite underhandedly not to call the sisters to tell them she was gone. It's a special program, don't you see? One they were just trying, and if Thérèse did any wrong she'd not get help again. And girls like her don't manage without help, do they? She'd also given up on *vous*, and maybe if she hadn't I'd have made a different answer. "Of course I am," I said. "I will telephone the very moment you are gone. Don't think you'll get far." Thérèse considered me and the import of my words. Then she shook her head and closed her eyes. As if the wayward girl was me! I opened the front door for them myself, and then I stepped aside.

At first while they were walking I imagined calling up the sisters and telling them precisely what I thought about their large, abandoned girl. How I'd done my best for her, but when someone hasn't any manners nothing's going to suit them. And how she'd damaged me. At the same time, and I can't tell you why it is, I also felt the way a person does after they have made a lovely meal and the guests are getting up to go. That sad, sweet peeling into darkness that makes you think you'll do it all again. And how you wish that they would stay, just a little longer.

It was another green, dull day, a whitish sky like thin, gray milk, and the girls stood out quite sharply. When they reached the very end of our long driveway Petra turned around and waved at me, with that strange smile on her face, which was both Hermann's and Sylvie's. Though just then it didn't look quite like her mother's or her father's, and it wasn't Persian, either. Thérèse only turned her head over her shoulder, and maybe she smiled at me, too. The bells rang from the abbey for the morning mass. In the stillness, from the upper road, which is rather far away, I could hear a car. I didn't wave at them, exactly, but I did curl my fingers in my pocket. Well, I suppose I made a fist.

Petra waited, then she shrugged, Thérèse leaned on her arm a moment, and the two of them walked off. From far away, you know, they looked like two ordinary girls. Nothing special. Certainly not horrible, not from a distance like that, when they were growing smaller and I could hear their footsteps echo in the gravel, their cases dragging on the ground. You wouldn't have known at all as I did that Thérèse had had a child, or that it had been taken off to someone else, or that she was the kind of girl who'd drop her skirt so easy. She was having a hard time with her dancing shoes and swollen feet, but I supposed once they found the blacktop she would be just fine. I couldn't help but think: After all, they did have extra money.

When I went back inside, Gustave was sitting at the table with his demitasse and a magazine on Pharaohs. "They're gone, then," he said. And I said yes they were. Then he said the coffee didn't taste quite right, and I can't help it but I told him Petra made it, and that made me feel better. I went into the kitchen for the apricots. Tomorrow's Tuesday, I told him. There's a topiary tour. He groaned. "I wish you'd stop all that, Celeste. It's like throwing pearls to swine."

I stuck my head out and I looked at my own husband. Pearls to swine. There he was, the famous archaeologist, telling *me* about giving pearls to swine. I left him at the table and went in to make the pies. I must have gotten very busy with them, and that's why I never made the call. In fact it was already afternoon when I remembered. And the number for the sisters was all the way upstairs. And then, well, I put the pies in and washed up, and once it came to me that I'd forgotten, well, it seemed a little late. I did tell Gustave I *had* called, so he'd be relieved that I am not a person to be fooled with. I even told him, though I am not the sort of woman who will trifle with the truth, that the nuns were informing the police and would make them bring her back to Liège. He nodded at me once, then went back up the stairs.

Already I could smell the apricots get warm and soften in the oven. I went into the hall and pulled the cloths out for the tables. I could iron them and get them fresh before the pies were done. I set up the tables in the field, not too far from Gustave's beasts. Later on I'd clean the two rooms in the tower, make them fresh again.

The pies came out quite well. I arranged them in a circle on the kitchen table and covered them with cloth. Then I went out onto the patio with a glass of bitters and some ice and a novel I had longed to read. The sun came out at last. The petunias were as sturdy and as bright as I had hoped they'd be when I'd watched the urns in winter. I could smell the chamomile and very slightly, too, my baking. I opened up the book and before I started reading I thought how pleasant it was going to be when lots of children came to look at Gustave's zoo. If they would finish off the pies, and thank me, and promise to come back.

❦ Wondrous Strange

A Kingdom to the North, 1992

The mediums of the Thursday Club dealt commonly in ghostly things: the disembodied voices, thoughts, once or twice the ephemeral likenesses that hovered, in best suits or favorite aprons, by the sofa or the door, echoes of the dead, all in all, the dim but urgent stirrings of humans human-born. The Medium Fontanella, the founder of the club, heard the ghost words in her head, responded to them, and, stylishly, lugubriously, related most of what was said. She could speak back to them, too, asking questions that the shades would sometimes answer. Maxwell Black the Scribe did automatic writing, bringing the old energies to life through the channel of his arms. He loosened his fat wrists and lifted up his pen, himself hearing nothing, thinking nothing; the revenants used his hands and showed him what to write. Maxwell Black produced remarkably neat, impressively coherent missives, which, once he had come to, he read aloud in measured, even tones. Max and Fontanella were the leaders, the most versed.

Eva Bright, no special clerk like Blackie, not as skilled as Fontanella (she could not *converse* with spirits, and she never, ever *saw* them), occupied the second tier. For souls she was no more than an unruly mouthpiece. When Eva let her mind go blank, opened up her throat, the spirits, without censor, spoke

❧ *43* ❧

their thoughts right through her, while she remembered nothing. She was learning, had potential. She was getting better.

Susan Darling, amateur, the newest of the group, had smaller, more diversionary gifts. She listened for the needs and dreams of objects and found things that were lost. She was like a parlor trick. The real heart of the Thursday Club was the funneling of *ghosts,* their messages from the beyond: of *human* flotsam, that was all.

On Thursdays, the function room above the Overlook Café became a center of communications, a human phone booth, post office, and microphone for the Rogers, Junes, and Mikes who'd died with things unsaid, or who, unable to observe the fleshy march below without wishing to meddle, required a human slot for their two cents or five. For more than seven years now, until the astounding show that upset everything and made a mockery of Max and Madame F., the usual guests from the Beyond had been possessed of ordinary age: they'd reached seventy, or eighty, sometimes a bit more than that, but never very much. Or theirs had been an interrupted span: *she did not see thirty,* for the woman-in-a-crash; or *taken far too young,* a dear child surprised. And young meant five or nine or ten, not two thousand years. Old was ninety-five, not—as the most recent visitor insisted—*more than twenty* centuries lived out under the sea. Indeed: Eva Bright, Fontanella's protégée, had been possessed (or so the manly, foreign voice that issued from her said) by no ghost, but a djinn.

A sea spirit from Africa, who, while Eva's body shook, while she stood and waved her arms, gave his name through her loosed mouth as Sheikh Abdul Aziz, and furthermore averred:

he had never been a child; he had landed in his fishy home on the Indian Ocean floor by some equatorial islands when King Solomon himself—the very one all Christians know—had flung all tricky djinn from the north to the far south and banished them from Galilee, Jerusalem, and Sodom.

And this djinn who spoke through Eva Bright was not come on a fluke, not an accidental visit for hello-here-I-am-and-now-right-back-I-go! Sheikh Abdul Aziz had come up for a reason: a message for one long-standing, solid, prim, and docile member of the club, an avid follower of ghost news, an admirer of mediums, who had never had a message in her life. A Mrs. Flora Hewett. This madame, Sheikh Abdul Aziz announced, could by following his lead cure her ailing husband, George. By doing some incredible, appalling, extraordinary things (involving jewelry and rose water, and the slaughter of some goats), all of which he detailed using Eva Bright's tight vocal cords and lips. In the dizzy wake of which, Eva Bright, exhausted, had fallen to the floor. Astonishing, indeed. What were they to think?

Aftermath

When Eva had come to, the room above the Overlook Café felt quieter and cooler than a full room ought to be. She had the sharp impression that almost everyone—and there'd been thirty, forty, a healthy, eager crowd—had gone. On the floor, laid out on her back behind the mediums' table, she had been upended. She was looking at the ceiling: brownish blooms, a water stain. At the edge of her left eye, the crystal chandelier, asway. Beyond that, the peeling strips of wallpaper (chestnut-patterned), which no one ever managed, or remembered, to bring down. Her mouth hurt, yes, her mouth hurt, and her arms and hands and ankles (itching in their soft, not-made-to-itch brown socks) and each one of her toes (hot and trapped in her well-laced walking boots), and her heart was beating fast. In the aching confines of her mouth, incomparable, distinct, the biting taste of cloves.

When Eva turned her head, she first made out the shining sphere of worried Maxwell Black: at the lower end of him, the pointed, polished twinkle of his brogues; farther up, the silk glow of his shirtfront. Behind him, in the wings, portly Fontanella, painted eyes agog. These two, Eva's oldest colleagues, used to seeing her take on the voices of the dead (in these past months someone's redoubtable aunt Celia; next, thoughtful cousin Jim; a longshoreman named Trevor), were looking at her as though she'd unbuttoned her blouse without a reason or begun braying like a mule. In shock, Fontanella, dedicated to the maintenance of what she thought a proper medium's poise (usually unruffled, never too sharp or hilarious), was bathed in a slick sweat, and speechless; Blackie—pencil snapped in half from the surprise—waved two wooden wands. "Nella," he kept saying. "Nella, did you see?"

Eva, still reclining, limbs like lead and pupils full of light: "What is it, Blackie? Tell me. What on earth just happened?" Toupee out of place, aglow with chalky sweat, Blackie stepped towards her and knelt slowly. Faltering, he explained. When it was her turn to commune, he told her, she had not sighed slowly as was usual (they all knew Eva's modest puff, a low sound like a whistle). No, she had groaned out loud, "And very loudly, too." He opened up his throat and tried to show her what he meant, but Fontanella, from behind, stopped him with a hiss, as though a groan too much like those given in the trance might provoke Abdul Aziz, turn that switch back on. Blackie acquiesced. Nella was his sweetheart. He did not like to displease her, so he turned to whispering and tried to sum it up.

He spread his hands along his thighs and leaned closer to Eva. In an accented ("Oriental," he said) English, Eva's channels had tuned in to the wishes of a spirit. "Listen, Eva. Not a shade, it wasn't. Not a *proper* ghost." He turned to check on angry, exasperated Fontanella, who was already stepping away, undone and annoyed; he went on, voice a little clearer.

Taking charge of Eva's mouth and will, he said, "A Mohammedan!" (so it did appear) had introduced himself: "I am from the islands off the coast . . ." Blackie's imitation, blurred and nasal, *Ah-frick-ahhh*. "The coast of Ah-frick-ahhh. Bahr al-Zinj!" he said, and then again, much louder, in an imitation, "Bahr al-Zinj!" He snapped the fingers of both hands. As the pencil bits skittered to the floor, Blackie paused and looked at Eva doubtfully, as if *she* had caused them to. He did not know what to think. Amazed, he said, "Sheikh Abdul Aziz, Eva. You gave us his name."

Eva, with the discomfiting but growing sense that she was being told a story she had always known but had never heard a person tell, begged him to go on. Did she remember that? Her throat hurt, yes, as if she had used it harshly, in an unaccustomed way. That odd tang remained with her, a hot numbness at her gums. And in Eva's ears . . . what tune was that, what words? *La Illahi ila* . . . Wondering, she said the words out loud. Blackie, suddenly impatient, not sure he should trust her, snapped, "There is no God but Allah, yes, I *do* know what that means." Eva was surprised. *She* didn't. "Et cetera, et cetera," he said. "Mohammed and so forth, yes, you did recite it all." He wiped at his damp brow with an embroidered handkerchief and then went on.

The coastal force from far-flung seas had next addressed himself directly and by name to Flora Hewett (who was *there,* who had stayed behind, and whom Eva, if she craned her aching neck and peered under the table's dark green cloth, could see: a frozen woman on the other side of the long table, red cardigan a vivid slash in the ill-lit, greenish room, white hair shocked among its pins, hands massaged by hearty, flustered Fontanella). To return her husband, George, to health, so said the interrupting *thing,* Flora Hewett must acquire a silver ring, drape herself in light blue cloths, sprinkle rose water about, obtain a white goat and a black one, and—"Do you remember, Eva? Listen. *Kill* them in the garden. *Kill them*," Blackie said. "Moreover, by a well, if at all convenient." Blackie said these last words with distaste, as if Eva had somehow intentionally demeaned him. "Does Mrs. Hewett have a well? I mean, does she, Eva? I'm telling you, I don't know what to think." He seemed almost afraid. Fontanella called to him, and Blackie turned away.

"Wait," said Eva. "What am I going to do?" Blackie looked at her. "Do?" Now his face was pinched. About to rise, he curled his nose at her, as if she had begun, uncouthly, to smell.

"You'll *do* nothing at all!" He placed a plump hand firmly on her arm. "For one thing, Fontanella's quite upset. She's sure you made it up. And *I*"—his voice was not unkind but it was firm—"*I* don't know what to think."

Eva, struggling to sit, caught a pearly comb that had jumped out of her hair. "Don't go yet, Blackie, please." Eva's very face hurt. She didn't know how she would get up. Blackie pulled away a bit, evaluated her with a tufted raising of his brow. Fontanella's voice sang out for him. "Maxwell! Maxwell, come away from there!" Blackie sighed, said softly, "Look, my dear, we'll go over it tomorrow." Fontanella called for him again, and with a final, puzzled look at Eva, Blackie scampered down the steps.

Little arty Susan had come out of the toilet then, where she had gone to throw cool water on her face. Strands of ghostly hair—she was pale, this girl, the color of coal ash—clung wetly to her cheeks; the butterfly tattoo that trembled at her neck seemed ready to flit off, for real, at last. She held her head at an odd angle, stood there as if listening for something she could not quite hear. As she moved, careful, to the stage, Susan did not step; she crept. She peered at Eva from behind the mediums' table. She had something to tell her. But, hearing Fontanella call ("Susan Darling! Come here *now*. Immediately!"), Susan gave instead a small, halfhearted mewl and skipped back to the main floor.

Knees atremble, rushing, liquid, legs not quite her own, Eva stood up then and understood that she was being left. Fontanella, black hair out of place, matching blouse alive, looked almost electric. Plump hands desperately at work, palping, sparkling, tapping, kneading in the air as if something had spilled out of it that must at all costs be returned, she told her murmuring charges: "We shall now remove ourselves. Get far from this damn *show*." And so she and Blackie led a nearly catatonic Flora Hewett firmly down the back steps of the Overlook Café, each clasping a still hand, while Susan, childlike and unmoored, clutched at the lace trim of Fontanella's scarf. Before the street door closed on them, Eva heard Fontanella's voice. "Ah-frick-ahhh, indeed. Who does she think she is?" Then came Susan Darling, tender and unsure. "What could that have been, do you think?" Blackie saying, "Calm yourselves. At this moment we don't know," and last, soft but unmistakable, Flora Hewett's tread, gloomy, solid, thoughtful on the steps.

Alone in the old function room, Eva tried to move her feet, found that she could, yes, after all, keep her knees in place, and began folding up the chairs. As she gathered the strewn paper plates, folded them in halves, and tossed them in the waste-basket, she thought of Flora Hewett, whose job this usually was, the cleaning up of fruit punch, sugar packets, and the tea bags, when the mediums' work was done. Flora Hewett had been doing that for years. Eva sniffed. What had she allowed herself to say? What had she done to Flora?

She folded up the long green velvet cloth that marked the mediums' table and slipped Blackie's record from the player back into its sleeve (*The Messiah*, it had been this time, which everybody liked). *What a thing*, she thought. *What a thing to happen.* As she shut off all the lights, the chandelier bulbs ticked. In the dark, Eva closed her eyes a moment, stretched the muscles in her back and legs. She ran her tongue along the tunnels of her mouth and felt something—not quite tangible, an unnamed thing—fall softly into place. *So be it,* she thought. *Sheikh Abdul Aziz.*

Flora's Evening

Flora Hewett, oldest paying member of the Thursday Psychics Club, was reliable, firmly of this world, practical and dull. Because she had no talents of her own, she had always liked the scene, all those people, from every walk of life, gathering to listen to the dead. It made her feel that things went on far beyond the confines of what most people believed, which made her less afraid (she *was* afraid, sometimes, when she thought about her age, that dimness she could sense sometimes encroaching from the edge). The Thursday Club also made her feel that she was needed. At the meetings, she felt recognized, in some small way important. It was she who had come up with the idea of regulars beginning to pay dues, to do away with entrance fees, so that there would be a budget, ensuring rental of the function room from the Overlook Café without any interruption. It was Flora who had thought of bringing snacks and some refreshments, and who, having thought of it, did bring them: the weekly tray of sandwiches and cakes, the urn of boiling water for the tea, the plastic bowl of punch, more recently the sparkling water for the younger ones who had begun, that winter (Susan Darling in their midst), coming from the Art School.

She had not missed a day in years. And yet, despite her excellent attendance, she had never, no, not once, been selected from the Other Side as the target of deep news; after the initial disappointment, she had come to pride herself on this; it meant, she thought, that no one in her family had been secretive or cruel, or done to death by hate, that her life and her loved ones held no hidden drama. She had taken the position left her: a source of strength for anyone who'd gotten a hard message from Beyond and needed a hand held. She came with tissues in her purse, cologne in a spray bottle, and lavender pastilles, which, she very much believed, calmed a person down just as well as brandy. She gave comfort where she could, and, after everyone was gone, she collected up the plates and cups and went home with her trays. The Thursday Club had always been a joy for her, a hook to hang her days on. But since her George had taken ill and now lay so incomprehensible and helpless in his bed, the Thursday Club was also the one thing that had, predictable and regular, helped her keep her head. Above the Overlook Café, Flora always knew, she'd thought, what she could expect.

So when it finally happened—so publicly, and strangely, as it never had before—Flora had both stiffened and dissolved; gone leaden and still; dissipated in the air and been returned in a new and unfamiliar shape, rubber or basalt. All those people staring at her as if she'd brought it on herself, or, and this was worse, as if *they* should comfort *her!* Someone had put an arm around her; another squeezed her hand. And someone, some-one—and she had no wish to know who, a black-dressed girl in work boots or a wild-haired boy in rouge who did not under-stand, a student, laughing, light—had whistled and applauded! She'd folded all her feelings close within herself and she had not moved a hair, even as The Medium Fontanella instructed all please but the principals to go calmly on their way.

She would have stayed fastened to her seat forever, chill and like a stone, had Fontanella and her partner, Maxwell Black the Scribe, not come to coax her up. The two of them, followed by peculiar Susan Darling—who had seemed to hover, weightless, in the background—had helped her down the stairs. "Don't you worry, Flora," Fontanella had said. "Don't pay Eva any mind. Don't you go and do anything about it." Serious Fontanella, fingers on the cold expanse that was Flora Hewett's face. Reassuring—this was Maxwell Black, bergamot and olive soap—"We'll sort this out, my dear. We'll get you some advice." The sound of the familiar voices had stirred Flora a little, and she'd managed, one foot before the other, to make it to the street.

As they went, they discussed the scene among themselves. Flora wasn't lucid yet, but, as if down a narrow stairwell, or echoing in a cave, some things they said came through. Fontanella thought Eva Bright either scurrilous or mad, that she'd gone *off her head*. That she'd done the thing quite consciously, on purpose. The weather *had* been strange, tourists throwing off their windbreakers, cats apreen in warm and clammy sun. Could that have brought it on? Fontanella thought it all in terribly poor taste. It was simply Eva Bright, that arriviste, attempting, because nothing real would do it, to make herself important, special. In any case, they trucked only in ghosts, she said, not in other beings. Not in djinn or demons. "We all go to Church!" she said, and "Other beings, Islamic ones included, are the Devil's spawn."

Maxwell, for his part, took a different tack. He did not think Eva capable of coming up with such a thing alone. "She's not that clever, Nella," he did whisper. And furthermore, he was a bit intrigued. A not-quite-human being! Did they not hear sometimes of hobgoblins and sprites? Of succubi and trolls? How *interesting,* he thought, that this should be a *djinn,* and that that djinn would come to them from *Africa,* which had, he said, he'd thought, not a thing to do with him, with them. "Djinn," he said, though it was nearly like a question, full of wonder, "are not in our cultural makeup. Are they?" Fontanella punched his forearm and gave him a dark look.

Flora wished they'd stop. She was tired of their voices. She wished they'd leave her be. If they had asked her, she would have had no choice but to say that unlike Fontanella, she knew that it was true. She, decent, plain old unsurprising Flora Hewett, *believed* immediately and without question in Eva Bright's Mohammedan djinn. *She,* careful, quiet Flora Hewett, knew, quite oddly—and not in the usual place in her own brain where she usually knew such things, like: I will make a pie, or I will purchase shoes—that she was going to take action. Whether Eva's mind had melted with the unexpected sun, whether Eva Bright had done this thing on purpose to bring attention to herself, and whether things from Africa belonged up here or not, it wasn't a mistake. *This* message was real.

Flora understood two things that she did not say. First of all, there was the fact that George Alexander Hewett had indeed been to Africa himself, had stayed there for a while. And secondly, perhaps the most important thing, Flora Hewett had been sent a sign, well before the show.

Before Sheikh Abdul had asked for her by name and in *that* voice, before Eva had even startled everyone and groaned, actually while Blackie read his final letter (Adam asks that Mary be good to his mother), a clear vision of her George had come to her. Not unlike a transparency, a watermark on the visual plane of things, it had remained there the whole time, even afterwards, while she sat still in her chair. Dear George. With a great smile on his face! Sitting up in bed and nodding! He had one foot on the floor and was about to set the other down. As if next he'd ask for breakfast. As if he recognized her. And yet in *this* sad and flattening life, he'd not sat up, not said a clear, sweet word for weeks!

Flora Hewett had never had a vision—some daydreams, as a girl, later on mistaking dogs for postboxes sometimes, birds where there were none. But never anything like this. She was sensible, distinctly closed to Other Realms, not given to hysterics. Why would she see George right there in front of her, hovering, looking his old self at last, well before the spirit rose in Eva, if there were not something in it? *Dear George,* who—though he was a hard man, though he was not always solicitous or tender—was nonetheless the light of Flora's life, the only man she'd had!

Remembering it so clearly was going to make her cry. Surrounded by her guardians on the sidewalk, Flora had the unmistakable impression that Fontanella wished she *would* cry, that Fontanella would have taken pleasure from offering her handkerchief and saying, "Now, there, there," and, while Flora liked to share her tissues, too, she took them from no one. She squared her shoulders, dug a fist against each hip, and insisted she was fine. She shook them off at last once they'd pointed out her car. "Yes, I have my keys," she said. "Good night." And they had reluctantly let go.

In the old, familiar seat, hands clutching the wheel though she'd not started the engine, Flora finally cried, hot tears that filled her eyes and slipped over her cheeks as though a dam had split, face so wet that she could not make out the words on the chip shop's lit-up sign, though it said "Hassan's Take-Aways" and she looked for it each Thursday because it was how she knew that she was near enough to the Overlook Café to find a place to park. She felt marvelment and hope. *George was sitting up in bed! George was looking well!* Had she seen into the future? How she wished he *would* look well again.

Bit by bit, her tears ebbed, and in the quiet were replaced by a limpid, lucent glow, the chip shop in hard focus. She knew her certainty was fragile, the kind that follows shock, but hold to it she would: She would do it. Whatever this Abdul Aziz demanded, she would do it all.

It helped that this odd message—Flora's first!—had come from Eva Bright. They had never spoken much. Flora did not *know* her, really. But Eva Bright had been her favorite of the mediums from the start. Eva Bright had a fine face, not yet in middle age but wise, which she did not accentuate with heavy makeup or with fat, prismatic pendants to make a person think, Ah, that person deals in ghosts. Eva Bright was always ordinary, reassuringly so. Modest. Normal. Interested in ghosts because everybody was. She did have some small gift, but she did not seem, as the other two appeared, interested in costumes or in marketing, in making a to-do. Maxwell Black in his old-fashioned, nearly dandy suits, with that walking cane the head of which was a globe in a bird's claw, and Fontanella, painted, scarlet, purple, black. And could those be real names? Flora did admire the scribe and medium's flowing, tailored costumes, yes, but was it not a bit over the top? She had not yet made up her mind about slender, wraithlike, ashen Susan Darling, who could sense vibrations, sounds ("and hearts," she said), in *things*. "Darling" *could* be real, of course, but it could also be a gimmick, to make everybody like her. Enjoyment, Flora thought, was one thing. Trust was quite another.

Once at home, she stood without turning the lights on over George's bed. How tired her man looked, even in the moonlight. How different now from what he'd always been—so active, such a figure! The square jaw she had always thought so handsome looked too angular these days. His flesh seemed to be thinning, sinking. He'd lost so much weight.

George's hands hurt her the most. He had little feeling in them, hadn't had since falling in the garden, falling without even tripping on the bench or on a rock, or on the slope that held the flowers—*falling*, simply, snatched towards the earth by something no one understood. He'd done so much with those hands! Built things, played chess with the neighbor, helped Flora with her puzzles, smoothed out folded bills he took from sticky envelopes that always gave her trouble, but which, with precise and steady fingers, he never found a bother! And now he seemed a shell.

Watching George made Flora wish to cry again, but she didn't want to wake him. And, she also told herself, did she not have hope, now? She wanted him to sleep a sleep of angels, a full, deep, fearless sleep from which he might awake refreshed and be *himself* again. Without taking off her clothes and slipping, as she usually did, into a nightgown and the bed jacket she had years before crocheted for herself, Flora lay down next to him and listened to him breathe. She took one of his slack hands in hers and pressed her cheek upon it. His skin was like a violet's.

Africa, she thought. It was the one period of his life that George never discussed, his time in the army. He *had* been out there (though Flora had no idea where that "there" was, on a map, what country it had been), and that, whatever doubts the other mediums had, made it oddly right, this Sheikh Abdul Aziz approaching her for ailing George's good. She'd only seen the pictures, had not liked to trouble him with questions, and she had let it be a mystery, his secret. But could something from so long ago, she asked herself, some *animus* (was that the word?), have chosen him back when he was young and crossed the sea to find him? How had the spirit known his name? How had it known *her?* Flora closed her eyes. George's breathing (regular, thank God!) rose and fell in waves. She curled her fist against his shoulder, as if to hold him up, and tried to fall asleep. Africa. Spirits. If *she* had met George at some foreign seashore long ago, or seen him walking down a street, would she not, too, have traveled distances to find him? Would she not, too, have remembered his sweet shape, longingly, for years?

Eva's Night

Eva Bright had never gone to Africa. She did not even know, she thought, a single person who had been there, let alone an African, or anyone who said that they were such. If only she'd been conscious while her visitor had talked! If only she'd been able to discuss the thing with him, the way Fontanella could with the shades who came to *her.*

At home again that evening, undressing for bed, Eva wished, as usual, that she were a better medium. Eva, Fontanella often said, was too raw yet, not entirely trusted by those who had passed on. She had come to her gifts late. In her upper thirties she might be, but in Fontanella's view, she was "Still an infant, just a baby in the jamboree of souls." Saying this, Fontanella would reach out with her short fingers, those hands that Eva sometimes thought were really well-kept paws, to brush the stern brown fringe from Eva's brow. She'd tap the combs that Eva wore, one on either side, as if drawing a spell. "You'll learn from me," she said, "in time." Sometimes reassurance of this sort was not really enough. Often, Eva bristled. But she knew that some of it was true: she had so much to learn!

It was Fontanella who had started up the group ten years before; without her there would be no weekly meetings at the Overlook Café, no introductory lectures on the many paths to spiritual peace (this week from the writings of Patanjali: the way of *pratyahara,* listening to silence). She was the metaphysicist among them, an excellent clairaudient, the most capable of all. Long inducted, so she said, from a girl into the realms of the Beyond, The Medium Fontanella was more than a mere conduit. She knew exactly what was happening to her each and every time. She could help the speaking souls if they needed her assistance. They came when she called. "Rather like a mid-wife," she would say, "I guide, I prompt, I soothe."

Without the audience hearing, Fontanella could, with her inner voice, say, "Can you repeat please, dear?" or "Do you mean this or that?" And receive clarification. She could also, if she saw a need, step in and stop the flow—if the message was too difficult or painful, if it was clear to *her,* The Medium Fontanella, that the receiver was not in any state to hear it all so plainly. If this happened, Fontanella rolled her eyes and held her hands up in the air and said, "My dear. Please wait. You are too strong for me. We cannot understand. Just a portion, please." And the message would be tamped, reshaped as she wished, a morsel that was right.

For example, instead of something horrible and dark, like a message from a sister who'd passed on to a sister who still lived: "Your husband beats your boy and plays with him at night, and Samuel won't blossom till you've left the cruel Frank," Fontanella might instead relate the following: "Your sister Anne is well, she loves you very much, but she has something to tell you. On no account tell Frank. Next week, leave your son with friends." In the days between, she would make a visit to the mother of the boy and inquire as to the setup of the household. If the husband was infirm (news from the Beyond is not always the most recent), or if the wife depended on his pay and had no relatives to turn to, it wasn't right to say it all at once. There were foundations to be laid; she kept a list of numbers one could ring up for assistance—as to women's shelters, suicide prevention, the legitimate addictions, counseling for grief, antidotes for poisons, and the rescue of wild animals who strayed. She kept these up to date and put them to good use. Wouldn't it be wonderful to know so much, not only about ghosts, but about the way the world of living beings worked, that one could be a force, somehow, for the good? For really bringing it about instead of, as Eva felt she did, simply taking messages that she herself did not recall accepting?

In the neat brick house she'd grown up in, not far, just around the corner from the Overlook Café, Eva couldn't sleep. Her mouth still tasted strange; her head was like a blender's bowl, the contents pressed up, sticky, to the sides, the middle all afroth. Cloves. It brought to Eva's mind the dentist's office, a sharp memory of being very small with her mouth open and a tall man dressed in white telling her that she should brace herself, prepare for a great pull. Cloves. Isn't that what they were for, for numbing tender gums? *Cloves,* she thought. Cloves and something else. What was it? Eva closed her eyes. Cinnamon? Cardamom, perhaps? How odd. Such spices were not what a person thought of, were they, when they thought of Africa. Did they even grow there? Cloves made Eva also think of muscle rubs, somehow of Indonesia. Cardamom brought Christmas cakes to mind. But Africa? She'd have thought of lions first. Bananas. But who was *she* to say?

In bed, she breathed as slowly as she could. Twice, her fingers seemed to dissipate, dissolve, she forgot which thumb was where, and she was able to convince herself that her head was where her feet were and her feet up by the lamp; she'd nearly lost the central, orienting sense of her material body's place. But she could not take that freeing, satisfying leap: her body held her back, her leg twitched, or her dissenting heart did, and her eyes opened again. It was getting late. Outside the world was dead and quiet, thick, the motionless damp green of an unseasonably warm night before the first birds clear their throat. Three o'clock. Then four. Eventually, from between the heavy curtains she could see the day arise, a glowing purplish light peeking at the tassels.

She gave up, rose to wash her face. Through the kitchen window, she saw the sky outside come white; below the paling sky, the Channel (that dull blue, so reassuring, the dark color of slate) was giving up its mist. A black fleck, a cargo ship, emerged on the horizon. Closer in, from her own street, she heard car engines starting up, shop-front awnings lifted on their cranks. A motorcycle rattled and droned past. She wished she had an atlas.

Africa. Another ocean farther on. Islands. *Amazing,* Eva thought. Then, *Wonderful.* Did it matter who the bringer was, a sprite, a soul, a spirit? Blackie said she'd given out *instructions,* something to be done. How very odd, how new. It was, she thought, a gift.

George Hewett's New Ailment

In the bed he'd shared with Flora for nearly thirty years, George Hewett, shivering and mute among old pillows and hot water bottles, was a bony raft, barely buoyed by the sheets. He had not spoken since his fall. Had not made any sign of recognition or desire, raised a hand or whispered, even blinked at any question. But it was not a stroke. He had not had a heart attack. Doctor Howard said so, over and again. He was simply, inexplicably, suddenly, infirm. At first, the weakness irked him. He might have been over seventy, it's true, but that had been no reason, since his entry to what others called old age, to succumb to anything, or to behave as though preparing for an exit. "Right as rain," he always said. "Stronger than a bull."

Until taking to bed after that odd fall in the garden (that fast collapse! that suck! that flattening to the ground!), George Alexander Hewett had been an able man who lifted things, dug holes, climbed up ladders and down, walked three miles each day. He breathed as regularly and strongly, he had liked to tell himself, and Flora, as the old Athenians had, muscled legs apump, racing with that flame. He was strong. Age was nothing to him. Until falling in the garden—he could see it, still, just there by the plum tree, not far from the well, the way his knees had buckled and his spine, how the world had warbled and gone black—George Hewett still felt forty-, fifty-five. He was used to jumping spryly out of bed, so naturally that the word *spry,* reserved for the surprisingly adept, never came to mind. He'd been a man who did things, who had traveled; he had even, it was said, and so Flora believed, fought bravely in the War.

At first, his inability to get ahold of things, move them with his hands, or to take steps on his own to any place he cared for, infuriated him. He couldn't rise from bed, could not balance his own head on his neck, and he couldn't even push away the blankets when he felt too hot. Oh, he'd been very angry. After several weeks, however, and more marked as days went on, a kind of inward settling, a silence, had occurred; he'd begun to see things differently. A slow but certain shift.

Perhaps, he thought, there is a goodness here. Perhaps he'd fallen ill for something. Perhaps—this idea startled him, so like Flora's alchemists, who dealt in messages and in what she'd once shyly called "holistics"!—perhaps his body, this body that had stood him in such dear and marvelous stead, was bringing him a message, a request for a hiatus. There was something nice about so much lying down, a little giving up. It let a person think.

At the moment, he was glad the house was quiet. Flora must be in the garden, weeding, watering things, he thought, her flowers. These he could recall: daisies, foxglove, and clematis, other bobbing things. *Her flowers.* He was glad she wasn't in the house. At present, he wished, most of all, to listen to his thoughts in his own familiar room. The great mahogany bedstead, across from it the two Somali chests, the velvets from Kasai, the model dhows atop the dresser, the spears he'd hung up on the wall against Flora's misgivings, Flora's knitting on the chair, the lovingly dried poppies, salmon-colored, flat in their wall frames, the flower press and papers on the sill, the fireplace to his right side, the wainscoting, the lamps—he knew it all too well and he was finding it distracting, static in his mental ears, a clouding in his view. He shut his eyes against them, but he could see it all, still there, on the screen of his own eyelids, though he was really trying, eagerly, to observe a different thing.

George was not, he thought, about to die. His wish for

silence and for being able please to shut out the known world, was not the precursor to an old man's dream of death. No. Not a thing like that, no easing, slowing down because life had been too long. Lucid, free of all reminders of his actual whereabouts, he wished, rather inexplicably, to find some-where else instead, some "where" that, oddly, he was certain he contained.

Something in him opened. If it was a place, what was it? What had Flora said the night before, in sleep, when he had come awake and found himself staring at the rafters, sweat-ing, listening for birds? She had murmured George's name, then something about Africa. George sighed, wished that he could bring his two hands to his face and rub his cheeks and chin. Indeed. He had been there, of course, it was where he'd spent the War. But that was before Flora, and he'd never told her much. He was not the sort of man to ask her what she'd dreamed, or to think too hard about what went on inside her, behind that softly wrinkled skin. Her murmurs, nonetheless, had touched something in him.

As he began to think of old, past things, he heard Flora coming in through the back door, pulling off her boots and hanging up her hat. In her slippers now (that well-known, able padding of his wife's reliable, hard feet), she moved past their door but didn't, George was thankful, come inside to see him. He imagined her in the front room, standing at the window. In his vision of his wife, the window at her back was filled with the Atlantic, with a wide horizon framed in swathes of mist. What could she have been dreaming?

The Mediums Visit Eva

At ten o'clock, the other members of the Thursday Club (Fontanella clutching Blackie's arm, Blackie on his cane, accompanied, at a respectful distance, by shy, strange Susan Darling) appeared at Eva's door. The three filed sternly up the stairs.

Fontanella sat down first, and in Eva's yellow kitchen chair began breathing in and out, loudly, through her nose. Blackie sat beside her. Susan Darling stood. Fontanella closed her eyes and tapped her palms against the table's polished face. She was not in a good mood. Eva, noticing again how long Fontanella's purchased lashes were, how they brushed the very edge of the medium's rounded cheeks, thought idly of the tassels at the edges of the drapes. After a long silence, she pushed the plate of Orange Buttons towards her. Fontanella heard the motion, opened up her eyes, and, because she could not help herself, took up a fat biscuit. But she gave Eva a sharp look, as if to say, *Don't think these biscuits move me.*

Blackie covered her free hand with his. "Nella, dear," he said. Something prim and tender in his voice caused Eva to picture them in bed, fully clothed but pressed against each other, fingers interlaced, Fontanella calling Blackie *Max,* and Blackie crying, *Nella, Nella,* as he frothed into her gowns. Blackie said, "Nella, dear," again. "It's possible, you know, just, that Eva *didn't* make this up. So please, behave." Fontanella chomped her biscuits greatly, swallowed, and did not wipe the crumbs from her tight lips. She sniffed, and said to Eva, "*I* didn't want to come, you know. *He* made me."

Eva felt a turning, sharpness in her stomach. Her ears rang. The biscuit in her fingers broke damply in two. "Fontanella," she said carefully. "I don't know what you mean." Fontanella rolled her eyes. "Eva. You don't really think we should believe you?" As Eva sighed and Fontanella glared at her, Blackie pulled out a chair for Susan, so that she was not seated at the table properly but next to them, in front of the big window, behind her sky and sea. A shuffling of wind raised her ashen hair, revealing her tattoo, which was, thought Eva, the same color as her veins, pale green, violet, and blue, like the girl herself and her light, arresting eyes. Eva looked at her and was not certain where she stood.

At Eva's silence, at everyone's, Fontanella sneered. "Eva!" she said. "Come on. You *sounded* like an Arab. Where did you pick that up, I wonder? Skulking by the docks, were you? Very good, it was. Almost like a man. Like a *Suhl*-tan. Like Ha*roon* Ra*sheed*." Blackie, whose love for Fontanella had kept him quiet for a while, stepped in then. "Nella, *Haroun Rashid* was Persian." Fontanella shrugged. She dropped another sugar in her tea. "Well, like a sultan, then."

Beside them, as if in another world, Susan rearranged her hair and looked down at her feet. Blackie shifted in his chair. The silence was exasperating. Fontanella set her cup down with a clatter. "Eva, this is hocus-pocus. Mumbo jumbo. Wanga, juju, junk. It doesn't mean a thing—aggression only. You made this up to shock us. For a joke. It's your resentment of me, don't think I don't know. You want to do things nobody else can, and this was the only way for you to do it. But to invent a thing like this! You've really gone too far." Blackie patted

Fontanella's hand, but he did not quite agree. "We don't know, yet, my dear. We don't know that at all."

Fontanella made a caught sound in her throat, looked elaborately away from him and plucked once at her blouse. Her nose puckered and her eyes. She seemed about to cry. "You did this for attention, Eva. You've made it all up. I can't believe it of you, it's so stupid and so cheap!"

Blackie sighed, preparing. He'd meant to speak first, after all. He hadn't meant for Nella to go wild. He cleared his throat. Was stern. "Listen, Eva. Here's what we've come to say. You upset Flora Hewett very much, you know. She's never had a message before this, and, I'm sure you can imagine, this one was a bloom! A whammy. Really. A foreigner, not even a shade, apparently. A messenger, two thousand years old, an actual ancient from lands we've never seen!" Eva set her teacup down. She *had* been thinking about Flora. "Yes," she said. "Poor thing."

Fontanella interrupted her. "Poor Flora indeed. You must leave Flora alone, Eva. You mustn't speak to her. You've done enough already. This was an awful joke on your part. Something you did on your own. And if you didn't sit right here" (she pointed at the table, at the counter and the windows) "and *practice* it beforehand, then it was your own subconscious speaking. Releasing your aggression towards me. Because I know you're angry with me. You wish I'd tell you that you're wonderful, when really you're just learning. You're an amateur. I can't believe this of you." She breathed fast through her nose, wiped her powdery face. "Blackie—though he *isn't saying so*" (her eyes blazed hotly at him) "also has some doubts. He does.

Where should Flora Hewett find a goat? Not even one but two? It's crazy. It's something *you* made up."

In the stillness left by his love's outburst, Blackie carefully explained that he himself was not sure what he felt. "Eva, listen." He looked sideways at Fontanella as if he feared that she would strike him. But he had to tell the truth. "I don't think you *could* have made this up." Fontanella threw her hands up in the air, then, boiling, crossed her arms over her black lace-covered chest and stared at him. Blackie did his best. To Eva, he said, "We each have some books at home, you know, describing rituals and things, of people far away. I'd like to consult these." He also, he said, knew an anthropologist in Leicester, an Africanist, he thought, who specialized in native cults and witchcraft. He would telephone today. "I'm sure that Nella," Blackie said, voice soft, eyeing his love carefully, "will be patient for a little while, with *me*." Fontanella blinked at him. "Generous, old soul that she is," he said, reaching for her hand, "while I do a little research."

Fontanella, though she did not agree with him, was soothed by his sweet voice and his gesture. She did not take his hand, but her next words were more measured. "If Flora Hewett calls you, Eva, you tell her in no uncertain terms that she must not try anything herself. She must wait until next Thursday. And you yourself must *not* try to contact her. You should leave her alone. Pretend that nothing happened." Here Blackie agreed. "If it turns out that this really was a djinn, my dear," he said, "then I—with Nella's help—will try to contact him next week. This Sheikh Abdul Aziz. When we have more information."

Eva listened. But, as clearly as she knew the teacups in her cupboard and the records on the shelf, she knew this: she had not made it up. It did not matter what had come, or who had brought the news. She had *not* put on an Arab voice, a man's voice, consciously. She had in her own free mind never once imagined slaughtering a goat. A brain was a strange thing for sure. But was it *that* peculiar, without some interference from a force outside oneself?

But there was also something else. What a fuss over something she had done! It made Eva feel chosen, for the first time in her life. If Flora called on her, and even if she didn't, if ordinary, helpless, unintuitive old Flora needed Eva's help, she would give it to her. "Look, Fontanella, Blackie," Eva said. "And you, too, Susan, though I don't know what you think of this at all, I need to be alone, if you don't mind." She rose and reached for Fontanella's cup. "If you've had enough to drink—and Fontanella, you should take the biscuits home—you'll show yourselves out?"

Although Susan Darling stood up first, because she did not need to be told twice, once up on her feet she paused. She passed a hand across her face, and, as if checking it for something, drew a slow thumb down her nose. Eva, puzzled, studied her. Blackie, too, was watching. Perhaps she'd not heard a single word they'd said. She steadied herself at the windowsill and then looked at them all and blinked. And next was pulling out a Walkman from a Guatemalan bag, already heading for the door. As Fontanella turned to ask where she was going, Blackie said, "I'm disappointed in you, Eva. You might be kinder to our Nella. She's a fragile soul, you know." When Eva didn't answer, Blackie sighed. He took her hand and squeezed it in his fist, not caring if he hurt her. "You mustn't think this is any kind of game. You'll *wait*. Promise us, promise us you'll do exactly as we said."

A Talk Near the Well

To Flora, Eva Bright, bathed and dressed in blue, a light scent of balsam on her, that heavy fringe in place above her ordinary face, with its plain and midsized nose and those steady, unobjectionable gray eyes, looked wonderful. "I'm so glad you got my call."

Flora didn't want to talk inside the house, not where George could hear. She pulled Eva towards her and motioned towards the back. The hallway smelled of lemon, bleach. Flora's head turned as they went by the bedroom. Eva looked at the closed door, the sheen of polish on old wood, the doorknob's porcelain shine. "He's very sharp, you know. It's not as if his mind were gone. He hears nearly everything." Flora paused, made a fist and dug her hand into the pocket of her housedress. "That's one thing that's no different." Eva nodded at her, knowing that she didn't understand, exactly, but to show that she did want to.

In the garden, Flora pointed to the plum tree. "That's where it happened, where George fell." Eva noted the dark fruits on the ground, some rotting already, gutted by the birds. Higher in the foliage, unripe plums still dangled, sunlit, yellow, bluish in the air. Flora waited for her by the round stone well, leaned lightly on the edge. "We do have one, you see." A well! Eva hadn't known. Stepping forward, she felt something, a kind of quiet awe. She leaned against the well's high edge and looked into the water. Far off, low, Eva saw the sky, reflected in a cameo, a cloud. The distance made her dizzy. "Come, let's sit," said Flora. Around them, the cobbles gave at their periphery to flower beds: echinacea, chamomile, creeping blue petunias, violet clematis. *Old man's beard,* thought Eva. Flora motioned to the bench.

Eva began softly. "Was it awful for you yesterday?" She touched Flora's arm, then pulled her hand away as lightly as she'd placed it. "I don't plan these things, you know." Flora didn't look at her. She fiddled with the housecoat's hem. "I know how it works, Miss Bright. I'm a regular, you know," she said. Eva smiled at her. "Of course you are, Flora. I know that. It's only that I'm sorry it all happened so fast. I wish I could have stopped it, slowed it down somehow." Eva pursed her lips, wished again that she were more experienced, and said slowly, "Fontanella said you were terribly upset."

Flora didn't answer. She was remembering herself, how still, how heavy she had felt. "I was, I suppose. Yes. Who wouldn't be?" She nudged a fallen plum with the tip of her brown shoe and looked beyond the flower beds at the untidy expanse. How did all the others feel, the members of the Thursday Club who *did* get messages, some even once a week, who had *relationships* with shades? They would know, thought Flora, how one should proceed. They made a habit of these things. But no, perhaps they wouldn't have any wisdom for her. Flora's message was the first to come from such a stranger, from a force that was not human, from a person—if one spoke that way of spirits of the sea—one had never known. "It's a . . ." she searched a moment, mouthing the word once before she spoke it. "Djinn, is it?"

Eva looked up into the plum tree and farther out into the sky, which was pale and close, a powdery, brisk blue. "Yes," she said. She felt wistful suddenly. "From Africa. But I haven't any news. He hasn't," Eva said, "come back." An inky fruit snapped from its twig, landing perfectly in the far lake of the well with a tiny distant pop. Down the lane, a door slammed. "Flora, look, I have to tell you this," said Eva. "Fontanella. And Blackie—Maxwell Black, I mean—they think that you should wait another week. Fontanella thinks I made the whole thing up." (*That I've got something against her,* Eva almost said, but she thought better of it. Flora didn't need to hear it. And this wasn't about Eva, or about the others. This was about *George.*) She went on. "And Blackie isn't sure, really, what that spirit was, and he thinks we should know first. He'd like to do some research. Then he wants to try to speak to it again, himself, have an explanation. Would you like to wait?"

Flora's hair, in perfect, heavy, yellowed waves of wax, shimmered in the light. Her mouth fell slightly open. She was listening to something in herself. Her heart hurt. She wished to save her husband, and she'd do anything at all, get that tea from China and do headstands if she must. "Miss Bright, George is doing badly. The doctors aren't a help. I don't want to wait. Whatever the thing wants. Whatever the thing says. Goats or diamonds, I don't care." She stopped. She caught herself, as if surprised by her own certainty and ready to disown it. "That is—if you think it's all right."

Eva took Flora's hand in hers. "I do think it's all right, Flora.

Yes, I really do." She stroked Flora's crooked fingers. "Listen to me, Flora." Flora's pale eyes widened. She planted both feet firmly on the ground as if to brace herself, for anything. Eva spoke then evenly and gently. "Flora, I believe in this. I am going to help you get what Sheikh Abdul has asked for. We'll do it together. We'll try it, as you say. We're going to see it through."

Hearing Eva Bright's commitment, that Eva didn't think her mad, Flora told her everything. What she'd seen while it happened, how a transparent panel showing George had hovered in her eyes. That George *had* been to Africa, had been there in the War. That it wasn't as far out as everyone had said. What if he *had* been touched by something there and it had come to help him? People *were* touched by all kinds of things, surely Eva could feel ghosts when she entered clients' homes, surely Eva sensed that the ordinary world everybody saw wasn't all there was. How different could Sheikh Abdul be from a shade? Did it really matter? "I don't know," said Eva. "Maybe not at all." Flora rubbed her feet against the flagstones, a busy, rushing sound.

"My George," Flora said. Her eyes were dry, her tired face was clear. Eva asked, "He makes you happy, then?" Flora looked at Eva in surprise, as if all husbands made their wives so. Then she nodded slowly. "Oh," she said. "You haven't ever had one. You don't know what it's like, do you?" Eva shook her head. A leaf from the high plum tree wafted down and onto Flora's shoulder. Flora plucked it up, examined it a moment, then let it drop on to the ground. "I do so want him back.

"I do wish, sometimes, or I used to," Flora said, "that he'd say more things to me, that he'd ask how I was feeling, you know, those kinds of things that women like and men find hard to do. As if they were just looking at the outside parts of you, not really looking *in*." Flora looked down at herself as though there were a window at her ribs; she laughed at herself then, as if at a child. "But he's been good to me, you know. A rudder. A strong man can be that for you, a good presence." Eva cocked her head, as if the very word "presence" might call a being up. Releasing her companion's hand, she said, "You'd be lonesome without him, wouldn't you?" Flora shook her fingers out into the air, as if casting bad things off. Her words were like a warning. "Yes, I would, indeed."

Susan Stakes a Claim

Susan Darling was Fontanella's newest protégée, the favorite. Shy and awkward but remarkably determined, Susan had, just three months before, gone to Fontanella's cottage and asked for an audition. She'd begun her demonstration by touching Fontanella's mantel photographs and telling her, without any clues, who the people were, and what they meant in Fontanella's life. Other adepts could do that, of course, it was not extraordinary. *That* someone could learn. But she had also located, without Fontanella telling her that she'd been seeking it for months, the purple powder puff that belonged in Fontanella's dressing room but which, oblivious, she had kept in hand when she went out into the parlor to the telephone; the puff had fallen from her fingers down behind the bookshelf. "Purple," Susan Darling had intoned, fingers at the books. "I sense lost purple here." Fontanella was amazed. "What?" she said, and then, delighted, smitten, "I've never seen the like." Susan Darling only smiled.

She was further talented in ways that none of them had ever come across: she did not simply locate wayward things, but engaged in the discovery of unsuspected objects that *wanted,* she would quietly insist, to be with so-and-so, that *needed* to be owned by someone who had, until Susan Darling told them so, never thought of owning such a thing, or (this happened often too) exclaimed that they had always thought they *did* want just that thing, but they had never seen it in real life, only in their dreams, how *did* Susan know?

In art school, Susan specialized in wood-block prints and etchings, which Eva thought was apt—all that digging in the corners, scraping, poking with thin tools; how different was that from biting one's own fingernails, or scraping wax from tabletops, which Susan, twitching, always seemed to do? She was reputed to be talented. "Quite the artist," Fontanella often said, too proudly, as if Susan's skills were hers. When she said it, Susan blushed and fluttered, smiled a low, sweet smile.

It made Eva uncomfortable, to witness that odd friendship, and it made her, though she hadn't really spelled it out, think less of Susan Darling, who appeared to take Fontanella's views so seriously, and next make them her own. She was so pretty and so young—there was also that. If Eva did see her in town—at the boardwalk or the market, coming from the library, Susan was usually accompanied by other students in their twenties, a gleeful, agitated bunch, among whom Susan stood out like an alien fairy. So admired and artistic, Susan would surely not have time, thought Eva, for plain and solid serious women like herself, in walking shoes and combs. And so when Susan rang the bell, Eva—who had just finished the dishes, was thinking of her overcoat, which would likely be too hot, and of Hassan's Take-Aways—was surprised.

Before Eva could speak, Susan asked, in a low voice, "You're not going out, are you?" Eva thought at first that Susan had been sent to check on her. "And what if I am?" she said. She was not a person who spoke harshly. But there was something afoot, a new anxiety that had risen too close to her skin. "Blackie sent you, I suppose? I expect you'll give *Nella* a report." She saw Susan cringe, but she would not take it back. She let her words hang in the air—Susan standing on the walk, one ankle curled around the other, one knee bent, her head lolling to the side, hand reaching blindly for the lintel as if she might be blown off by the wind, and Eva, dish towel at her hip, sleeves rolled up above her sturdy elbows, angry. Susan tried again. "No, Eva. You mustn't think so. No." Eva leaned against the doorjamb, watching her, trying to get a fix on why the girl had come.

Susan closed her eyes. Her hair—so blond that it was nearly white, the sort of color children have but are intended, aren't they, to grow out of—fell forward in two screens on either side of a violent, perfect, middle part. She was breathing through her nose. Was humming, nearly, then whispering to herself. "No, no." Eva watched her. "Susan," she said. "Susan!" Susan didn't answer. *What on earth does this girl want?* Eva had nearly lost all patience with her when the tortured buzzing stopped and Susan raised her head. And when she did so, Eva saw the girl in a new light. There was such an openness in Susan's face, a shine to it, such clean tears in her eyes, that Eva was quite taken aback. "Susan!" Eva said, more softly, and moved towards her. "What's happening to you? Hey, are you all right?"

Susan set both feet on the floor and let her hands drop slowly to her sides, no longer weird and wobbling, rather, very straight and ready, like an arrow or a flute. "Oh, yes," she said. "I am." She looked Eva in the face and, unhesitatingly at last, loosed her fine bell voice. She said: "I don't believe that you have played a trick. I don't think you are ill. I don't agree with Nella. I don't want to hurt her feelings, but I'm not on her side with this. I was right there, too. I saw you. I heard Sheikh Abdul Aziz. And I would like to help."

With a look around them to both sides of the street, a scan for Fontanella, Eva pulled the girl deftly inside and took her up the stairs. She gave Susan a drink of water and asked that she explain. "I don't quite know," said Susan. Here she smiled a bit at Eva over the thick rim of the glass, and with the sea behind her, the way the light shone on all that ashen hair, Eva thought, as everybody did upon looking again, and close, that Susan Darling was astonishing and beautifully fragile. She was very young. She did not warrant Eva's harshness. And her words, in a strange way Eva recognized, made a lot of sense.

She didn't know exactly what she meant, she said. She only had a feeling. "And I know that I'm not given to, you know, *feelings* in the same way you and Nella are—" Eva wished the girl would stop shortening Fontanella's name, it made her think of Blackie and The Medium (*Maxanella!*), pasted in a kiss. Susan sensed it in her: "*Fontanella,* I mean, Eva. Anyway, I don't have access to the future, not in terms of what somebody should do, or what is going to happen. And I generally don't have feelings that are to do with people. Or with people's stories—as *Fonta*nella does, you know, when she senses that not everything is right, or that some man has cheated on his wife, or is so attached to her and frightened that he can't let her move on." Eva hadn't ever heard Susan talk so much, or so plainly, except behind the mediums' table, when she was at work. Outside of the Thursday Club, she'd thought of Susan, it was true, as *Fontanella's rabbit*. And yet here she was, voluble and eloquent, speaking clearly in her kitchen. She went on. "All my feelings have to do with *things*. So I'm not sure why I'm having this one, except that maybe I'm about to find something, or some *thing* will find me. But I am. It's been coming on since Thursday. Since—" Susan did pause then. "Since you—since Sheikh Abdul—asked Flora for *rose water*."

Eva refilled Susan's glass. For a slight girl who didn't seem to exercise, Susan drank a lot. *Perhaps she's like a plant,* Eva thought, and the idea made her smile. She also thought, *Rose water.* Susan had much more to say. "I know rose water isn't hard to find, so of course that isn't it. But there was something there. And what happens to me when I'm about to find something for someone is that I get a sort of headache, here." She lifted a wan hand to the center of her forehead, where her straight nose began. "It got better here, this morning, and at first I didn't think much of it. But it came back when I left, and it got worse at home, and later on at Nella's—Fontanella's—the pain kept getting stronger, horrid, which it only does if I'm in the wrong place."

Susan looked at Eva as though surely she'd already understood. "And so, I had to leave, you see. I knew I shouldn't be there. So I left. And I walked and walked around, and I went down to the water because that can clear my mind sometimes, and the pain got softer then, more like a dull throb, which is just as it should be—the water's quite near *you*—and then it led me here. I'm here now. That ache is altogether gone now. And I wanted you to know."

Eva was aware of thinking that Susan had some courage. Was admirable, even. What did they have but feelings, after all? What else did mediums go on? Their work did have rules, of course, and guidelines, ways of being done. But in the end they couldn't ever *prove* that they were working with the truth, the kind of fact that can be captured with a ruler or a gauge, or trapped inside a jar. Her own feelings about Sheikh Abdul Aziz—that he had torn into her body, made her mouth taste strange, and that she had no choice but to do his will—well, these were hard to justify, unless a person simply trusted in herself. And this—what she had thought was not possible for Susan, who seemed simply to follow Fontanella and do whatever Blackie said—was precisely what the girl had done. Followed, so to speak, her nose. And shown up on her doorstep. "George Hewett *has* spent time in Africa," said Eva quietly. Susan smiled. "Well then. That makes it even better, doesn't it. Like it's really *meant*."

Eva asked, "You're not worried about this Sheikh Abdul being a djinn? Two thousand years old, I think he said. That isn't troublesome to you?" Susan shook her head. "It isn't. Who are we to say what's out there? Spirits, forces, goblin? Phantoms? We don't know anything at all." Eva was almost convinced.

But she did have to check. "You really haven't come to spy?" This hurt Susan's feelings, Eva saw it—the recoil, the biting at her lip. "I haven't come to spy," the girl said very quietly. "George *has* been to Africa. And there's a swelling in my head. I'm here because of this." She gestured to her brow. Eva liked the firmness in her voice. "Yes. All right," she said, and Susan looked so pleased that Eva touched her arm and left her hand there, on the thin girl's cool, soft skin.

George Hewett in Africa

Hitler's war, they called it in those parts, as if no one else were in it. But if by war was meant the crush and broil of battle, heat and flies and blood, then George had not exactly been to war. If asked, which he was less and less these days, since men his age tended to stay home and the young people didn't really care, George agreed that he had "fought in Africa." He would then make a face that told inquirers that he had said enough. *Ah, he saw great battles,* they would think. *He shot men dead cold.* And they could easily imagine that the kinds of stories he might have would be too hard to hear. *El Alamein,* they thought, confused. *The Rufiji Delta.* Perhaps even *Gallipoli.* Pleased—for that was what he wanted—George would say no more. But the real truth of it was that he had not fought even once. War, for George, had been a lot like a vacation. He did have a rifle, yes, which he carried with him sometimes on his rounds, and which he cleaned and loaded at the drills, and yes, he'd had a uniform. Which suited him. But that uniform had not once been drenched in blood or guts, he'd not fired his rifle even in the air, or at any living thing, and he'd seen no wound caused by a cannon or a bomb. What *had* George Hewett done?

Garrisoned on the coast, right beside the sea (that Indian Ocean, yes, where Sheikh Abdul was from!), George Alexander Hewett had had the calmest and most pleasant, the most free, time of his life. His duties principally consisted of keeping track of Greek and Polish prisoners, making sure they left, or stayed, ration cards in order. He did not travel far or wide at all. He did not take hard rides in a tank, did not see a grenade. He spent three fat, wonderful, phantasmagoric years in what, when he allowed himself to think of it, had been something like heaven. How wonderful it was. He was young, handsome, and more far away from home than he had ever thought he could be. And this place! These places! Unbelievable, to him, how different from his own. The ocean was a lighter blue than any he had swum in as a boy, clean and clear and filled with colored fish. The fish! He'd always liked his seafood—and out there, well, there were fish he'd never had before, and squid, and octopi, tiny orange shrimp the length of a boy's eyelash.

He had not been interested in local lore, not either in the language, which (even taking pride in his refusal) he had stubbornly not learned. Seeking out, instead, the broadsheets from the army, the dear BBC, he'd barely thought about the local news. Of the natives, George did not ask any questions. He was not the sort to truck with them, the narrow men who plied the others with hot weed or offered boys and girls and women in the narrow streets and alleys. He'd never either gone into a local home to sample homemade foods, nor spent any time inside a smoky, street-side shack. He'd not formed any friendships. And he had not really wished to. That whole world had been far beyond his ken. But it had surely dazzled him. George Hewett, from a well-fed, comfortable distance, had principally observed.

How watching all the people had been fun! From the balconies of office buildings, from the ramparts of the fort, from a corner in a square: how they moved, how they bore loads on their heads instead of in their arms, how they flicked their wrists into the air and made sharp cracking sounds, how on the sidewalk women transformed tight and furry wads of kapok into smooth, soft mattress stuffing, how little girls and boys, and even sometimes men, could climb up tall papaya trees with just their feet and string. Such interesting variety. He had been amazed at the colors of the natives' skins, how dark they were compared to him, even with his tan—ruddy, dark-haired George, whose mother had one summer said he looked just like an Indian. He was nothing, he thought, like them. Some of them, he'd seen, were purplish! Others a warm brown so like the bark of pine trees that in some lights they seemed almost green! Still others like shoe polish—some black, some tan, others more like oxblood, and then still other shades which were like nuts of various kinds. Oh, he'd liked to see them move! It was a pleasure he had also felt once, when, on a visit to a distant camp to count the refugees, they had passed through the savannah.

Elephants and rhinos, warthogs, waterbucks, impalas, the giraffes, the dik-diks, and the hippos! So amazing in their way. Other men had shot at them, taken trophies home. Other men had laughed about their kills, had taken a wild joy from it, had likened Africans to animals. George hadn't been like that. There'd been nothing wrong with his behavior. What harm was there in looking? What harm was there in simply looking at the world, if a person did not touch it? Such a simple joy. He'd felt very like a king. He spent three years swimming, eating, resting on his balcony, and feasting his hot eyes. When he left, so he might recall that sweetness, he'd bought souvenirs. The chest, the spears, the model dhow, the velvet. Though they'd not be enough, he knew, would not do it justice. On the boat back home, that long and stuffy journey back to ordinary seas that looked like soot and junk, back to a world where he might really be required, where he would have to speak and ask and get all kinds of things wrong, George Alexander Hewett had felt a wrenching in his heart, a silent creeping fear. A lovely chapter closed. And he'd been right to be afraid: he'd never felt that way again.

Flora, dear, ignorant, amenable, unobtrusive, reassuring Flora, did not treat him like a king. Did not parade before him, or amaze him. She washed his shirts and ironed them and mended things for him; she cooked for him and kissed him on the cheek and asked him how he was and he'd found comfort in her limbs. But that had meant involvement, soothing her odd doubts, fixing things for her, telling her where he was going whenever he went out. It was not bad, not irksome, he did know that. But it was not the same. How, when he allowed himself to think of it—that sea! those sights!—he did, really, miss it.

Had he ever, passing by the shore, tripped the heart of living man or djinn? Well, no one knew for sure. And if George knew what had happened, he was not able to say. From his bed, he'd certainly gone somewhere else, had lain there in deep silence. But what he'd seen or felt, he was, still mute, keeping to himself.

Fontanella

Eva's telephone rang three times that night. Fontanella called her twice, worried, aptly, it turned out, that Eva might have taken matters into her own hands. Blackie had called once, when Nella had despaired, and said, "You try, Max, my love. The girl listens to *you*." But there had been no answer. They tried Susan Darling's next, where there was also no reply, but Fontanella was not so worried about that. "Dancing with her friends," she said, "or somewhere making *art*." Nella did sound wistful, so Blackie entertained her by putting on her tango records and holding out his arms. They danced. Fontanella kissed him. And while Fontanella trucked with Maxwell Black in the cottage's back room and told herself to forget all about Sheikh Abdul Aziz, a well-planned partial meeting of the Thursday Club took place quite without her at Flora Hewett's house.

Flora Taking Charge

Eva had not expected Flora's parlor to remind her of the function room, but Flora, on her own, had taken steps to make the space feel special. She'd made sandwiches for them, cucumber on day-old buttered white, and set the tray on the piano, by the window. Beside it, a new cake. She'd brought a green cloth out—not heavy, forest velvet, as Fontanella's was, but still, a cotton sheet that she had draped over the sofa. "I thought," she said to Eva, "that it shouldn't feel exactly like my home." Flora's thin voice dwindled, and Eva understood that although she was working very hard at being cheerful, it was also difficult for her.

Flora, it was true, was gambling. What if it didn't work? Much better to allow herself to think, *It wasn't in my house, it wasn't in the parlor that we planned to do these things.* They were in it together, yes, but it wasn't Eva's husband, glazed and withering in the dark room down the hall. "You thought right," said Eva. She explained that Susan would be coming, and Flora laughed, a little giddy. "All right. If you think so, Miss Bright. We're in no position, are we, to discount someone's *feeling?*" Eva smiled at her.

Susan was dropped off by a young man on a motorbike. They saw it from the window, fey, lithe Susan raising a long leg over the seat and wobbling for a moment in the drive, looking gravely up at Flora's house as though it were a hospital where she had come to carry out a visit. Flora worried for a moment about Susan's companion. He had a fuzzy, unkempt bush of bright red hair, red even in this twilight. His long-sleeved periwinkle shirt was fluid, lacy at the cuffs, nearly like a blouse. "You don't think he'll come in?" she said to Eva. "I wouldn't like a man here, I don't think." She caught herself. "Except for George, of course. And"—she laughed again, a tinny, brittle sound—"your Sheikh Abdul Aziz."

As Susan righted the back strap of a sandal with a finger, one knee bent, lifting up her foot, the boy stretched from his seat and offered her a kiss. Susan, Eva was impressed to see, was not having any. She slapped the air behind her, shooing the boy off, and, steady on her feet now, came up to the house. Her clear, smooth voice rang out. "Wait for me!" she shouted. "Down the road, not here." The boy shook his head at her as though giving up on something, threw kisses with his hands, backed out into the street. The buzz and drumming of his motor sounded out as Flora got the door. "Susan," Flora said, a little doubtful still. But Susan smiled at Flora brightly, thanked her for allowing her to be there, and then—this pleased Flora most, relieved her of her doubts—went, very naturally, happily, straight to the piano, where she said, "Oh, cake! I'm always hungry for it!" and lifted up a big piece to her mouth.

And so the three began. Eva, setting down the sandwich she had taken, thought, *Sheikh Abdul, if you can see us, if you're here, please try to steer us right.* They prepared to make a list. Flora said she knew of a good jeweler in a neighboring town, open on the weekend. If someone—Eva?—could agree to check on George and make sure he was all right, she would like to go, to find the silver ring. "I'm supposed to wear it, aren't I? I'm assuming it will stay with . . . us. Afterwards, I mean." She was refusing to imagine that there would not *be* an "us," if George did not pull through. "So it's right that I should get it?" Though Eva silently sought the spirit's help, when no news came she did think, yes, that Flora ought to get the ring. With a look at Susan to make sure Susan felt all right about it, too, Eva said, "Yes, do."

Eva spoke up next. There was a market on the docks, Gitanjalee's, she thought, where spices sat in sacks and colored paintings of bright deities dolled up the grim walls. She would like, if it was all right with the others, to go there for the rose water, unless Susan thought *she* should. Susan, for her part, was listening to her own forehead for guidance. "That's fine, too," she said. "I'm not here for that one." Flora nodded, though wasn't sure what Susan meant. "That's just so, dear," she said, because it helped her to agree. Eva patted Flora's thigh. She knew now, as if something in her mind had cleared without her notice, what these things were for. "The rose water, I believe, is to be sprinkled on the ground out there. You know, around the plum tree and the well." Eva gestured vaguely to the back end of the house. To Susan she explained, "That's where George fell ill, you see." And Susan, wrinkling her eyes, said, very seriously, "I remember. Sheikh Abdul *did* mention the well."

Flora said, "Of course." On the list they made together, Eva wrote their names beside the objects they had claimed. "Blue cloths," she said. "Who wants to do that?" Flora brought her hand up, like a child responding to a teacher. "I'll do it," she said. "I'm to—I'm to *wear* them, aren't I?" Eva nodded. Perhaps Sheikh Abdul *had* come to her somehow, though she felt her usual self. "Yes," she said. "That's right." Eva looked at Susan and gestured with her pencil to her nose. "Susan?" Susan shook her head. "Not that either, no." Her eyes were focused on the list in Eva's lap. "Well," said Eva. "We've nearly got it all." Flora frowned. She plucked a loose thread from her hem. Eva sat still for a moment. The hardest thing—and they all knew it—the hardest thing was next.

Eva coughed. She gave Sheikh Abdul a chance to twist her

tendons, flood into her mouth or head. She rolled her eyes back for a moment, in the way that Blackie did when making ready for a text. She breathed in through her nose and shook her wrists about. Something in her chest unclenched and balled up, unclenched itself again. Then nothing. If he *had* come, he was gone. "We have to talk about it," Eva said. "If we're going to do this thing. Flora?" Flora had begun to pull out other threads from her own skirt, her fingers flexing sharply, pinching, snapping up and back. Eva drummed the pencil on her knee. "We have to talk about the goats." Flora shook her head.

"Flora?" Susan, without stopping to think—generously—slid from her place on the sofa and came to crouch at Flora's knee. She placed both her hands on Flora's twitching ones. "Flora?" Eva waited. She knew it would be hard. "Yes," Flora said at last. "I know." She'd do anything, she told herself. Anything to help her George. And she'd killed chickens as a girl. She'd seen sheep and pigs done, too. *Anything,* she thought. Even kill a goat. But it wasn't easy thinking of it. Not easy at all. "I can do it, yes. I'll do it if I have to." She would need, she thought, an awfully good knife.

Flora's hands slowed beneath the calming influence of Susan's stroking thumb. Susan, like a girl beside her mother, laid her head on Flora's dimpled knee. Her hair fell loose across it, caught up, a white fire, in the glow of Flora's old brass lamps. "Shh . . ." she said. Something in the sound made Eva look up sharply, study the girl's face. "Shh," she said again. Flora, too, was watching Susan Darling. Susan's eyes shut very tight. She lifted her pale hands from Flora's speckled ones and brought them to her cheeks. Her fingers kneaded lightly at the domes of her shut lids, then, in one swift motion—which startled Flora, rather—wrapped one arm around Flora's thick, soft legs, as if clutching for support. She seemed now to be humming lightly, breathing with marked force—the way she had at Eva's doorstep, the very way, thought Eva, Fontanella did when she wished to concentrate. Flora looked embarrassed, awkward.

At last Susan sat up. She moved onto her knees, and, very quickly, sweetly, kissed Flora on the cheek. "That's it," she said. She granted them a bright, very wonderful girl-smile and slipped her fingers gratefully across her butterfly tattoo, as if it had helped her. Then she squeezed her nose and held it at the bridge. Her eyebrows rose and fell in a slow stretch. "Yes, that's it. I'm in charge of those. The goats. Please leave that up to me." Giddy, sure, Susan seemed transformed. At the sofa beside Eva once again, she looked for just a moment as if she might kiss her, too, but Eva turned her head and made a note on the supply list. She was glad Susan had come. *Goats,* she wrote. And beside that, *Susan D.*

When they left, Susan gave Flora's arm a squeeze and kissed her once more on the brow. Flora touched her hand. "Thank you, dear." The two of them walked out into the twilight, Eva's slow tread thick and measured on the ground, and Susan Darling's, headed for the motorcycle boy, as if her feet were bare, as if she had no feet at all.

Fontanella

In the days that followed, Blackie stayed at Fontanella's cottage to give her his support. Nella was distraught, confused. Did not comb her hair; did not know what to do. She'd left messages for Eva Bright and Susan, and had not heard a word. She had so hoped that Eva would come round, apologize at last, admit that she had made the whole thing up, beg to be forgiven. She'd counted on it. But now she imagined Eva sitting by her answering machine, listening meanly, even laughing. And not hearing from Susan hurt her feelings, too. Didn't Susan love her? Didn't Susan owe her her accession to the Thursday Club's rare ranks?

Blackie knew when Nella needed love. He'd spoken with his expert. And it had turned out that after all there *were* all kinds of beings out in Africa, invisibles who flew, mizimu in the gardens, sheitani out at noon to woo a human spouse, marubamba with hoofed legs, and yes indeed, a tribe of underwater Arab djinn, who often made pronouncements on dry land. These facts, he was told, were well known in the field. The expert had himself assisted at possessions. He'd gone on, but Max had heard enough. Too much information might make him do something that Nella would not like. And so, although he himself was now convinced that there was more to this than met the eye or ear, he kept his thoughts to himself and simply wished the days would pass and that George Hewett, somehow, would get better. He kept Nella supplied with sweet biscuits and hot tea, and sat beside her in the bedroom, where, though he stopped now and then to look over the notes he'd made when he'd talked with that professor, he mostly petted Nella's crumpling face. They were right to worry, be concerned, in any case. There was plenty going on.

Flora on Her Own

Flora woke up beside George the day after the meeting in the parlor feeling somehow new, refreshed. Stronger than she'd been. She'd squeezed George's body to her own and kissed him—as Susan had kissed her—wetly on the brow. "I'm going to fix this, George," she whispered, and, did she imagine it? George smiled in his sleep. At nine, Eva came and Flora walked with her to George's room. "Take care of him," she said. "He won't need much. Just keep those bottles fresh." She put on some lipstick and made certain that her stockings were not rumpled at her knees. Daring, she did not take a sun hat.

It was good for Flora to get out of the house. Apart from the Thursday meetings, and three times to the supermarket, where she bought as many things as she could think of so she wouldn't have to go out again for something stupid—dish soap, toilet paper, flour, something she should have thought of—since George had fallen ill, she had not gone out at all. She'd not visited the library (where she liked the gardening section, and sometimes picked up novels) and she'd not even gone to Church, which she and George had always done together. She didn't want to go to Mass alone. People noticed things like that, especially when a couple was what they thought of as old. "One down, one to go," they'd whisper, or "Poor old Flora Hewett, all alone now." They'd think George was dead. And she couldn't make herself be anywhere that thought would arise. It wasn't true, she told herself. And she was not about to get used to thinking that it might be, that he could leave her any day.

So, having opted to go out of town, to Paliston, where no one knew her, made Flora feel glad. Light. As if (though she felt guilty thinking it, it was such serious business, after all), as if she were giving herself a small treat. She had no trouble locating a place to park. In fact, the curb right before the jeweler's shop was free. This was definitely unusual, and she took it as a sign. She marched into the shop and told the jeweler what she wanted. "A silver ring," she said. "A good one, but a plain one. Silver, that's the most important thing." When she stopped to look at him, the salesman's youth surprised her, nearly still a boy, he was, black-haired, freckled, a sweet blush at his cheeks. Twenty, twenty-one. There was something nice about his manner, as if he liked the jewels he sold, respected people's wishes, and did not try to sell them things they really didn't want. He heard her as she said it. "A right plain one. Let's see."

It didn't take her long to make her choice. She knew full well as she plucked it from the satin-cushioned tray that this ring was nearly like a wedding band, a good thick ring that was supposed to weather things. The kind of ring that one could drop into a drain by accident and recover with a wire without fearing it would keep a telling mark. She thanked the boy, was grateful. He even took the time to snip the thread that held the tiny tag, slipped the chosen ring into a small blue velvet box. *Blue,* she thought. And that made it all the righter.

She found that she was strong enough to want to walk the half mile to the fabric shop. It was warm outside, still that thickness in the air that had come in with the winds on Wednesday last. But Flora didn't mind. She was going to be courageous.

And although George had never said much about those years in Africa, and she couldn't hope to ask him anything until he was speaking up again—if, *when*—she *had* seen some programs on the television set. It was hot in Africa. She'd show George and Sheikh Abdul that she was more than equal to it. To anything they wished.

Later, out of breath but carrying three yards of light blue linen (linen, she had thought, was natural, and fibrous, and expensive, the right kind of cloth for something elemental, as she'd come to think this was), she was nearly ready. She thought of Eva back at home, sitting beside George. She wondered what was happening in the bedroom. She *missed* him. But it was precious being out in the fresh air and under the bright sun. She made one more stop: she saw a chocolate frosted cake behind the window of a tea shop, and went in. She would fortify herself. *Africa,* she thought. *Dark chocolate.* By the time she'd placed her order, Flora knew that part of all this cheerfulness was horror, that she was putting off the return home, to see how Eva'd faired, putting off the wait for Susan's news—goats could not be easy. *God!* thought Flora. *Goats!* Could she really kill one?

Eva Confronts George

It didn't take Eva very long to sense that there was something in the room with George—though she was not sure if she herself had brought it in, or if he had called it up. She had just sat down in the armchair by the bed, just begun to look at him, when her mouth stopped feeling like her own. Unbidden, unexpected, that sharp taste had come back, though it was hotter now. Cloves. What was going to happen?

She looked over at George, narrowed her sharp eyes. Was he really asleep? She could hear him wheezing, could see the stray hairs of his now unruly mustache ruffled by the air. She scooted over, pressed a water bottle up against his arm. At first, the old man didn't stir. But next, he startled her. His head turned, very clearly, with a snap. Eva gasped, jumped back. George Hewett's eyes were open. Open and unblinking. Was he coming to himself, returning? Eva leaned in closer to him and passed her hand near his face. George Hewett didn't blink at all, seemed to look right through her. Eva, her own breath coming fast, thought, *His eyes.* Discolored, this pair was, the whites aged darkly, with occlusions, some the color of burnt onion, trailing at the edge. The irises like pond muck, all opaque. "George?" He did not respond. Eva watched, chest tensed.

It struck her that Flora Hewett's husband looked, indeed, not unlike Fontanella did when she was channeling, or even Blackie just before the pencils darted to the page. Perhaps he even looked like *her,* when she was in the throes. Strange—the postures that in one person signal everything is as it should be, can, in someone else, be exactly wrong. As she watched, her hands began to ache. A tingle started at her fingertips and worked its sparkling way slowly to her elbows. "George," said Eva. She didn't, as a rule, try to open herself up when no one was around. She didn't like that it was true, but she relied on Fontanella, Blackie, someone else who knew how these things worked. What would Fontanella do? "George," she said again, this time loudly, anxious.

Eva Bright was not a person who was easily afraid. She did deal in spirits, after all, she walked in life aware that death was present, that death was just the other side, a different take on things. And she'd come to think that Sheikh Abdul Aziz was just another mystery, another facet of the thing. A spirit, in some fundamental way, just like any other, like herself, like Flora, like Susan Darling's ardent red-haired boy. She was not afraid of Sheikh Abdul Aziz, no, that wasn't it at all. She was amazed to find that what was frightening her was very definitely *in George*. What was it? Was he trying to speak? Did he *see* her? Eva brought her face to his, though this made hers go cold. "George," she said. "Please. Can you hear me? Do you know I'm here?" Her arms continued tingling, she felt a headache coming on, but all over her skull, not a *finder's* ache like Susan's, something harsher and complete. George's pupils shifted then, and he very briefly fixed his eyes upon her, sighed. His air coming from his mouth smelled of marrow and hot dust. He blinked, once, twice. "George?"

Eva found herself now actively desiring Sheikh Abdul Aziz's presence; if he were with her, in her, she might be protected, Eva thought. But from what? From withered old George Hewett? Could that be? Could George, through the force of his own will, have designed this whole affair himself? She was irritated, angered by the thought. "George, is all of this your doing?" Eva asked. She knew her voice was shrill. Eva moved in closer, lifted her hot hand and set it on his shoulder. "George?" The old man's flesh felt stiff, too full for a sick man's, and unyielding.

Eva's head was spinning. *Does he—is he—*this thought would stay with her, despite her wish to be a good force in the world, despite Flora's love for him—*is that even George?* It occurred to her as it never had before that old men could be frightening, even in this state, even weakened, with their good health hemorrhaging away, even on their deathbeds. "Sheikh Abdul Aziz!" she shouted. As she did so, the feeling in her hand returned all at once, and George Hewett's head fell back onto the pillow. Eva's skull felt soft again, familiar. When she looked at him next, George Hewett looked very nearly harmless, ordinary. Old and weak, for sure. Not a man to fear.

Susan's Wondrous Ride

Susan, if excitement meant a journey, physical, to real-live places one had not gone before, had the most interesting time of all. The young man with the motorbike had come to visit her the night before, and, because she thought that he was sweet, because she hoped that she could trust him, she had allowed him—Julian, his name was, which she thought a good name—to kiss her on the mouth. Because the kiss had pleased her (not too much at once, *respectful, even*), she had granted him permission to spend the night sleeping on the floor of her front room, and in the morning, when she still found him nice and good, she asked Julian to take her to the countryside, where she needed, she told him, to find out about goats.

Julian was the sort of boy for whom the stranger a girl was, the less explicable, the more outrageous her requests, the better. He'd already understood by watching Susan from afar that she was such a girl. But this—waking up to slender, white-haired *darling* Susan, dressed already in a wonderful transparent sheath the color of pistachio, strapping on a glossy pair of high-heeled yellow sandals, an intent look in her light eyes, telling him very firmly in that warm, melodious voice that Julian had to help her find a goat or two—was far more wonderful than anything he could have come up with himself. He did not mind the aching in his arms from having slept, so cramped, against the wall; the dust and lint in his dry mouth were nothing. "Sure," he said. "Where do you want to go?" Susan had said, "Never mind, just take me," in such a serious way that Julian, in his mind another kind of taking, felt his heart careen.

He'd had the bike for years. He'd ridden with a girl in tow before, of course he had. But never one like this. He felt almost as if the mystery of his birth, the jagged, mismatched steps he'd taken until now, were suddenly as clear as the bright day. He'd go with her to the moon, he thought, to the hot core of the earth. And so they went, Susan clinging to him on the back of the loud bike, her thin thighs pressing at his hips, but light, just like, Julian thought, her butterfly tattoo. They were on the highway for a while, passing the old factories and car parks, construction sites that seemed somehow abandoned, although surely things were being built; the air held drilling sounds and thunks, the pounding of tough tools. Next, the broad country-side emerged, a wide, dark green expanse, broken here and there by square patches of fawn yellow. Stone walls lined the edges of the fields, bands of poplar trees. A wonderful, low quilt.

When Susan said, "Get off the highway now," Julian did,

and next—and this was thrilling on a good motorbike like his—they were trotting along country lanes, leaning into curves. Though Julian didn't care what Susan was looking for, he'd do anything to find it. It was a delight to feel her tender weight behind him, the long flow of her hair, which darted forward in the wind to mingle with his own red fluff, and—a charming torture—pricked him. Oh! He hoped her hair left welts, all along his jaw. They rode along like this for quite a while, until Julian quite forgot that Susan had a goal. The sun grew high above them, hot and white, and, despite the movement of the air, whipping all around them, they both began to sweat. As far as Julian was concerned, Susan's sweat was liquor.

Suddenly she stopped him. He felt her hands in slaps along his arms on either side, heard her telling him that they had gone too far. "Did you see the sheep back there?" He had, a cluster of them on a slope. "Do you think that there'll be goats? Julian, I think I saw a goat there." Julian didn't think she could have seen it if there was one; they'd been going so fast. "Susan, are you sure?" His questioning annoyed her. "Look, I really do think they have goats up there. Please, Julian. It's important. Do you think you saw a goat?" The more he listened to her, the more Julian thought Susan wonderfully unhinged. "I don't know," he finally said. Then, gently, "Shall we go up and ask?" Her answering smile and the hot squeeze of her hand on his happy, melting shoulder very nearly killed him.

They did go up to ask, or, that is, Julian did. He parked among the weeds beneath a teetering pole and waited for Susan to dismount. Together, they stood a moment near the wire fence, beyond which three generously furred, vaguely golden sheep stood idly in the ragged shade of a modest apple tree. They didn't see a goat.

Susan looked worn out. Julian, however, was not going to give up. Not if finding out whether there *had* ever been a goat here would make Susan Darling grateful. He called, "Hello! Hello!" and kicked purposefully at things, a rusted can, the stones, the root of a low tree, as though the kicks could bring the owner out. Susan walked around him in a circle, hands pressed to her face. They were moving towards the farmhouse (a stone thing, nestled at the bottom of the slope), just beginning to head down—when suddenly she stopped and told him to go on alone.

Her voice broke. "I can't go any further." Julian turned, held out a steadying arm. He didn't mind feeling confused, he thought, about whatever Susan did. "All right," he said. "I'll ask. You want two goats, right?" he checked. "A black one and a white one?" Susan's breath was coming out unevenly, and she'd grown rather red. But she did nod, push his hand away. "Listen, you're sure you'll be all right?" Susan urged him on. "I'll wait right here, Julian. Don't you understand?" He did not, of course. But he was dutiful and determined to please her. He would be her hero. Quickening his steps with several looks over his shoulder to make sure she was still standing, he went on to the farmhouse, where he did find things out.

He was back after a half hour with a canteen of fresh water. He'd found the farmer home, he told her. They'd talked a bit, he'd learned some things, but the news wasn't very good. Susan drank the water greedily, drops of it abobble at her lips and chin. "I knew it wouldn't be," she said. "I knew." She was patting her own brow now, fingers damp with sweat. "It's all wrong, this is. This isn't what I meant."

Julian didn't like to hear her so disheartened. He placed a hand on her thin forearm, cupped her elbow with the other. "It's not wrong," he said. "We just didn't know enough about it." Goats in these parts, he told her as she drank—she seemed only half there, he was not sure she could hear—were mostly golden brown. "Guernseys, mostly," he said, proud of his results. "Some Toggenburgs, about five miles down the road. They don't really come in white, you know, not really. Splattered. Muddy-colored things." He liked to hear himself describing creatures he had never once set eyes on, was imagining already a new series of paintings in just these splattered, dreamed-up, muddy-colored shades. Life-sized, it would be, a gift for Susan at the end of term.

"The only white ones are called Saanens, and according to the farmer—a Mr. Mackey, that's his name—he's not seen one for years." For the black goat, Julian said, now stroking Susan's hair, there was a bit of hope. "Really?" Susan said. She did not believe him. But she wanted to, she did. Why did she feel tricked? She felt blind for having come out here. She didn't understand it. What *was* it, what was she meant to do? Julian was explaining. "Anglo-Nubians, right?" He had a good memory for facts. "That's a mix, this Mr. Mackey said. 'Dual-purpose,' milk and meat. Mixed from Egypt, India, and I think he said Ethiopia. 'Got long ears,' he said. Oh, and this: 'upright and very proud.' They do come in black, 'not infrequently,' he said. Black, right? Susan? Is that what you wanted? He thinks there may be some an hour off. He'll telephone and ask, he said, if you just want him to." Susan was looking off into the distance, violet eyes fixed on the horizon. She bit her lower lip. "Ethiopia is in Africa," she said. "Isn't it?" Julian had to think. "I think so. Yes, I think so, why?" Susan didn't answer. He tried to put his arm around her, but she stopped him, cold, eyes hard. "Don't touch me, Julian, please. I really need to think."

Julian shrugged and shuffled off, slowly. He wasn't going far, just down the lane a bit. Against the fence in a green bush he found a trove of blackberries. He searched for ripe ones, turning now and then to see how Susan was. At last, Susan screwed the cap on the canteen and wiped her mouth with her long sleeve. She came to stand beside him. She'd been crying. "I'm sorry, Julian." He uncupped his hand over her flat palm, filling it with berries. She ate one. "But we've got it all wrong. It was stupid of me. This whole thing, this coming out here, asking you"—she seemed to realize that he had made an effort, and she patted Julian's arm. "Look, you've been really great. Really. I know you've tried to help. But here's the thing," she said. "My nose is hurting me so much! My head! We've got to get away from here. Please, Julian. Please. You've got to take me home." Julian did as he was asked, thinking all the while that this was really love. That he wasn't going to trade her. With a girl as wild, as special as this Susan, Julian told himself, there was no telling what would happen, and ordinary rules just did not apply. Love! It meant being willing to be hurt, trying things and failing, until he understood. But he did want to know. "Susan. What about the goats? I mean, you don't expect to find any in town.

These Nubians are out *there*." He gestured past the farthest trees, far into the west.

Susan, clearly still in pain, did her best to answer him. "Julian," she said, trembling, holding out her hand so he could steady her as she raised a leg over the seat. "I really can't explain. All I've got on my mind now is a bicycle. *A bicycle*." She fixed him sweetly with her wonderfully vague eyes. "Don't you understand?" Susan knew she often gave ordinary people the impression that she had lost her mind. She knew what it was like, the way a person who had started thinking that they liked her could all at once cloud over and move on, disowning any interest they'd felt. She didn't want him to cloud over at all. She had wanted to please him. He'd kissed her nicely, after all, he gave her lifts from school. She would have let him kiss her later, even more, might have let him sleep with one hand on her bed. She would have stroked it in the night, held his fingers to her face, maybe even licked them. But now—she'd put him through so much! "Do you think I'm mad?"

A shadow passed over the sun, and Julian's eyes and face looked dark. He smiled at her and touched his knuckles to her cheek. "Of course not, darling girl," he said. "It's me that's mad." He did put his arm around her then. "I'm crazy for you, Susan, don't you know?" Susan murmured something low into his chest. "This bicycle," said Julian, feeling very brave, "I hope it's built for two."

Flora's Stumble at the Chip Shop

On her way back home, Flora neared the Overlook Café and had an inspiration. The chocolate cake, she knew, had given her a surge of energy. The supplies she'd carried in the shopping bag and which now took up the seat beside her were making her feel strong. Could she trust herself? *Hassan's Take-Aways,* she thought. Weren't the Hassans Muslim? Did they not, like Sheikh Abdul Aziz, believe in Allah and Mohammad? And did not—she had seen this on TV—Muslims often kill their animals at parties, before a fancy barbecue? Did they not quite expertly kill sheep and goats and camels? Could she go to them and get some information?

Her first idea was that the Hassans would naturally know these things and more. But she thought twice: not all people believed in things they couldn't see, after all. Even Muslims might not be ready right away, to believe in unseen spirits. Should she try? She clasped her hands before her mouth and pressed her lips against them, then decided. Yes, why not? She needed something from them. She would ask them, just, if they'd recently slaughtered a goat, and if so, what sort of knife they'd used, and where could Flora get one? What harm could it do? She felt far gone already, a little more, a little, couldn't hurt.

She parked across the street, wondering as she got out of the car and smoothed her blouse and skirt how she would begin. Should she mention Sheikh Abdul? Perhaps he was already known to them? Perhaps the Hassans were related to him—maybe he was their ancestor, in fact, not a djinn at all. Perhaps they should be invited to the Thursday Psychics Club.

But she hadn't ever gone into the Take-Aways, only parked beside it. She did not know what the Hassans looked like. And was Hassan the family name or was there only one, like Jim?

She crossed the street and slowly, steady, walked up to the window. The sun was bright, and she had to hold a hand up, a visor from her forehead to the glass, to see. In the glassy gloom, a slender easel held the laminated menu. Fish and chips, she saw. Kebabs. Were kebabs made of goat meat? Beside the easel, on a doily-covered stool, a clutch of plastic roses, livid pink with candy-yellow hearts, stood tall in a vase. She liked that, roses, even made of plastic. Someone who put roses in the window had to have some sweetness in them, Flora thought, had to care about soft things. Oh, *how* should she begin? Perhaps she ought to ask for them: *Excuse me please, but who put out the flowers?*

In the restaurant, someone moved. She caught a flash of navy blue, a work shirt or a blouse. *All right,* she thought. *I am going to go in.* A cowbell on a leather strap thunked out its hollow ping as she pushed her way inside. It took a moment for her eyes to clear, adjusting to the blanched fluorescent light. "Hello?" A round young woman sat behind the counter, the dark blue was her apron. A textbook, maths, lay before her by the ancient, hulking till. A pencil in her hand. Efficient-looking, well filled out, and smart. Eighteen years, perhaps. Nineteen. Flora thought, *So many young ones in my life!* and she tried to find some strength in her own wisdom and her age. She took a small step forward. The girl looked up. "Yes, may I help you please?" She had watery green eyes that turned down at their outer edges, a high-domed brow and a pugnacious rounded chin, dark hair pulled tight from her forehead in a single, perfect braid. Flora touched the countertop and, apologetic, frowned. "I don't know if you can," she said. The certainty she'd felt outside of the shop, when she had stood across the street and looked up at the sign and thought, *I must,* seeped out, as if from her shoes. What was she doing there? Flora looked down at her feet. "What is it you want, then?" The girl's voice was clipped and sure, not harsh, but businesslike. Not welcoming. Not the sort of Muslim Flora had imagined—though it's true, she hadn't before this imagined one at all.

"Well," said Flora. "I wondered. I was wondering, you see. Wondering about goats." Oh, she must sound absurd. The girl looked hard at Flora. "Goats? We don't have goat here. Beef kebabs and lamb. No goat." Flora felt her face go red. Her hands worked at the short strap of her purse. "No, I mean. I—I don't know what I mean. I wondered about knives." The girl leaned forward on the counter. "Plastic knives along the wall, see? Right there by the napkins. Menu's on the wall," she said. Flora nodded at her. "Yes, I see. But"—she wished the girl would look at her with understanding, something other than that young look she was wearing, of impatience for the old. It was a look she'd seen on other students—on the art students, for example, who'd come into the Overlook because they thought the séances a hoot. This made her think of Susan. Susan wasn't like that, was she? Perhaps if she began again, found some way to explain. The girl continued looking at her, and Flora stood there, foolish, hands now twisting in the air. At last the girl slipped off her chair and disappeared a moment, into a side room. Flora heard her voice, calling someone, a male voice shouting back, "Just wait, yeah?"

The girl's father came out, or Flora thought he was her father. He had green eyes, too, a long nose as she had, and that same heavy chin, though he was lean, looked hard. Perhaps he was her brother. "Yes, madam, what is it you want?" His voice sounded more patient than the girl's, and, Flora thought, perhaps, perhaps she could ask him. Something kind about that mouth. But when she tried to speak, she found that nothing came. "Chips, then?" the man said, moving towards the fryers. "Something for your tea?" He was trying to be helpful. The girl had gone back to her maths. "No," said Flora. "Thank you. It was—I was foolish to have come." Something in what Flora said made the man smile and lean towards her. "Among the blind," he said, "a one-eyed man's a king." The girl looked up and rolled her eyes, as if her father, or perhaps he was her brother, dispensed these kinds of things all day, and she wished that he would stop. But Flora felt forgiven. She felt, almost, that Sheikh Abdul had spoken, was telling her to wait, to leave the Hassans be and wait. His ways would be his own. The proper knife would find her. She'd see what Susan had to say. "A king," she said. "Yes. Thank you." The girl picked up a calculator, and the thin man wiped the counter with a rag. The cowbell's rattle as she left made Flora think of stairwells, of journeys yet to take.

Goats

Susan telephoned to Eva in the evening. "No luck," she said. "No luck yet. But something odd has happened. I can't explain, exactly. You're going to have to trust me." Not much later, Flora called to tell her how she'd fared. The trip to Paliston, the ring, the cloth. Even that she'd had a piece of cake. And when she explained to Eva that she'd also been to Hassan's, Eva's laughter—not unkind, not *at* her, but at the oddities of life when one believed in very nearly every kind of thing—made Flora feel much stronger. Eva said a strange thing then: Susan didn't think that in the end, they were going to need a knife, but she couldn't explain why. Flora, thinking still about one-eyed men and kings, said good night and tried to let it go.

George slept well, through morning, and when Flora went in with a cup of tea, she was able to hold her husband's head up and pour some past his lips. When she replaced the water bottles, he startled her, amazed her, by speaking out her name. A soft, old sound, his endearment. "Flo." Then he was gone again, asleep and murmuring to himself. Flora felt some hope. She thanked him, rubbed his hands and kissed him on the forehead. Later she went out into the garden and looked down into the well.

Eva went out to Gitanjalee's and on her way back home stopped at Flora's to drop off the pint bottle. A cloudy plastic thing with a photographic label: bright, clear roses in a vase. "They even have a gallon jug, I saw! Although," she said, subdued, "we won't, I think, need that much of it." Flora took it from her carefully, as though it were a fragile thing that she might drop and break.

In the morning, Susan, who had let Julian sleep not on the floor beside the bed as she had planned, but next to her, beneath her single sheet, because she'd been distraught and felt that she could do with nice long arms around her, got up and made some coffee. She had work to do for school, and so did he—a set of still lifes, an empty glass in various lights—but neither of them felt prepared quite yet to leave the other's side. They sat together on Susan's orange sofa and made halfhearted sketches, smiled shy into the room, and now and then Julian squeezed her hand or touched her serious face. At three o'clock, things fell into place. Susan's nose began to pound, a sweet pulsing in her head, just as a girl who they both knew, a burly sculptor named Amanda who often went on camping trips alone, came rapping on the window.

Amanda, loud, big-toothed, arms and face and legs haloed in dark down, was upset and in a hurry. She wished to know, did Susan have a pump, because she'd been riding past and noticed that her tire had gone flat. And she had a way to go still, was going on a trip.

The moment Susan heard the words, the dull headache she'd been having fell away at once, so suddenly she gasped, and she felt very hot. Julian, newly worried in his nervous and dramatic way that the girl to whom he'd given his whole heart the night before might even have a brain tumor or some other rare romantic ailment, hurried to her side and asked was she all right. She waved him off. "Let Amanda in!" she said. "It's here. The thing I need is here." Susan held her head, pressed a fist against her nose.

A generous girl with strong arms and good fingers, Amanda

offered Susan a massage. "A head rub, that'll help," she said. But Susan didn't want one. "I feel very well," she said. "Please bring in your bike." Amanda, thinking this meant Susan Darling *did* have just the pump, ran outside with a glad cry and brought the big thing in. "Where is it, then? I've got places to go, you know." They both looked to Susan for an answer, but Susan had receded, a vague look on her face. Those light eyes of hers aflutter, closing, opening, with her gasps. "Susan!" Amanda, brusque, impatient, was not as yielding with her friend as boys tended to be. "Look here, Susie. I need to fix my flat. Where is it?" Susan looked up slowly, drew her eyes along the floor near Amanda's feet, next to Amanda's bicycle, up the tire, darting to the handlebars, then, as if afraid of what she'd see, to the thick neck of the thing. Amanda's bicycle was white. And right there at the top of the front fork, the logo she'd expected. "It's right there," Susan said. "Don't you see it?" She held out her hands to Julian, smiling, pale brow smooth at last. "'Mountain Goat,' it says." It did. A silver, rugged, bilious, thick-horned, unbelievably good goat, poised to climb the world. Susan came towards them, so languid and so happy that Julian nearly swooned and Amanda couldn't sputter at her, and she wrapped them both in her long arms. "Wait till I tell Flora."

It wasn't quite what Eva had expected. But she'd begun to feel that she no longer knew what the best thing was to do, that she was absolutely without rudder or compass. She'd had the thought, in fact, that everything since the previous Thursday was so strange and so unfathomable that it was best to simply go along. She felt *carried,* as though she herself, the woman people knew as Eva Bright, the woman she sometimes spoke to in the mirror, calling herself "Evie," as her mother had once done, was not in charge of anything at all. That morning over her own cup of tea, she'd called lightly for Abdul, as if he'd join her at the table and talk about the weather. At Flora's house she had, for no good reason she could name, determined that the pint bottle of rose water should sit out in the garden, right against the plum tree, until its time had come. And Flora had accepted Eva's judgment without any question.

"Are we mad?" Eva had asked her. She couldn't help it, though she knew she shouldn't let herself be weak in front of Flora, that Flora needed *her*. Flora had looked very steadily at her and said, firm and slow and hard, "No, Eva. We are not. You're doing this with me. We're doing this for George." And Eva had been grateful for what was really a reminder: Flora needed Eva to stay with her, to believe in it, one hundred percent, to see it through, no matter what. And if "no-matter-what" meant listening to Susan Darling, who said the goats they needed had two wheels, thirteen gears, and nuts and bolts for flesh, well, Sheikh Abdul Aziz had never had flesh either—and wasn't *he* about?

Preparations

On Monday morning, Flora went down to the bank. She no longer cared what people thought. This time she dressed in black. This was serious business, and she would look as grave, as solemn, as she needed to. The dress was one that George had liked, with a low neck and pearl buttons, a collar with gray piping. She put on a black hat, a pillbox one she'd kept from her young days, and stockings, and black shoes.

Outside, that spell of heat not spent, the air was still too warm, but Flora didn't mind. Sweating in her finery made her feel everything more keenly—the discomfort, the excitement, and all of her desire to have her husband back. At the bank, she did not stop to stand under the fans. She went right up to the desk and withdrew the needed funds. It didn't matter how expensive the bikes were. She was doing it for George. When she had thought of buying goats, she had known that they would not be cheap. Livestock was important. Livestock could give milk and meat, and the females could have babies. It was right to have to pay a lot.

She met Susan at the bike shop. Julian, lank, regretful, hung around the corner. He'd insisted, he'd just had to come. At Flora's doubtful look, Susan said, "It's all right. He's harmless." Once they were out of earshot, Susan added, "He'll even help us, if you want." Flora nodded. She didn't care about him anymore. She was resolute. "Let's go in," she said.

Susan took her arm. "They've got what we need, Flora, they do." Susan had been there since dawn, focusing her mind, making doubly sure, if it was possible, that this was really the right thing. It was, she thought, it was. She knew it. The sensation at her nose was dull, a comfort, a reassuring weight. She felt absolutely right. Perfectly in tune. Through the window, she had seen nearly right away that the cosmos was uniting with her, hugging her to its own vast and sinewy heart. One of each in stock. A white goat and a black one. *The Saanen,* Susan told herself, *is the white one on the left. A little Swiss, just right.* The Anglo-Nubian—*mixed up from Egyptian, Eritrean* (she had double-checked), *and Indian, Jumna Pari, Chitral goats*—*is the dark one to the right,* she'd recited to herself. *Everything, yes, everything's in place.*

The assistant was surprised. Flora, Susan: a weird, unlikely pair, the long unnaturally white girl so very thin one wondered could she even manage a bike's weight, and the big old shapeless woman dressed in formal black—surely she'd not manage the top tube, not in that straight skirt. Did she really mean to ride? But it wasn't often he sold two bikes in a day. "We'll take these," Flora announced. "We'll be paying cash."

Outside, Susan called to Julian. "She was wonderful!" she said. "You were, Flora, you really were. Just great." She kissed Flora on the cheek. Julian relieved Flora of the bicycle she'd managed to wheel out, and Flora saw that Susan had been right to bring him. Boys were good for something. How had she expected to get these to her house? Susan, stronger than she looked, was doing fine with hers, the black one. Julian, big-haired though he was, was remarkably polite. Solicitous, in fact. "If you like, Mrs. Hewett"—she was touched that he didn't call her Flora—"Sue and I can ride these to your house. We'll come this afternoon."

Eva was already waiting on the walk, a box of tools beside her. She too was in black, a short-sleeved blouse and trousers, and it had occurred to her when she caught sight of herself in the mirror that perhaps she'd been a little harsh, dismissing Fontanella's costumes as so much foppish show. Black *was* serious, wasn't it? There was something powerful about it. Unwavering and strong. She got into Flora's car feeling needed, a person with a task. "Let's go," she said. "I'm ready."

The Strangest Afternoon

While Eva, standing in the garden, surveyed the layout of the grass and well and tree, Flora took the aspirin from George's bedside and swallowed two with water. She slipped a lavender pastille into her mouth, then reached out for the mentholated ointment. She eased the mixture from its tube and rubbed it on her hands, her forearms, and her ankles, wiped her hands around her neck. "I've some work to do, my dear," she said, though George was gone from her again, asleep. She squeezed his hand, put the ointment back. Nearly ready now, she kissed her George's face, stroked his smooth old hair. "I'm coming, dear, just wait," she whispered. "I'll be right beside you. You're not finished yet."

At one o'clock, they gathered in the parlor. Flora brought out her blue cloths, and Eva, not quite sure what she was doing, nonetheless wound the sheet three times around Flora's chest and shoulders, leaving room for her arms to come through. Susan had—she'd just known she might need them—three safety pins on her, and these with Eva's help she fixed to Flora's garb so it would not come loose.

While they worked, Julian rolled the bikes into the garden, using the back gate. He propped them up against the tree, the black one's handlebars firmly jammed into the white one's. *Locking horns,* he thought, and shook his head. He waited on the bench for the three women to come out, thinking with each moment that passed that he hoped his life with Susan would be just like this, for years—eventful, wondrous strange.

Eva came out first. She took a great many slow breaths, held her mouth a little open, listening with it for Sheikh Abdul Aziz. Nothing came to her, no taste, no shivers. But she felt deeply calm and right. She told Julian to move aside please, could he stand close to the house? She plucked the pint bottle from its nest among the tree roots and twisted off the cap. Standing balanced on both feet, heart centered, she peeled the padded silver foil off from the mouth and waited for a moment, then began to walk a circle, round the plum tree to the other side of the stone well and round again, dribbling as she went. The smell of rose water was light and soapy. Sweet.

At the bicycles, Eva paused a moment. Should she sprinkle them as well? Why not? The liquid formed bright beads against the chrome. She found herself standing in the very middle of the circle she had made, an unseen, perfumed ring. She dabbed water on her face, her elbows, and her wrists, and then she called for Susan. Susan gave Julian a smile and raised her fingers to her lips for him, sent them forwards in the air so that her little kiss would reach; then walked steadily, as if on good, thick, muscled legs instead of gliding, floating as she often did, to brave, strong Eva Bright. Eva dabbed her, too. Next, Flora, who had come out of the house, sailed out towards them, wonderful in blue. The perfume mingled with her ointment. "That's right," Flora said, looking at them all. "That's it." She took their hands in hers. "You'll let me do it, won't you? All alone?" Eva kissed her on the cheek. "Of course, she said. Sheikh Abdul asked for you."

∞

It took all afternoon. Flora Hewett, hunkered at the plum tree, took the bicycles apart with the tools from Eva's box. She worked on both of them at once, starting with the Nubian, moving to the Swiss, and back again, so neither would feel slighted. *You will come apart together,* Flora thought, *as equals.* She started with the fork in front, loosening the hub clamps, locating the nuts, then pulling out the tires. She then moved to the back. She pried the tires off the wheels and laid them one atop the other, four black, nubby circles, which she pushed towards the well. She plucked off the front bolts, then worked on the rear cage, then moved back to the front. She struggled with the toe clips, then the pedals.

She was hot in her blue outfit, the black dress underneath. Her skin itched and tingled, her tight hair thickened and went damp all along her skull. Her pillbox hat fell off, tumbled towards the daisies. Flora plucked it up and put it on again. She worked slowly, carefully. She would not stop to rest.

It grew difficult, towards the end. Her fingers were on fire. Her knees hurt. The chains came loose with a clang, and Flora, suddenly upset, threw these towards the base of the plum tree. She was angry, angry, beneath that somber calm. It wasn't fair losing a husband, and she wasn't ready to. She wasn't going to, she thought. She *wasn't.* She hadn't come this far, been ogled at last week's Thursday Club as if she'd lost her mind or brought a bad thing on herself, consulted with a djinn, gone out to the jeweler's, and made a great fool of herself at Hassan's Take-Aways, to stop this thing in midstream. She was going to finish it. She'd do it if it killed her.

Eva, watching beside Susan (Julian, wisely sensing that this was not his to behold had long before slipped into the house), wondered if she ought to help. The sun was setting. Flora's hands were shaking. Now and then she pressed a fist into her hip as if to keep her legs in. "Can she do this by herself?" Susan wasn't sure, but she thought that they should let her. "If it gets too hard," she said, "we can ask if she needs help." But Flora heard them, and their words upset her further. She *did not want* anybody's help. Wrench in hand, red-faced, her blue cloths loosening around her, she turned to them and shouted, fierce as they had never seen her. "This is *mine* to do," she said. "The spirit asked for *me*. I'm doing this for George, for me, for George and me. So George will come through this. You will leave me be." She took a huge breath, one great gulp, turned away, and she started to work faster. Her sloping shoulders quaked, her arms. "Shall we go inside, you think?" Susan asked. "I'd like a drink of water." Eva nodded at her. "You go on, then. I'll wait here for her. Poor Flora."

Inside, Susan went to Julian and let him hold her hand. He could see that she was thirsty and he poured some water for her, thinking as he did so that his Susan—if she'd let him call her that, he would have to ask—was something like a flower. *Like a rose,* he thought.

They listened as the telephone rang out and the answering machine clicked. It was Fontanella. "Flora dear! Flora, I do hope you'll come on Thursday. We're going to try again, you know. We're going to work this out. Blackie's got some *infor-mation* for you. Flora, are you there? Oh, Flora! I haven't heard from Eva Bright, have you? Flora! Flora? Don't do this alone." Susan closed her eyes and leaned back into Julian. She did like how he smelled. Like good earth, a little bit like sky.

Eva kept her eyes on Flora, and, bit by bit, something seemed to happen. Flora's sobs subsided. She stood looking at the bikes, their parts strewn all around her. Eva thought, *Yes, breathe, Flora, that's right.* And as she did so, she could feel a tingle at her toes. The next came to her unbidden and it was a surprise: *You are strong, my love,* she thought. She had never once referred to any clients as "my love," as if she and they were bound together by a sturdy, tender care. But it occurred to her, genuinely and purely, that she really did love Flora. That she really hoped, oh, yes, that George Hewett would get better, that he'd rise out of his bed and hold his wife or move the furniture or take a broom to the front steps, whatever husbands did. No matter what she'd thought of George when he had risen up and frightened her, when he'd stared blankly with those discolored, yellow eyes. Whatever he had done in Africa or not, whether he'd been followed by a djinn through all these years, or had brought it all himself, from some cruel place within him, as a joke on his own wife. Whether he was mad, or simply feeble, very much his own mysterious, ordinary self.

As the sun grew dim and the bloated seaside sky went fat with evening blue, Eva found that *she* herself, *she,* Eva, wanted this to work, and she felt aware, as well, that *this* wanting was hers, not Sheikh Abdul Aziz's, and that made her feel strong. She didn't know if Sheikh Abdul was with them. If he had simply come to tease them and then disappeared for good. If he'd ever come at all. But she didn't think it mattered, suddenly, although she knew that for a woman who dealt primarily in ghosts and who had long believed in what she did—had never thought of hobgoblins or sylphs—not minding was strange. All she could do was this: she willed her words to Flora, harder. *You can do this, dear. It's only yours to do.* All the strength she had, she tried without moving an inch to send to Flora Hewett's limbs.

Flora moved painfully about. She did not stop until the two big bicycles, their makeshift mountain goats, had come perfectly apart. She began to sift through their tough rubble, determining an order. Then she moved the pieces from their piles beneath the tree into the flagstone circle. One by one, she hefted them into the air and dropped them down the well. The chain sang as it went. The tires blubbered. The bolts went soundlessly. The top bars were larger, a bit awkward, but she sent them down with a great shove and a cry. Her pace was even, sure. The handlebars, both sets of them at once, were last. They rattled, grazed the stone inside, before striking the black water—a far crashing, like the coming of a sea. When she had finished, Flora looked down at her hands. They were nicked and bruised and splashed. Blood on her right thumb. The ring. She looked down at it and sighed, then brought her left hand up and kissed the spirit's jewel. Shucking leaves and grass, she adjusted the blue cloths and straightened her black hat.

And next she turned, came carefully towards Eva. "That's it, then," she said. Eva watched her, didn't speak. Flora said, "I'd like you all to go now." The tears were sticky on her cheeks, pink traces of face powder gathered at the creases of her mouth. Her nose and eyes were red, but she looked steady, firm. Alert. All pearl buttons buttoned. Eva nodded. She waved at Susan through the window. Julian, a red blur, turned towards the front door. "Thank you." Flora raised her hand, those twisted fingers, her sharp bones, a glint of silver light. Behind her, no plums fell. The primroses were closed. "It's time now," Flora said. "I'm going to see George."

Theft

There and then not there, the bus came like a prowler through the not quite dawn's thick fog. It—Jahazi Coastal Seven—bobbed a bit, coasted on, and rolled into a bare, wide space under a shattered lamppost at the edge of the old bus grounds. Beneath the mist: a wide expanse, droppings, litter, shards. Other things unseen. The world so dim and cold. Ezra, thinking of the uncle and the house, of comforts and of things he knew he had, advised the passengers to stay in their chill seats. "Not safe, out there. Sleep, now. Stay, please." He was half-hidden by the dark.

But for the few who knew their way, felt brave, and had nothing to carry, the travelers, hard to see in that night gray (seven of them, eight?), remained. Four of them were strangers to this place; they did not understand a thing, but did as they were told. The others, not as raw, knew Ezra was right. "At six. At six you can get out." Ezra settled in the aisle. Sharp face hidden in the crook of a thin elbow, he lay on a jute bag near the driver and the steps. With his fingertips but without moving otherwise, eyes closed, he pulled the cuffs of his white shirt—the only light, close thing that most of them could see—over his curled fists; a sleep gesture, receding from the world and turning in. The driver, sleek and thickset Iffat, since the last stop in the darkness more silent than a stone, seemed already asleep. Iffat breathed but shallowly, lids an unshut seam. He had—if Ezra'd only caught it!—the air of a performer. The others did as they were told, dozed fitful for an hour.

Four rows down and to the right, Lucy, unused to travel without guides, twitching and alert and not as rugged as she had been when she'd agreed to getting on (hours back, nearly a whole day!), knotted and unknotted her thin hands. Her skin itched. She felt soiled. Her dry eyes would not close. She pressed her face against the window and saw the world beyond it brownish, greenish, bruised, purple at the heart. Through the panes—plastic, mostly, to replace good glass that had broken long ago—she could vaguely see the ticket stands, cargo boxes tipped up on their sides, locked and double-locked against the city's temperamental night. Farther out, the dimly moving shapes of watchmen, stiff and sore, stretching necks and arms; even farther, shifting and ablur, a few daring, careless seekers, poking, shuffling in the bins. (The words *night crawler* appeared. *Crawler-crawler-crawler,* Lucy thought, then stopped.) Beneath the awkwardness of it, how she felt exposed though no one cared to look at her, beneath the chafing and the way her very scalp hurt, she was proud of having booked her journey back to the big city for the airport, without help from the hotel. (That manager who had betrayed her!) *But when was daylight in these parts?*

It was hard moving alone. The landscapes, so refreshing to consider when a person has a room and key and knows there will be breakfast, had on the road seemed altogether different. And they were: pale earth followed by gray rocks, mounds of them like eggs, tinged pink at the cheeks; later the red soil, a climb, a steep and sudden fall, thick pine forests and green valleys; eventually the darkness, which was liquid, more black and more glassy and more hollow than a dream's. No longer that light coast, the sweep of sand and sea, the palms; the low hotel, its rooms facing the beach, doors opening on bright green tile and sand.

Lucy had not known how hard the bus would be, how many people could get on in one thick and shifting wave and push one to the side, even if a passenger had paid for a whole seat and had a ticket stub to show. A ticket stub was nothing. She'd been glad when, well before the city's heart, most of them had left; in the emptiness she'd thought a calm might settle on her. But the air, which she'd desired, was also bloated from the night. She could feel each follicle along her legs, the joints inside her skin, as though they, too, had swelled to fill a void. She wished the mist would clear.

At six, the day was pearly and aglow, at last, as promised, coming right. The mist, thin curls dying in the light, broke nearly all at once; the first crows cawed and clacked. Burly Iffat woke—as if he hadn't been asleep at all—and stood up like a shot. He cast the passengers a darting look, bent to pull the handle, watched the door come free. He nudged Ezra—Ezra, who'd really, deeply been asleep—with his heavy shoe, then jumped. His landing on the ground out there—spryer than his shape—was thick and sharp, a complete sound, ballast dropping hard. From below, on earth, he said, "Ezra, weh. You handle this for me, right? I'll be back." He had something to do. If Ezra could just get the luggage down and help these last ones off. "Nothing to it." Going to protect himself, finish up a deal, he was, but Ezra couldn't know.

Iffat's wild dog smile showed a missing tooth, the creases at his eyes. The dawn light through the pinpricks in the concha of his ears showed white, a dot of day on each side of his head. The dots moved with his smiling. That smile, the blades of light (Ezra didn't like it), made him get up fast. "All right. No problem," Ezra said, and Iffat, leading with his chin, lifted up his head to say yes you know your place and that is very good. Like a cheeky man who jumps from bed while a dreaming lover lolls, he slapped his hand against the flank of the old bus, and then was on his way.

Lucy saw him—Iffat—right his woolen cap and, before rounding the corner, stop to check his watch. Over a big shoulder, he looked quickly back, at them, the bus. Observant in her way, Lucy thought: *he's strong, he knows where he's going.* She had the vague idea that she would like to move about the world like that, slapping things good-bye and striding off, just so. *Taking,* Lucy thought, *precisely what he wants.*

Ezra, standing at the head, suddenly their leader, rubbed his skull with both his hands, scratched his narrow throat and that flat chest beneath the collar of his shirt. "All right, all right, it's morning now," he said, to let the sleepers know. "Welcome to the city! That's right, you've arrived." Lucy didn't need to be told twice that it was time to touch the ground. She was aching to. The clammy air. The way the leather of the seat was sucking at her skin, even through the cotton dress. Something bit her ankle. Her joints cracked as she rose. The local passengers pushed forward while the strangers, Lucy and the other three, made ready with their awkward feet to step into the aisle.

Ezra dropped to earth himself before the passengers streamed out. Poor Ezra. Bus touts, ticket boys (though he was a man, of course, or about to become so), oughtn't have to deal with such a shock and stir. He slipped the key into the luggage lock, turned the shiny handle, and lifted up the door. And felt his heart shoot to his shoes and up again, racing past his eyeballs to the far sky of his head. Alone in that big space, one green banana rolled. Tufts of nylon string come loose from someone's stolen pack. The luggage hold was empty. Around Ezra, the locals who had landed, too, made sharp sounds in their throats. Then there was a shout.

Lucy moved into the aisle and started down the steps because the big white man who had sat not far behind her (head cocked, lizard-eyed) had said, "Ladies first" just there. *He's sweating,* Lucy thought with a quick glance, then, unsteady on her legs, found herself outside. The other passengers agog, upset. *What's happened?* After those first cries, a roar. A show of fists. Hard voices. One man, bright, long-sleeved in a red shirt, brown trousers so well starched their creases had not felt the trip, stood, feet spread, threatening Ezra, yelling for the driver. Another in a city suit—poisonous dust-pink, Kaunda-style, neat pockets up and down—smacked the air and shook his head in warning; the woman, old and wrinkled, bent over in black cloths, said the word "police." The two men reeled and wound, hands out towards the hold: that emptiness! They slapped at the bus, too, but not as Iffat had; they slapped those flanks as if they'd like to roll it on its side and turn it on its head, smacking a fool's face to have that fool make sense.

Lucy felt the white man, corpulent and damp, suddenly impatient, hurtle down behind her. She landed in a hurry, pressed herself behind the open door. The other strangers, two long boys—beards on their young chins, red bites, scratches, on their knuckles and their knees—stepped out, a little ginger, sure, but braver than she was. They took up a position farther out, to see what they could see.

A jarring of the bus-skin, human spine on metal. Thump. Thick scratch and smoke of sand when a body falls upon it. Red Shirt and Kaunda knocked stunned Ezra down and held him to the ground. Red Shirt knelt towards him, elbows in his chest; the other one, Kaunda, standing tall, from his regal heights stepped on Ezra's leg. Beneath a glossy wingtip, Ezra's knee twitched hard. "You did this!" they said. "We trust you with our things and this is what you do? Thief! Thief!" Ezra jerked and snapped. *Like a fish,* thought Lucy, cool, something frozen in her; she did not even gasp. The woman egged them on. Red Shirt dug an elbow under Ezra's ribs and punched the bus tout's sorry face. From above, still standing, Kaunda kicked his side. Ezra crumpled, flailed, was not ready to fight back. A murmur: "I didn't know, I didn't know." Another punch—Ezra's lower lip split, and the blood brought on a pause. Curious and put out, the big white man appeared between them. "Now just a minute, here," he said, and because Ezra's mouth was streaming and the man was thick and white and wider than them all, they paused to look at him. "You don't understand," one said.

The white man blinked and frowned, was about to speak. From Ezra's place, the intervener's chest (pale blouse vast and pasted to his flesh, a rumpled linen suit) looked like the high sides of a mountain, and his face like a red fruit—a mango, purple at the cheeks and at the curve of his bald head—pate agleam with the same light that had streamed through Iffat's ears. Ezra didn't move. Would this one kick him, too? He could sense the white man's feet, how big they were, the brown snout of his shoe.

Before the stranger could respond, decide what he would do—he'd said, again, "Now just a minute, here"—the old woman, who had watched and cheered the punching on, veered around, called out, "Jamani, there he is! He's come with the police!" Ezra was aware of a black flash, the woman in her cloths ajump, this way and then that. She was shouting, she'd had produce down there, fruit, things that she could sell, and what had this man done, this stupid, stupid man? She'd tell everyone, everyone, that's right. What else was she to do? Ezra's view, between their twitching feet: Iffat, playing a mean part, with an officer, a copper man in tow.

The untried passengers, new and unaccustomed, felt a dart of hope: a copper! *The driver has come back. This matter may be righted.* But the locals understood. No order, justice, here at all. Iffat, shaking his thick head like a person who is baffled. The copper at his side, short sleeves neatly pressed. That paunch! Remarkable, thick avocado nut still lodged in a half, those bright thighs, plump, beaming like a well-fed homing bird's, the buttocks that could be distinguished even from the front, outer edges of a bulbous moon on either side of the short legs—oh, they understood his walk. That mean slapping of heels. And most of all: the sunshades.

See how carefully this copper has decided on the glasses. Why wear sunshades at all, so early in the day? Ask yourself:

who wears them? Lean men tinged in gold with pistols in their pants, gangsters in the films—America! hot dreams!—men with aeroplanes to fly, extravagant new suits, and men, yes, just like this. The two perfect silver pools, revealing nothing of his eyes, showed themselves instead: these seven people round the struggling ticket boy, the flattened tout, that Ezra. Where two eyes should have been they saw their own horrid huddle, shrinking, swelling in the lenses, tiny, warped, upset, and that vision did this work: *Here you are, you eight, thinking how enormous is your loss, but you are minute after all, right here in my eyes.* Bad enough, indeed. And yet another tell. Why, like a perfume, a loathsome titter in the air? How was it that the sound of them was laughter, though both their mouths were closed? *In. On. It. In on it.* The two of them. The driver and the copper. What was there to say?

Before they got too close, the locals took their chance. They knew how this worked. No need to give their names. Make things worse, it would, make them future prey. They knew: the theft had happened long ago, perhaps hours before when in the blackness they had gotten out to pee or eat, and others sleeping still. Not everybody's bags, just these, these aimed for the last stop. They'd go.

Kaunda, who'd kicked Ezra so hard, gave the boy a weighing look, and saw then one more thing, which made him sorry for the blow: Ezra was an innocent. Ezra hadn't known. He bent and pulled the bus tout by the elbow, leaned him up against the bus, then spat onto the ground. No culprit, this, an idiot, bleeding like a hen. "You get out of this," Kaunda said. "You're working for a thief." He took the wrinkled woman's arm. "Let's go, Ma, there's nothing to be had here. Let it go, let it go like wind."

While the copper, who was close now, said, "Jamani, what's the hurry? What's been going on here?" the locals headed off. "We're fine, sir. Fine. No problem." Another bus theft, oh. And while it was much worse for them all because their things were more precious, it was also, if in only a small way, better: there was the awful tang of having lost their things for sure, and then the steam released of having turned their anger on the boy, and then the kick of how they'd all been had. But then, and then, because the mist *had* really lifted firmly now and there could be porridge somewhere, maybe, and still some loved ones living, and they did know their way, there was also this hard and mitigating thing: a laugh. A laugh at those four white ones who didn't know how this worked at all.

Ezra coughed, one hand at his side against the lip of the black hold. The man whose face was like a mango gave him a sharp look as if to say, *Stay there,* then sputtered at the officer, "Who's responsible for this, my man? An outrage!" To Iffat. "You call this a business? What am I to do?" To the awful pair. "Where can we complain?" The policeman gave him space: he was allowed to collar Iffat. There was a game to play.

In her other life, in Philadelphia, in America, which was very far away, Lucy helped to run a shop. An experienced service girl, she was good at looking blank, at maintaining a still face no matter what went on behind. The noise had been a trial. *Are they hitting him?* she'd thought, and then, because she was self-absorbed, could always feel her insides like a house, or ship, its struts and pillars more demanding than anything outside her: *My holiday, that it should end like this!* The big man seemed aboil. His heavy face, ruddy from the start, was flushed. A down of sweat clung to his mottled jaw. Beads flew. A look that Lucy did not like passed over his face. She tried thinking of her suitcase, which she understood was gone, but didn't dare to take the other step—*what was in it*—because she knew exactly what and couldn't face it then. She thought, most loudly, *I mustn't fall apart.*

The other men, a pair, no, *boys,* white, too, languid-limbed and furred, had hair that had not, Lucy thought, been washed in weeks on principle, hair like women's, down their backs in tails, but thin. She thought: *They're balding at the brow.* On the bus she'd eyed them with disdain, was sure that they'd been high. Following their elder's lead, the boys edged in with narrow jackal mouths towards Iffat and the driver. One said, "We need our stuff back, man." The other said, "That's right. They took my guitar."

Ezra's head hurt, that swollen eye on fire. Iffat and the copper. He was not surprised, but his feelings had been trampled. Not a nice thing, not a nice thing this, this stealing from the customers, not good in the least if one hoped to keep one's job. Iffat was not, after all, the boss. The real boss was in this city, not far off, and there was another, that man's brother, in an office by a lake, and another brother on the coast, keeping all ends of these channels sealed, all right, and they were crooks in their own way, or worse, but not like this for all to see in the bus park after dawn. Picking pockets was one thing, was discreet, but this was crazy pride. Ezra thought himself a fairly honest man; alone, he could not have thought it up. But would he have objected? Why didn't Iffat *say,* cut him in, at least? Ezra's mouth: a leak, a line of blood or mucus slid over his chin and down along his throat like ice or boiling oil. In the other stillness that was the blooming of a bruise, his side shook like an engine. He watched. That busy clump of men; and a bit apart from them, not too far from him, the girl, still standing near the bus, a knocking at her knees, her hands at work before her, blinking like a toad. Traveling women like she was were less dangerous than men.

Ezra reached out to the bus flank for support. "I did not know," he said. Lucy didn't want an explanation. She simply wanted this: a room, a bed, and a closed door please, if she could only be alone. But she was briefly interested in him. She'd never seen a man beaten before, not like that, and hadn't he been horribly astir, legs spread in the dust, each breath like a plunge? His swollen eye, the stains on his torn shirt, combined to make him look—this thought was a dart, a quick fish rising and then gone—*ruined and sincere.*

When Lucy was alert, she was: good at spotting shoplifters, gauging how much money someone had to spend, knowing had they come to browse or buy, or to hide from something else. But that was Philadelphia, in Mr. Kershaw's Germantown Boutique on Walnut Street, where she had worked for years, where she knew how things stood. And this was quite another place. She did not know how to take him. Though her eyes were focused on his face, she saw (instead of the high cheeks, sharp nose, long eyes set far apart) the moments of the bus ride in which he had appeared. Had this man not shelved all their bags himself, commenting on which was heavy and which was so worn it might break? Did he not have the key? Was he not a suspect? But had he not also, startling her as she moved through the aisle and reached for balance to his headrest, offered her some baobab fruit and nuts?

Lucy couldn't tell. She did not care at all for the sweating suited man or for his undulating voice, which was thick and serious in the middle of his words but knife-sharp at the edges, and she did not trust the boys. She had, from the first, felt ogled by the driver. As for the pinched, plump officer in shades? Though she herself had never broken any law, she did not for all that have any faith in the police, did not like the thought of *answering to, explaining.* The tout was small, as she was. He'd been beaten, suffering, was not part of the group, and for the moment at a disadvantage. In her own and different way, wasn't she, as well? She wished none of it had happened, that she'd stayed longer on the coast, found another place and were, instead of all of *this,* waking to the heady smell of seaweed. Toast and eggs and tea.

Ezra mustered up his breath and said how lucky they had been, how they might have been held up or perhaps killed, and how some busses were *hijacked* and the travelers dropped off in the wilderness to make their way on foot, if lions did not eat them. His low voice was soft. Beyond them she could see the sky, the buildings, the city rising up. The two tall boys, greasy T-shirts plastered to their chests—*caved in,* Lucy thought, then thought how cold caves were—danced as if on pointed toes. "No, man, no, man. What about our stuff?" It was a chorus now, *our stuff,* unlined faces crumpling, mouths opening again and closing, heads ashake and all their dirty hair with a dull gleam, swaying down their backs. The young one said, again, "They took my guitar!" and the companion slapped his hip to emphasize the awfulness of it; hand like a tambourine. The older man's big chest heaved up and out and down; his fists clenched and unclenched. Iffat made thick soothing sounds. *Everything in my power my good sirs and there will be some forms.*

Ezra understood another thing: at any moment that same officer would turn to him and say, "And what does *this* boy know?" and that would be the end. Ezra, not all that wise to city ways, quite yet, did know what fall guys were. Iffat would remain in charge and Ezra would get fired.

Lucy fingered her own dress, just there by her thigh, and although something was threatening to rise in her, something she'd feel later—shock, an outrage that she did not quite understand—she told herself that it was not so bad. She was gifted, too, at reciting little formulas that sometimes kept her steady. *I still have money with me, and my ticket. I can still go home.* Aware of Ezra at her side, Lucy worked her toes in her flat shoes and saw something at last: those three could plant themselves beside the empty yawning of the luggage hold all morning, saying, *No, man,* and *Preposterous,* all day, and it wouldn't change a thing. Lucy turned to Ezra, quietly, and said, "Excuse me, please. But is there a hotel?"

Ezra pointed at himself; he couldn't put his weight on his two feet without a little help. Could she give a hand? Though the effort cost her—of being in the world at all, and of helping someone (the words *presence of mind* ran through *her* mind like rabbits on a mill)—Lucy pulled him forward, one hand in the bus tout's, the other pressed tight to her belly, where beneath her buttoned dress the money and her papers hung still from a bulky canvas belt. "Hurry, please," he said, although he limped, moved towards her like a broken cart. "This way, follow me." And while the fat man in the linen suit said, "I'll file a complaint," and the two thin boys said, "Yeah," and no one looked to see, the two of them shoved off.

On Railroad Street, as though they had consulted one another and agreed that they would not lay him out flat, Ezra's injuries let up on him a bit. He was able to take stock. His face hurt, but the leaking at his lip had stilled, in its wake a steady pulse. He saw the street before them through one open watering eye. The other like a clamp on the right side of his head. Through tears he could not control and which he wiped at now and then with the soiled sleeve of his shirt, Lucy, next to him, came in and out of focus. She was, by nature, a slow and careful walker. And although his side hurt, and he couldn't move as quickly as he liked, her pace—stilted, one foot before the other as if afraid the pavement would snap back—disheartened him. Though she'd given him a good excuse—*he has not run away but is assisting our poor customer, who has had a serious shock*—he wanted to be rid of her. He had the last house wall to build, the uncle to take care of, other things, a man who made him sweet. There was Iffat to rethink. *My aching side and eye.*

To calm himself, he counted off her traits. Her hair, he thought, was the color of red earth, tied back in a short tail that was thick, might crackle if you touched it, like a brush, or wire. Even through his tears, she was clearly freckled, which disgusted him a bit, but skin couldn't be helped. The fresh blue of her dress, which did not change, no matter how he blinked, did please him. He began to feel, as he did not for the three whom they had left behind, a little sorry for her, though not much. Probably she'd lost, what? a camera, some jewelry. She'd have more of that at home. She couldn't know how lucky. But still. He was not unkind. She was in need of buoying, too. "Come along." He urged her on with the low sweep of a hand. "It's going to be all right."

A sign: "Abuu's Guest and Rest." A white housefront, rising up four stories high, at every floor the drooping leaves of potted plants above a balcony's edge. On the street, the entrance to a stairwell. Lucy looked at Ezra. Sore, he raised his head to show her, tried to lift his arm to point. A cry caught in his nose. He winced. Perhaps a rib was broken. Lucy did not know what to make of Ezra's stopping and his frown—that swollen eye like beef, skin sunlit like a slick—the grunt. The stairwell loomed, green shadow. She felt for the first time specifically afraid. Screaming, she thought, would not help. Her fear showed on her face—a tightening at her narrow mouth, a stiffening in her arms. Ezra felt a patient thing inside him fold and cede to something else. He had a fleeting image of her breasts, which he thought were not large, and in his mind a moment the idea of her belly and her legs rose and left him cold. *There's nothing there,* he thought, and it almost made him laugh. But then he thought she couldn't know he hadn't taken all the luggage, hadn't helped someone in the darkness with the latch. Understanding made him tired. *I don't want you,* Ezra wished to say. *I am not a thief.* He wanted to lie down. "You're here," he said. "That's it." He left her on the steps.

Lucy watched him go. In the street (hot now, dust-filled air glowing with the day) men and women, bicycles and carts, more busses, cars, were hefting into life. The street looked strange to her, not one of her own avenues, with elms and cobblestones and pharmacies and homeless men she knew, bag women with caddies, and not either like the coastal streets, Indian, Arab houses on a seafront, dhows in the far blue. This was something else: the city that she had been told would not be nice for her. She did not want to be out there again, could not have found her way back to the bus stand, much less to a different hotel, alone. She thought about how Mr. Kershaw or one of the girls at the boutique might act. Much brighter, much more capable than she. Helen, touching up her lipstick and showing with a twirl a good bit of her leg: "Into the frying pan!" she'd say. Fiona, who was elaborately gloomy, who liked tarot cards and smoke, would have added, "It isn't in your hands," and sadly ushered her up the shaded stairs, to destiny. She heard Mr. Kershaw, too, explaining that fine girdles like these, standard ones in the old style, could not be had elsewhere, that they came direct from Austria, and that tradition wasn't cheap: "What else can you do?" The beaten man was gone, she could barely see the top of his bent head over the early crowds of people that were filling up the walks, seemed to come from nowhere. "That's it," he had said. She closed her eyes and went.

෭෨

Ezra understood these places: the street-side premises of Jahazi Coastal Travel, the back door to the private office where bus touts went for pay, Iffat's place above the bus stand restaurant (the Zam-Zam, which was always busy), and the walk down Railroad Street, where backpack tourists stayed, and where he'd taken Lucy. And he knew the other bus park, past the railroad yard and clothing market, where people came and went in minivans and pickup trucks from places that were not part of the city. He knew this place and the other, but the town that lay between these few familiar points made him quick and anxious. Whatever Lucy might have thought, the city wasn't his, and was not safe for him. No time to nurse his wounds. No telling what else might befall him if he fell or stumbled here.

Ezra had come out just three years before, and, when he wasn't on the bus, lived on the far edge of a sprawl called Ukilala, along Ujenzi Road—a narrow thing, well graded, Ujenzi Road kept traffic moving to the west, inland. Goods and people crammed and packed and skidding, speeding heedlessly elsewhere. Now and then pedestrians and goats were killed on it because the drivers were in haste. Many chickens died. It wasn't legal building there. People without permits or associates built in Ukilala, because, apart from the fast road, the city didn't care for all that land, its people; it was tricky to police, it didn't really count. Permits were expensive, difficult to get. But, presence being two thirds of a battle now and then, you could begin without one, lay down a foundation, make a home among the trash heaps, wait and see how long it would remain.

The uncle had come in from the countryside after a drought, had sold most of his cows and come out there to build. Once the house was done, he'd bring his wife, the grandchildren, anyone who languished in the village. Ezra'd come with him to help, and together they were making this: a three-room house with a front stoop and a courtyard on the inside, for gathering water in a cistern and for cooking when the girls were safe and sound. The uncle had been thrilled with Ezra. Ezra helped him find things, learned to bargain for cement, where mangroves could be gotten cheap, or, failing that, where fences were not good and where it would be possible to steal a pole or two. The house was good, and very nearly done. The next thing was to finish the far wall, put frames into the windows, and after that, a rope bed for the uncle and his wife to share, and a grass mat for the hallway. Home! *At least there's that,* he thought. The uncle would take care of him, and if not him, the neighbors, Tillat the seamstress, maybe, with her tricky hands, Gideon Juma from the radio shop, or, best of all, perhaps, Habib, his friend who lived next door. *Habib.* He would be all right.

The blood was drying now, and those wet tears had stopped. He grew accustomed to the world seen through one eye: the spaciousness of this part of the city, which was almost an out-skirt, nearly calm, unpeopled, just before the rise. Blue sky unlike the color of the woman's dress, much deeper, opaque with rains to come; house crows, black flecks in the acacias; a flame tree in full bloom. He sensed the other bus stand by the sounds—gun of engines, creaking, slamming, fleet boys, cardboard trays of hard-boiled eggs balanced on their heads, their footsteps in the rubber thongs a rhythmic thudding on the ground, the sharp clapping of coins held loosely in their fists, money calling money; and the shouts: Majengo, Pirika, Hanakitu, Ukilala! Drivers and the bus touts (who did work like his, but whose drivers couldn't steal as Iffat had, because the trips were shorter and the riders magpie-eyed, had less that could be shopped) grumbling, calling out. He saw the colors, too, the painted sides of busses: here, not the cleanly stenciled strokes of paid sign painters who'd studied for just this and could make any word look suited for high trade, but curly washes of wild paint, "God's Best Bus," "Hassan's Happy Line," "Hallelujah Host!," and, Ezra's ride, "Ufakiri Speed." All around, women's bright, fresh dresses, men's brown cowboy hats and patterned shirts, the schoolkids dressed in green. At least his feet were fine. His feet knew where to go.

Ufakiri Speed had just come in, and there was lots of room, most people heading in, not out, at this hour of the day. The driver knew him and he helped him up, said, "I'm so sorry! You be careful now," but didn't ask for more, kept quiet, had seen worse in his day. Ezra, creaking, groaning, too, took a window seat. Once he'd bathed and gotten sorted out, he thought, he'd sit out on the stoop and his uncle would come out to drink coffee, and they'd talk and work things out, look at how things stood. Later he would get a message to Habib. Ezra sighed, the van came into life, and next his grateful ribs and tired chest closed gently round his heart and let him fall asleep.

Upstairs at Abuu's Guest and Rest, Lucy, though her throat felt oddly tight, was conscious of relief at the sight of a big woman. Abuu's wife, wide-browed, round-cheeked, clean, perfumed, alert, was manning the reception. "Hallo, you're welcome!" she called out. Lucy's voice was shrill, unsteady. She managed: "Is there room?" The woman motioned to a set of keys behind her, hanging from a hook among a row of other hooks. She had no trouble telling when a person was unsettled, she was keen that way. Looking steadily at Lucy—because steadiness can spread, from one person to another—she asked for a deposit, which Lucy took a long time to hand over. There was the dress to be unbuttoned, slyly, at her waist, and the search inside the pouch, the crumpled bills, which she could not look at in advance but held balled in her fist as she zipped and buttoned up. The woman took her passport, eyed it, closed it, gave it back. "Lucy," she said, with approval. Her voice was like a balm. "You came on a bus?" Lucy nodded, kept her mouth closed. Aware now of a sharpness in her bowels, a trembling in her throat, she was afraid to say too much. It was the suddenness of things, the fact of luggage disappearing in the night, things taken when you didn't even know. Wasn't it quite *wrong* to think something was safe only to find a gaping when one looked, an empty hold, with *nothing?* "Yes."

The woman dropped the pen she had uncapped and slid down from her stool. She moved slowly, too, but she was large and graceful. Lurching softly, holding her own back, then touching the long counter for a moment, she came around to Lucy's side, made a *tsk* sound with her mouth, and placed a hand on Lucy's elbow. Lucy leaned against it. She saw the empty bus-hold and her vision blurred, tenebrous dots. *What's happening to me?* Lucy's voice was thinning, but she heard herself: "I think I should lie down." She wasn't thinking straight.

She tried to focus on the woman's fine, plump feet moving in their sandals, tried to think, *Bright shoes, that red,* watched the woman's ankles at the hem of her black coat. With the prospect of a room at last, with quiet, with an able woman showing her the way, all the brittleness she'd felt tamped down, *prevented,* at the bus stand was right there in her limbs, a cracking. *It isn't in my hands,* she thought, feeling her heart race. *What else is there to do?*

They walked along the balcony. Lucy, dizzy all at once, looked over the low ledge into the atrium. A bicycle down there, a palm tree in a tin, the cistern and a tap. Cracked basins in a pile. The details steadied her. Down the hall, the woman snapped a padlock down and drew the tongue aside, pushed inwards with her foot. "Number ten," she said. Lucy came towards her. "Your towels." A rough, bleached stack dropped into her hands, a key settled on top. "Just there. Is everything all right?"

Lucy hadn't looked into the room, but it *had* to be all right. "Thank you," Lucy said, meaning it as much as some- one like her could, as someone in her state, thinking first of all, *I am going to sleep.* The woman stood and watched her for a moment, as if about to ask, *Are you sure you are all right,* but Lucy braced herself against the doorframe and said, tight face like a snarl, "Yes, that's all, I think." The woman's face closed then, and she turned back towards her files and countertop, one hand at her back.

Behind the double doors, Lucy-who-had-lost-her-things let her purse fall to the floor, unbuttoned her blue dress, which also fell, covering her feet. She stood very still a moment, in the center of the room. Her hands moved to her head and clutched it, paused, and then, dissatisfied, fluttered off like birds to land, arms crossed, on her shoulders, as if she would hold herself. She couldn't. Shivering and folding slowly at the waist, she felt the belted pouch and tried to loose its clasp, could not. Thought about her ticket, how *yes, yes, it's safe in there,* then gulped and felt her throat close and her lungs constrict and then begin to shake. She tried to think about the things they sold on Walnut Street: brassieres, housedresses in three styles, four kinds of underwear, all decent, girdles, for shapes that really needed them, for back pain, large ones for incontinence, with flaps, and nightgowns, long and buttoned robes in white, in pink and blue. She recited model numbers, *A23, A24, C62, P6,* found that she could not recall which were the sleeved gowns and which the undershirts. She closed her eyes, which—*like that Ezra's,* Lucy thought— were burning. Her hands moved down again then, rubbing at her throat, her bones, finding and then holding on to her small breasts as if she owned nothing else at all, and next she missed her bathing suit as if it were a child, and then was bent over quite in half and felt she couldn't breathe.

When Ezra woke up in the brightness—full day now, not too far from noon—Ufakiri Speed was halfway where he wished it. They'd passed the biscuit factories, the fields where prisoners labored, and the textile markets. They had gone up all the hills. Below them to the right, far beyond the miles of plantain groves and trash heaps, the city sat on a horizon, a blurry, distant clump, so small now that most of it could fit in his one eye. The aching in his side, which had subsided with his sleep, rolled up and came back. It rattled, tapping at his chest and hip like something trying to get out.

He tested out his arm and found it stiff, still sore. He felt a man beside him, a pressure on his other hip that came from the outside. His neighbor turned to him—Ezra caught a narrow plane of dark brown shirt, rolled up at the cuffs, a well-fed arm, plumping near the wrist, in a wobbling periphery the promise of thick thighs. "My friend," the neighbor said, in that way people have of bringing others into conversation, others they don't know. "You are now awake. What happened to *you?*" Ezra groaned, tried to smile, and at his lip a crust of blood cracked and he stopped. "It's nothing," Ezra said. The wrist and hand rose up and curled over the edge of the narrow seat ahead. "I was afraid to sit, when I came in," the man told him. "I thought you were dead."

The driver overheard. Hot laugh in the rearview mirror; he didn't have to turn. "I had to tell him you were sleeping. I told him, 'That one's always fighting, but nothing gets him down.'" It wasn't true at all. But the driver had a fantasy of fighting, liked the kung fu films, wished he could fight better, and admired people who withstood. And it was a kind of joking that made Ezra feel all right, better. He winced, but said, keeping his mouth small, "That's me. A fighter." "No, really, you all right? Are you going to a clinic?" When he said, "Ukilala," the driver and the neighbor shared a look and didn't speak. Ezra wondered if his voice was softer than he heard it. "Just to Ukilala," Ezra said again.

A bead of blood rose in the cracking at this lip, far juice from a dried orange. The neighbor shifted in his seat. In the rearview mirror, Ezra saw the driver shake his head and say, "O-o-ohh!" and the neighbor, softly, said, "I'm so sorry, sorry, I'm so sorry," as if someone had died. The movements of the bus shoved Ezra closer to the window, and he pushed against it with his shoulder. He heard: "Going to see the ruins, eh? See what's left behind?" "Don't tell me you lived there!" Then, because now they could believe he didn't know and saw that they should speak more kindly: "Were you right on the road?" Ezra's swollen face could not show his frown. "I've been on the coast," he said. "Now I'm going home."

The neighbor's silence was a weight. The driver pressed his lips together, tight, though one sharp wayward tooth, longer than the rest and jutting, showed there like a sign. The man in the brown shirt did Ezra a kindness. He turned and brought his shoulders round, pressed against the seat ahead of him, so that Ezra's eye could see his face when he said the next thing. A round face, well fed but not meanly so, not the kind of fat that was an insult or a sign of taking money from the poor. Round eyes set quite close. Eyebrows thick and sparse at once, dark dots in a line. Sweat on a wide nose. "Oh, my friend. Don't say you haven't heard?"

"What's that?" Ezra said, trying to lean in. The neighbor brought his hand down from the seat in front of them and touched Ezra on the arm. "They're widening the road. At dawn, today, you know." He stopped. The driver grew impatient, didn't like the way some people gave bad news in slow bits. "Listen, man. The Caterpillars came," he said. "Chop-chop. Tore the whole place down."

⟳

Before Ezra could think, Ufakiri Speed's left tires fell into a pothole and the bus jumped, veered too close to the edge, and for a moment the fast wheels were caught on the wrong side of the grade. The passengers behind them shouted, cursed the driver's inattention, and told him to do better. He brought them back up with a lurch, a triumph. "For myself, I thank God," he said. "Wide roads. That's what this country needs." He was angry, with the man in brown and his wide face, and with Ezra, who'd come in looking like he couldn't help himself, who'd collapsed in the first seat and gone to sleep so quickly. "Humans are not cows," he said. "*We* know how to suffer." Things were what they were. Poor Ezra.

At Ukilala, the neighbor helped him down, blessed him with a sad and gloomy look, told him to be strong, then went on with his journey. It was hot; the flies were coming out. Ezra felt one at his mouth. His head twitched. Part of him was glad he couldn't see it all. What the neighbor'd said was true. Permits cost too much, permits were denied, the city didn't want these people here. And that meant, every now and then, sometimes here and sometimes there, that bulldozers arrived and without any notice tore people's houses down. This wasn't news to Ezra. Nor to anyone. Operation Whatnot. All over the place. But that it had happened here, right here while he was gone, was another shock. The curbside was a shambles, there was no denying it. He was first of all aware of rubble at his feet, of jagged cement blocks all across the ground. The gouges, gullies in the earth.

The things he'd known at the bus stop—a strip of sand before the houses, where boys sold cigarettes and gum, stands for T-shirts and old shoes, were gone. A sea of broken stuff. Things not crushed—what had once been a wooden table, dry stumps here and there, split off from the top—were torn or cracked, on sides or upside down. Bottles, flour sacks, a broken chair, a crippled goatskin stool, a bright red dress with pleats, through its neck a gallon jug and splintered wooden spoon, shards of broken glass. A woman's yellow dance shoe, buckle loose, the stuffing of a pillow. A portrait of the president, its skewed frame partly covered by a Chinese metal bowl. Dust and rubble. Ruin.

Behind him on Ujenzi Road the cars and trucks whipped by, some busses, throwing up in clouds what had been torn down—the cement dust, the lime! The air tasted like chalk. If trucks could think, they would have had these thoughts: *more room for us, more room.* And it was true. A lot of room for trucks, now. Ezra tried to think: How far had they been from the road? Not as close as this, right? Uncle had insisted on the garden in the front, for the daughters and their girls—who lived for roses, didn't they, and jasmine? Had the space left for the garden been enough to keep the house alive?

He tried remembering with his feet. Here and there he saw things and knew exactly what they were. Along the way, a patch of what had once been Gideon Juma's radio bar: sesame sweets and kwassa, soukkous, kidumbak and taarab tapes, shortwaves, now and then a boom box, players for cassettes. The wooden sign he'd nailed up just below the little shack's tin roof was jutting from the ground (the slats, bright red, green, and gold) from a pile of what had, just the day before—*while Iffat was making plans,* he thought, *while I was counting cash*—been radios: now a mat of black plastic and wires, the glittering of resistors, red, black, yellow beadlets in the sun, a puddle of blue batteries. Tangled audiotape, shining like burnt grass. Gideon, Ezra thought, never left that stand, guarded that equipment with his life—who would want them now? The scavenging, he thought, could not have started yet.

He was struggling to find a clear space for his weight when Tillat the seamstress came to him, from which direction Ezra couldn't tell. But suddenly Tillat was there, holding up a cupboard door, a nice one, nakshi-carved with lotus flowers, bright brass handle at the edge. "Ho! Ezra. Where've you been? Where were you when we fell?" Tillat had been drinking. She was laughing, the three teeth she still had awiggle in her mouth. "Widening the road," she said, "widening the road!" She handed him the cupboard door, and Ezra took it from her, set it down. "The cupboard's gone," she said. "I still have my machine, thank God. But you know what?" Tillat steadied herself on his arm, not noticing his wounds at all. He felt her sour breath and took it in, as if the smell would keep him sharp. "I had three orders in and half paid for pretty curtains. Curtains. I'll never see that other half. For what windows, I ask you?" Ezra didn't speak. He was thinking of the luggage hold, of *this,* of Tillat's cloth, and even about curtains, of the things that happen that a person doesn't know.

Suddenly Tillat was gone from his one eye and Ezra set the door down at his feet and turned to look for her. She was not far away, behind him, holding her wide skirts high above her knees. He could hear her moan. That laughter. Her whimpers troubled him, for his own sake, and hers, too. Tillat was a force, a strong one, clearheaded even when she drank. If old Tillat was whimpering like this, what about the uncle, who was given now and then to dazes, to not responding when one spoke? What about the radio man, whose eyes teared up when the Kudra Birds or Morning Star sang sweet songs about love?

He called out to her. "Where's Gideon Juma gone? Still here?" Tillat laughed, this laugh so hard that she bent over and it sounded like a cough, a private falling down. "Still here? Ho! A part of him remains." She gestured to the ground with a thin arm, then with a wild look in her eye, she shook her wrist at him like a woman showing off a ring. "He left some fingers here, my love. I haven't found them yet." Someone, she said, squeezing the words out, someone—she could not recall exactly who, mind you—had dragged him to the clinic. "He was in here when they came! Drunkard, don't you know." In a sudden billow of hot dust, Ezra couldn't see her.

Standing in the midst of things, Ezra felt some thanks for his own injuries, which were broiling now, pulsing in the heat. Glad his side was hurting. *Pain enough right here,* he thought. Tillat, lifting up one foot and then another, began a dance among the radios. "What about my uncle?" Tillat didn't answer him, was reeling now, pulling up her skirts. Ezra closed his eyes. A barb curled in his stomach just below his ribs and he stopped a moment at a pile of cement moldings, hearts and stars and diamonds, disordered now, but high enough to lean on. His hand closed over them and he had to laugh a little, too. *Here's Habib's new wall.* Graceful Habib Pawpaw, who sold vegetables and fruit—bananas, guavas, coconuts when he had the luck to find them, papayas most of all, and who, a lot of people knew, made real money singing on the other side of town, where he called himself Habiba. Habiba Pawpaw, who made Ezra laugh, who talked to him as though he really liked him, and for whom the uncle only felt disdain. That sweet fruit stand was gone—but that fruit stand, and the square he'd kept free for the nursery he'd planned, had saved his little house. Habib's place was all right.

Ezra turned then towards the uncle's, wishing as he did so that both his eyes were closed. The garden had done something for them, yes. But now it was a pit, and the front half of the new, not yet finished house was gone—not exactly gone, but buckled and reordered, crumpled, not strong and square where it had been; huddled like a pack of just mixed cards or an accordion pressed shut against the inner courtyard wall. The three front rooms were lost. He did not take the time to think about Tillat—to think, *I understand now, I know why she was laughing,* why she was standing on the radios kicking at the wires, why her skirts were high. Ezra couldn't take another step. He started laughing, too, until he couldn't hear the trucks behind him anymore, until his one good eye had closed and tears were streaming from it, real ones now, not simply from disruption of the flesh. He knew that laughing wouldn't help, he knew this and he sniffed, spread his fingers out across his thighs and tried to hold it down. It wasn't funny this, at all. But his laughter rose like a sick thing. He couldn't help himself.

Habib Pawpaw saved him. In a high and lilting voice, like a bird calling from nowhere, Habib, who always said things twice, said, "Ezra, Ezra." That voice was aiming for him. Ezra felt it and was glad, and then Habib was right there next to Ezra, telling him and telling him to stop.

There'd been too much laughing since the morning, stuttered waves from gaping mouths and sneaking up in sudden barks and pops from others who did not think they were afraid, and Habib understood far better than some that even if you learned to shut it off, which you could do, it could take you over any time at all, even after years, and each time it rose up it was much harder to control. "Calm down, calm down," he said. "Basi, now, yes, basi." Ezra, laughing still, opened the one eye. All at once, Habib said: "Stop that or I'll hit you," and Ezra was surprised enough at hearing Habib Pawpaw—so gentle he kept food aside for cats and even gave them names—say he'd hurt someone, that quiet came at once.

He tried to look at him and to believe in what he saw: Habib was not hurt. Both of his hands whole. Feet right there where they should be at the bottom of his legs. A bit of blood on his white gown, not white now but brown. But Habib was neither bent in half nor weeping. His wandering eye still wandered. He was even smiling, and his sweet face, lit partly by the sun, looked almost as it should. "Ezra, Ezra," Habib said again.

He seemed to understand that Ezra was not well—had suffered other things than this, and that this, on top of whatever else it was, had made poor Ezra fragile. Habib moved in close and put his arms around him from behind to hold him up. "Your uncle is with me, with me," he said. Ezra could feel Habib's breath on his shoulder, soft, like cardamom and tea, and the way that Habib held him made Ezra feel as though he'd

been washed up by a wave, that he could rest, at last. Habib said
again, as if in a song (and this made Ezra wish to cry in a clean
way, with relief, instead of this hard laughter), "Your uncle is
all right, all right." Ezra heard *all right, all right,* and when he
let his weight fall back, Habib's sweet mouth crooned into his
ear.

At Abuu's Guest and Rest, although she did not know that that
was what they were, and could not have told the time, Lucy
woke to the powdery and muffled sounds of early afternoon.
A lot had happened while she slept—an entire morning in the
life of the hotel. A city's life, indeed. She'd missed: Abuu, the
woman's husband, stepping out, headed to the market where
he would be shopping for some time and next would sit with
other men like him to drink coffee in glass cups; the arrival of
the girl who did the washing and who cooked, that girl who
was a flirt. Lucy missed the sound of street boys high from
shoe-polish and glue saying hey now would she trade a sniff for
a quick fuck and the girl's loud laughing back. Her thumping
up the steps and next her sweeping all the floors, the scraping
of the brush, shuh-shuh-shuh-shuh-shuh, which Abuu's wife
told her to quiet down because the white guests who slept late
didn't like the sound. Laundry being done, the taps, their rapid
jet of water. The slapping, mossy sound of feet. Just before
eleven, floating on a sea of engine growl and rattle, radio tunes,
the prayer calls; a silence, then the rush-rush-woop of someone
sifting rice. The quiet of a mealtime. At one o'clock, the stores
closed. Taxi drivers stopped to rest if they'd been at it for a
while. The city sounds receded. Abuu took up the front desk

and sent his wife to sleep. The air went thick and slow, slept, too, and into this fat quiet, in the swelling median of a gentle midday pause, Lucy finally woke.

Excepting the thick money belt, which pinched into her waist, Lucy was still bare, and because the sheets had twisted in her legs, when she opened her stiff eyes she saw herself from breast to toes, and that seeing was too much. She winced. She tried to pull the sheet out, bring it back around herself, but it was caught fast at the far end of the mattress. Oh, she didn't like to see herself, just then, when something difficult had happened and she knew she would feel safest in her mind. She wanted no sight of her limbs, and wished, as her head turned, that she could not feel her hair. Her skin was cold. She hid her hands under her head. But such blankness is not easy to secure. Her mouth was dry, she wished to drink. She closed her eyes and made herself sit up. She almost looked, as she had done for two weeks upon waking, for her books, her bath bag, for a dress she would have set over a chair. But the morning's theft, the beating, the hot walk beside the tout, it all came back to her, and she remembered she had nothing. She almost cried again, but—hearing Helen in her head, the brash one, saying, "Just what do you think you're doing?"—didn't. Thought instead, *Stop it, stop it. Now.*

Mr. Kershaw didn't think much of it—he was Catholic, and didn't hold with magic, as he put it—but Fiona always said one's balance could be located through breath. "Our breath!" she liked to say. "The truest thing we have." Lucy tried to breathe as she'd been shown, from the low part of her belly, in and out and out. Fiona said the breath contained the soul, bridged the past and future. Lucy thought about her trip, how long ago it seemed that she had told the girls and Mr. Kershaw that she wanted a real holiday, a place one had to fly to, not the Jersey Shore, Niagara Falls, or Amish country, which she'd all done as a girl, under supervision. That wasn't what she wanted, not the sort of trip where someone else decided what she was to do, and hurried her, and told her to wash up. She was fully grown now, wanted something for herself, a thing she'd never done. "For me," she'd said to Helen. "On my own." Helen had congratulated her and Fiona had behaved as though Lucy were becoming interesting at last. And Mr. Kershaw had been proud.

It had been sweet, and good! She'd felt so brave at the airport! Helen and Fiona had surprised her there, found her just as she was heading to the gate. They'd brought her good luck charms. Helen, bright and laughing ("She's all teeth and bosom," Mr. Kershaw liked to say), had presented her with condoms, red ones wrapped in yellow cellophane and tied with silver string; Fiona brought a vial of bath oil. "Dragon's Blood," the label said, to keep evil at bay. The vial came in a purple velvet sack with a drawstring of gold braid. And they'd brought the nicest thing of all, a gift from Mr. Kershaw: a camera, an Instamatic that was not difficult to use. "He says he wants you to bring pictures." He himself had sworn he'd never fly again. "I am in America," he'd say. "And though it be a dream, in America I'll stay." But he liked to think about the globe; he was looking forward to Lucy coming back and showing them what it had been like. It did make a difference knowing there were people thinking of her while she was away. On the airplane she'd felt strong.

At the distant airport—where the air was yellow, hot, where she had shown her vaccination papers to a clerk before being allowed to cross the line into *another country now* and then moved to claim her luggage—she'd been fetched by a tour guide, a hefty man in spectacles with an impeccably white shirt. He held a sign with her name on it, and, in a moment of excitement, Lucy took out Mr. Kershaw's camera and asked to take his picture. The man (who introduced himself as Jonah, said he had four kids) allowed her to, even smiled for her. She took a picture of the minivan as well, of the writing on its side: "Goliath Tours." She'd been nervous and excited. They drove through the big city, just her and the guide, and she asked him if they'd stop there, if she could have a tour, but he told her that the city wasn't *nice,* and when she asked him why, said, "Not nice for girls like you." He'd slapped at a lone fly that had settled on the steering wheel and added, "Dirty. Criminals and thieves." He'd laughed a bit, smiled at her in the mirror. "Not at all for you. *You* are going on safari."

Oh, she had liked that very much! *The hut!* It looked from the outside like something from a movie or museum, but on the inside there had been a lightbulb and white walls, a cane chair and a desk, a bed with a mosquito net, which had made her feel that she was in a different, distant, and romantic place. In the afternoon, Jonah came to call. With the other guests, they drove out to a riverbank and watched hippos in the sunset. They ate on a big deck, where citronella candles kept the bugs away. Tilapia, she'd been told. And yellow juice called bungo. The other guests had been a blur. She didn't speak with any-one, and didn't want to. *I am with myself,* she thought, and this, coupled with the safety of the tour, the itinerary she had chosen and been granted, gave her a cool and private, precious feeling of achievement. They did other things: *I have seen giraffes* (these had struck her very much, how gentle those beasts looked! one of them reminded her, with its interminable neck, the way its eyes looked painted black, of Fiona, her strange head in the clouds) *and warthogs*. A sodality of lions (these did not look real, too many of them, nestled in a tree and at its base, as if on display, but she snapped the camera anyway, was secretly amazed—perhaps they looked unreal because she'd never seen a real one, didn't know how to compare). The ostriches had also pleased her, galloping—*I didn't know they were so fast!*—and she never saw a single one with its head buried in sand, wondered where that came from. *Ostriches are fierce!* she thought, and this made her stouthearted in the night when bush babies snuck in under the thatch and their wild eyes glowed at her before they shot off with a scream. *Ostrich, riches, riches,* she had thought. How nice that had all been!

And afterwards, the beach, where she had stayed almost a whole week. This sea was unfathomably wonderful, a horizon full of blue she could not have explained to anyone—a blue that made her feel her eyes were drinking, and her heart. She spent hours at a time immobile on the shore feeling *splendor,* though her bathing suit, which had pleased her when she bought it, was not as right as it had been when she'd tried it in the shop. She felt angular and strange in it, too pale, aware of eyes on her when local men and women passed by to sell trinkets. But she did not shrink from them. She bought a string of wooden beads to give to Helen, and, for Fiona, the carved

head of a woman; Helen liked adornment, and Fiona talked
of goddesses and energies, collected Pharaoh's cats. For Mr.
Kershaw she acquired postcards showing what she'd seen, and
some (because he wished, after all, to be informed about the
globe) of places she had chosen not to go—the lake full of fla-
mingos, and the mountains, and a desert that the card called
"Emerald," though she couldn't quite see why. The pictures
she could show them, but the postcards he could keep. She'd
amassed them in a paper sack that had a drawing of an elephant
on it, a huge one, stepping from a tiny map of Africa. Helen's
necklace she had wrapped up with the yellow cellophane (she'd
thrown the condoms out, *What had Helen been thinking?*) and
replaced the Dragon's Blood oil (no baths to take here) with
the woman's head, drawn the gold string tight.

At night, by the light of a Dietz lamp that hissed nicely in
the breeze, she had read two books: a novel about three girls
growing on a farm, their cruel father, and one girl's inconstant
lover, fooling her with that girl's youngest sister; and another
in which a blind man crossed the whole of Europe, touching
everyone he met with all his fingers so he'd remember who
they were. They had not been very special books, but she
had bought them at the airport when she left, after Helen
and Fiona had waved her off and she had crossed the barriers
and had nowhere else to go as she waited for the plane. She
had written her name neatly on the inner side of the front
flaps, and sometimes thought: *These are the books I took with me
to Africa.* A blushing in her chest, a happiness.

It had all gone very well until the final day, which should
not have been her last. She'd come back from a swim, hair

wet, freckled from the sun, to find the manager outside her room, a big couple in tow, a man and a woman from Chicago whose voices were too sharp, and sharpening, and loud. "I'm very sorry, Miss," he said. "But you were to check out today, or not?" She hadn't. No, she hadn't been. She'd made her reservation firm until the following day, when she would be driven by Goliath Tours into the city, directly to the airport, arriving in the evening in time for her flight. She did try to say so, but the couple wouldn't stop, and the manager, who'd seemed so kind at first, who'd seemed *so glad to see her,* suddenly behaved as though he didn't care at all. She'd felt everything inside her stiffen, crack. Afraid. Hadn't she planned right? Hadn't she been perfect? *Reservation. Preservation.*

The manager pulled her into what had been her room and touched her on the arm. "We'll pay for your bus fare, miss. But please. *These* people—they are not on a tour, like you. Full price, you see, I'll get from them. But you, you're no help to me. Please. You understand me, yes?" He'd tried to press some bills into her hand, but these she'd pushed away. She did not like anyone to touch her. Even Helen couldn't, and certainly she always kept three feet away from Mr. Kershaw, who was fat and breathy, and who made her feel too small. Once, Fiona had tried to read her palm, but she had not been able to withstand the probing of strange fingers in the dampness of her hand. The manager gave up at last, tossed the bills onto the bed, and left her, saying, "The van goes to the bus stand in an hour. In one hour. Believe me, you'll be out." Once he'd gone, she'd felt all ashake. She'd packed all of her things—the books, the dresses, the rubber thongs she'd bought for walking on the beach, the presents, the seven rolls of film, and the camera in the purse. She'd tried to smile at these. She kept her passport and her ticket and the money and she tied these to her waist. She pulled herself together. She stopped herself from crying, and she tried believing she'd be all right on her own. *I am with myself,* she'd told herself, over, over, on the way.

When she'd climbed onto the bus, when the grim driver with the beard and narrow eyes said, "You are going to the city?" and the bus tout, who was thin and did not seem unkind, took her case from her and pushed it gently in the hold, she hadn't felt too bad. She'd looked out of the window at the landscapes, and she'd thought about her things, how at least she'd gotten presents and how the moment she got home she'd take the rolls of film down to the pharmacy, and ask for them express. Everything would be all right, and it didn't matter what the manager had done. She heard Fiona saying, "It all happens for a reason," and she stopped trying to find one. Once she found a place to stay, she could wait there until evening and take a taxi to the plane. It couldn't be too hard, she told herself. But it *had* been hard, and wrong. And now at Abuu's Guest and Rest she was alone in a white room, without even a toothbrush—and how dirty her mouth felt!—without any soap or other underwear to use, and it would be the same dress on the plane. *My holiday,* she thought. *See how it turned out.* How terribly unfair things were. To be like this, *with nothing.*

Lucy passed her hands over her face. Aware of her own skin, now clammy, damp, she realized she did not know the time. The only thought, the one thing that kept her, Lucy understood, from screaming, was an image of the airport, and the plane. She would wash her face. She had towels, after all. She would manage all of this, somehow. Crying wouldn't help. She remembered Jonah then, how gentle he had been, and how he would have smiled at her and told her he was sorry for how everything turned out. She got up and put her dress back on. The woman at the counter would have to know how it was done. It couldn't be too hard, not after all this. *A taxi,* Lucy thought. *I'll need to find a taxi.*

Ezra's uncle *was* all right. When the bulldozers had come, he'd been outside for a shit. Their setup wasn't ready yet for that, and he didn't like to do his business too close to the house. He'd been squatting in the bush in the dawn light, distracted by the ants. He could very nearly see them, traveling in a line beside a heap of maize husks and the carcass of a bird. Because his ears were no longer what they'd been, he hadn't heard the sudden cracking sound of it—which was in some ways the worst part, the inexplicable and unpredicted crash and break of things—and although he was soon ready to stand up, he hadn't. Standing up meant a twisting in his knees, hip pain, and he couldn't brave it yet.

A chicken flapped into the trees. He watched it wind and smack its little wings as if it could really fly. While his own house walls were falling down, he thought about this place, the animals that lived here. It wasn't easy knowing what belonged to whom, and the uncle thought the owner would be looking for that chicken, but how like as not a child would steal it and take it home to parents who might look on such a theft as only what was due. And his mind had gone a little blank, then, slow.

Just as Gideon Juma dove for refuge underneath his counter, and the dozer rolled over his hand, just as Tillat ran disheveled and enraged from her own crumbling place, he'd started thinking of the village and his wife and how he missed the kids. He'd forgotten one old village neighbor's name—a big-faced man who had played checkers with great style and had a little yellow dog—and this failure on his part had stopped him. Why could he not recall it? Then, a half name on his tongue, he'd risen very slowly, wishing that a person could know always, all at once, everything they'd loved. No, he had not realized what had taken place until it was all over, when he came back, surprised, to find the house half-gone.

Of course he'd been upset. Of course he'd run towards it, sore legs notwithstanding, gone to look, and he had looked and looked and filled his eyes and for a long, hard moment tried to keep his heart from breaking and his liver from rising up to kill him. It hurt him, yes, of course it did. How hard they had worked! How much money they had spent! Beside this, other people's tiny pains were nothing. He'd sold twenty cows for this, and Ezra, too, had given money for cement, and helped him build the walls. It wasn't good. He wasn't grateful. This *was* no easy thing. But Ezra's uncle was a church man, and a good one, and he understood that things like this did happen. More than this, he was old enough to know that if you just stayed alive, something else could come about to make things a little better, before something altogether different and more awful rose to make you start again. And the quicker you could think so, the better it would be, or you might die from it. You very well might die.

He knew, too, that certain things could force you to be close to people whom you did not like. He did not care at all for Habib Pawpaw. He never had. He felt distaste for men who were like women. They disgusted him, indeed. He did not like his voice. He knew that Habib burned imported incense in his clothes, and that whenever Habib passed, the smell of roses hung thick in the night air; he knew the man kept cats—Aziza and Kitoto—and thought how wasteful that care was. He had no doubt as well that Habib wished to play in Ezra's pants. But he also recognized sometimes, and now, that things like this were nothing in a pinch. He'd turned around and seen Habib Pawpaw come out of his house—which stood, which stood! The young man shaking at the sight of all the rubble, the potted plants that had been crushed, the walls he'd meant for vegetables. And Ezra's uncle had gone over to him, said, "Habib, are you all right?" He was not really without feeling, no, he didn't like the man, but he did not wish him dead. And then he'd said, "Thank God, thank God." And here he did not lie. "It's good to see you whole."

A singer's ears are sharp. Habib heard fallen Gideon first, wailing from the site of his disaster, but they went to him together. It was Ezra's uncle who took Gideon to the clinic, two long miles behind the houses, across a brook and up the steep hill by the slaughterhouse, where goat legs all on end inside of buckets lined the road, and the earth was thick with blood. It wasn't all bad being nearly deaf; he didn't have to hear how Gideon keened over his hand. He didn't have to hear too much of other people shouting, telling what they'd seen. It allowed him to be calm. The clinic halls were overrun, but he left

Gideon there and returned very slowly. The uncle wasn't very old, but he was over sixty, and in the heat and all that dust, and with his brittle knees, four miles was quite a way. When he came back he didn't have the strength to go inside his house and really look at how shattered it all was. You took help where you could get it. Habib's vegetable and plants stand had been crushed. A mess. But the house he kept so neat, which he had painted blue, had not even bruised.

Habib Pawpaw could be very tender and solicitous with men who did not like him. He had invited Ezra's uncle in, and they had shared some tea. Habib did wonder about lineage, how Ezra let a person be themselves, yet his father's brother was so sour. But he knew, too, that neighbors have to help. Ezra's uncle looked done in, and Habib brought out his yellow plastic mat, the finest one, with a pineapple design, and told the man to sleep.

Ezra's uncle did not hear them come in, did not see the blood on Ezra's face and chest, or the way the boy was bent almost in half and could not move his arm. Habib was grateful for the silence. Ezra couldn't know how bad he looked, better he be cleaned before the uncle saw. Habib held on to Ezra's arm and took him to the taps and, while the uncle dreamed, began to care for him.

Habib often thought of men he liked as boys. Boys were cleaner in their hearts than men. Sometimes *he* felt like a boy. How wounded this one was! Ezra murmured softly when Habib plucked the shirt up from his chest, where blood had dried and stuck, and pulled the sleeves down from his arms. Habib poured water over Ezra, made suds with the black soap. When Habib pressed with two long fingers at the crust of Ezra's lip, Ezra winced and pulled away. The courtyard floor went pink. Habib found old cloths in his trunk, cloths he wore at night when he was going as Habiba, and he was glad his house contained some silken women's things. He tore one into strips. As Habib bandaged him, Ezra didn't speak. Habib said, "I've seen worse than this, much worse. You're going to be all right." Ezra mewled a little then, and Habib stroked his ear. Ezra's one eye closed.

Habib gave Ezra his bed. He promised he would find him aspirin, peroxide, if any shops were standing. Singing made you money, Habib thought. Singing gave you cash. He thought about the uncle and wondered if he knew, and this thought made him laugh. Before he left, he stood a moment on the threshold and watched Ezra fall asleep. The swollen eye already seemed much better in the dark, receding like a bloom. Habib would have liked a photograph of Ezra in the bed, but for that kind of picture you couldn't ask a passing photo man, you needed your own camera, and that was beyond dreams. Habib sighed, passed his hand across his chest, and let his fingers linger where he felt his own heart beat. An awful day, it was, for everyone. But things were better when you had people around. Sleeping bodies made the air sweet, so he always thought, showed a place was safe. The uncle, curled up on the mat, and lovely darling Ezra, who would have to heal, and who—here Habib felt tender—might stay there for days.

෨෧

In the evening, Ezra woke and asked Habib to take him out onto the stoop. "I want to see," he said. "I'd like to see what's happened, sitting down." The uncle came out, too, rubbing his sore belly, wondering would there be something to eat. Habib brought out a tray of tangerines, a gray plaid thermos full of tea. "Some for you?" he asked the uncle. And the uncle had to smile, although he didn't want to. *That man-woman!* he thought. But he remembered that you couldn't always tell just who might be an angel in disguise, a test from God to you. Habib had taken care of Ezra, hadn't he, almost like a nurse? Ezra looked all right, except for that one side of his face—fat and rippled like a green tomoko fruit, eyelids tiny like a clam in the middle of the swell. Still bad, yes, but not so broken. He'd ask him in a while what had gone on in the city, who had beaten him. But some questions could wait; Ezra didn't always tell him what was going on. One approached him like a dove. The uncle poured some tea from the cup Habib had given him into the saucer, held it to his lips, and looked into the road. One of Habib's cats came out, Aziza, a spotted rust and white one, thin but very clean.

Ezra's one eye let him watch the sunset. The cat jumped onto the stoop and sat beside him, worked her front paws on his knee. He thought about the bus park, the sly look on Iffat's face just before he jumped. He wondered about the white man and those two young ones, who had looked so dirty, as if they'd chosen to be so, and frightened. Their hair long like warriors' but that trembling at the lips. He wondered idly, too, about the woman he had left at Abuu's Guest and Rest, and why, though he recalled the white man's face and the two boys, and though he'd *looked* at her so hard and walked right there beside her, he could not see in his mind's eye exactly what she had been like. He didn't know her name, or where she hoped to go. By then, Ezra recalled, his chest had really hurt. He'd been most aware of his own mouth—a weight, it had been then, a swollen thing he carried with his face, not a part of it he knew.

In front of them Habib Pawpaw's wall was ruins, still a jagged sea, but purplish, softer in the slipping light. Ezra tried to make out hearts and diamonds in the bricks. A truck zoomed by, tarps flapping. Ezra thought about the bus again, how surprised the passengers had been. How when he'd opened up the hold and seen that emptiness he'd felt as though someone had hit him—and yet later someone had, and it hadn't felt like that. He wondered, very briefly, was *this* anything like *that?* Ezra didn't think so. No it wasn't. Not at all. This wasn't really a surprise. This was probably not even, Ezra knew, the worst he'd ever see. In his one eye, the rubble inked, grew darker, melted to the ground. Beyond the widened road, beyond a line of palm trees, the sun had gone quite red, the sky around it orange. Leaving their black trails, aeroplanes dug into the sky, some moving down to land, others reaching up. They watched one hum its way across, the steady blinking lights.

Then darkness really came. From somewhere not too far away, they heard a radio come on, a sputter, a song burst and a crumple. Then another crackle and a hiss as the dial turned. Habib passed a bit of tangerine to Ezra. The uncle asked for some. Looking at the two young men beside him, the nephew and the neighbor, something in him woke. A person never really knew what hit them when it did. Talking would take time, all that making of a story, for having it make sense. If you could survive it, that was the key thing. Habib spat out a pip. The other cat came out, ran after it, and stumbled in the bricks. Ezra shifted, raised a hand to test the air, set it down again. "Tomorrow," said the uncle. In his ears the rush of traffic was distant and subdued, something like a river. "We'll see it better then."

❧ *Sisters for Shama*

Indian Ocean Coast, 1989

Upstairs, Shama's family has eaten, and her man—an old man, now—is more asleep than dogs. Shama's children, grown-up kids with kiddies of their own, have waddled back to work on Sam Ouko Street and New Post Office Road. The grandchildren have scurried past my downstairs room, pointed through the doorway, made the usual faces, and gone outside to bark. Shama's husband's mother, so much older than her crumpled, hairless son that she barely ever sleeps, and so enormous she must roll into the kitchen seated on the footstool I gave wheels to long ago to ease her rotten legs, has settled by the taps and bats her little hands across the dishes and the cups. With all the crashing and the splashing, no one hears what I bestow on Shama in the darkness of my room: in exchange for Shama's food, I talk about lost children.

In Shama's youth, when I never noticed her, and she didn't think of me, Shama's spine was straight. Between that little-girlish time and the day she took me in, she has become a hunchback. Don't mind, I say, don't mind, although it troubles me. With Shama's pointed face protruding so far from her chest, her thickening mustache, that nice bosom, her soft long trousers and light feet, Shama is as pretty as a picture. When I tell her so she says she must remind me of myself, though I've nothing at the top and she is lighter than I am. "But both of us mustachio'ed," Shama says. She points at her own down and tips her foremost finger towards me, so I will think of mine. "Both of us grown old."

After I have eaten all the soup, or the chooko or pilau or whatever she has made, I lie back and talk. It's what I do for Shama, though she thinks it's all for nothing, or that more likely it's for me. Here's what everyone forgets: right here in this town, to her mama's second girl, Shama at the start was a baby's older sister.

For fifteen years the two grew up slim side by sister-side, until the younger girl woke up, and—leaving poor Shama behind without a blessing or a word—she vanished. Here one windy coastal day and gone the very next. Run off with a man? you ask. Eaten by a lion? Taken into slavery by a European thief? No one ever knew. Not a letter, not a line, not a jar of lime achari with a message in the lid. Imagine.

It's difficult, of course, to know what boils in someone else, but when you're old and still, as I am, and have such elephantine feet, there's nothing left to do but close your eyes and conjure. Someone else might ask themselves about the origins of cane juice and who invented that machine, or why they chose a coffeepot and seven cups for that fountain by the fort, but—other folk aside—*I* think about poor Shama's long-gone little girl.

An absent-sibling toothache, I believe, has bent my Shama's back, and I and no one else will be the one to cure it. I am the only person who can see that she is ever, ever sad. The sister-pain has weighed her jaws so fiercely it's caused a crushing in her neck and been too much for Shama's back to stand: this missing-sister gap become an ever-growing hump!

I know the little-sister wound still throbs in Shama's heart. In my room while she's upstairs, I imagine Shama weeping all the time, dripping tears in the karai to fritter up her feelings, or crying at the pillows on the sofa. All the dampness in the house, the mold that streaks my walls, I think, springs from Shama's eyes. Of course, when Shama comes to me or passes by and pokes a hand into my room, she looks perfectly at ease. No signs of wetness or of redness puff up Shama's peepers. Shama's very brave. I know better only, because, as I am sure you will agree, people who must lie down in the dark see what others can't.

Like I said, I talk. And so before too long I hope to find a made-up girl to outdo the run-off sibling and give Shama's spine a break. Or so. A hot-water story for the slivers in my Shama's sister-heart. Some time after I have talked in just the perfect way, Shama will speak out: "Oh! That one ended nicely!" Or "Yes, that *could* have happened to my sister!" For several days she'll think of what I've said and soon her crooked neck will loosen and her shoulders sit up straight. She'll think, *Ah-ha, there's happiness sometimes!* I will resuscitate, revise, give a real-life story to, and kick all sibling shadows out the windy door. But the thing cannot be done directly. I have been working on some options.

This is what we do: In the morning after Shama's kids have gone away to work and the grandchildren are all industrious at school, while her husband's mother shouts that there's no money to be had from feeding invalids and sinners, Shama brings me porridge. As she's thumping down the steps, she hums a little tune to drown out Bibi's voice. She doesn't stay to talk but goes back up to cook. After they have all come home and eaten and gone away again, she comes back down for stories, this time with thick food, with fish, and sometimes a fresh fruit.

Shama's grown quite stubborn and she stays with me till dusk. Then she goes back up to pray and wash and make another meal. Upstairs Bibi does the dishes to provoke from Shama a reaction: she ought to be asleep, instead, and leave those things for Shama to wash up. While Bibi soaps and shines the plates, or sometimes later —if there is a film—Shama puts her man to bed and comes downstairs again with waterbread and honey or pakoras if she has some, and she'll let me talk some more, until both of us feel sleep. There's time, you see, for making little sisters. And like I said, I've got some new ones at the ready. I'll make Shama listen close.

Dear Shama, I'll begin. I started as a child and grew. She'll laugh. "We all begin that way!" I'll wave my fingers at her as though at a fly, though of course she's seen my point. I've lied through all my teeth, Shama, and thus can love quite sharply. "Sharply?" She will sniff and squint her eyes. "If truth shows its fine face," she'll say, "all else will move aside." She'll settle happily against the wall, bring an ankle to her thigh, and with a shake of her high head will purse her lips at me. "No good can come from lies." I'm sure I don't agree, and I know Shama for herself quite often holds another view, but let's not get off course.

Sit still, I'll say. While I have not been everywhere, exactly (and who has, after all?), I have traveled in my time. Feats and quakings I have never once experienced I can perfectly imagine. Qualified, I am. And also, don't forget, motherless, and lost. Shama will take hold of my poor hands, and I will shake her off to show I'm hard enough for whatever is afoot. So look, I'll say, to capture her attention: before a boy can calculate his funds or wipe himself alone or speak out his own name, there is first of all a mother. A mother is the start. Shama won't think about her missing girl at first if I begin this way, with mothers and moreover with the mention of a son. Deflect, go sneaking! People who love sharply learn to hide their better tools.

I will spread apart my hands and bring them back together, to prepare the introduction. Mothers. Something to consider: now and then, indeed more often than we think, a boy has more than one. Before Shama can say a single word, I'll introduce the decoy. Slyly. Little Khaled, for example. Shama will take note. "Khaled," she'll repeat, a little doubtful at the first, and I will gesture with lips tight please be quiet or I'll stop. Khaled, I'll go on. Two-times-over talented, and a selfish boy to boot. Unlike but not unlike a thousand other boys, Khaled found himself with two.

Shama will give out a little sigh and tuck her legs behind her spreading hips, which, unless I speak surely, may shatter too one day from all that rolling loss. "Two?" Oh yes, the boy was very lucky. Two mothers! What a joy. More care, you think: All's well. Good for little Khaled. "Sure," Shama will agree. "Two mothers. Nothing wrong with that. Not a big surprise." But-but, I will go on, too much mother-love is only flattering on screen. Shama will curl her tongue between her lips and pointed upper teeth to affect a serious look. She'll nod. I'll keep my eyes fixed on her pretty, wrinkled face. By this point I will have her. We both like the cinema.

Shh. Now listen. Khaled's Mother One, who stretched and clawed and pushed and pushed to let the creature out? Ayeesha, good-looking and gifted. Grew up to be an actress (films, let's keep these jewels in mind). Ayeesha. She's the real beginning. And, I'll say to Shama, because things that start out far away don't look as though they're yours, Ayeesha lived in Egypt.

Shama now and then is skeptical with me. She'll pretend to be upset. "What foolishness is this, *yakhe?* In Egypt? Have you even been?" I have, I'll say, though Shama's forehead, which when at rest is not much bigger than my palm, will grow smaller with a frown. I have been to Egypt and to top it off have seen the oldest talkies. And what's more, I will remind her, though Shama says it can't be true, I have been a sailor-lover at all harbors of the Gulf. And so.

Egypt, in a sleepy town with seven date palms and a mosque, creeper roses sneaking in the schoolyard, and, as all small towns must have, a dangerous, deep well. Ayeesha. Just sixteen. A brainy girl, she was, good with shapes and numbers. Not badly shaped herself, Ayeesha was the kind of handsome that can tear a shirt in two. And she had (bad news or good news?) particularly fine feet. More handsome as the days went by, nice face, some curves, and pretty feet, Ayeesha was exactly on the verge of things. Her little heart was ready for some music.

"Feet?" says Shama. Despite the hope of hearts in song, talk of toes has stumped her. With a question on her face, she gestures to her ankle. Yes, I say. I motion to the lumps beneath my blanket, which, had I to wear them on my shoulders, would make me a hunchback, too. Nice *feet*. Now listen. Back to this girl's heart. "Oh yes." Shama's little mouth is round and twisted like a sugared noodle nest. Eyes aroll, she makes a show of grumbling. "Go on, then." Shama's own foot sways above her knee. "Song."

The first to pluck a tune with this Ayeesha's girly strings was a dreamy teacher in his twenties who now and then wrote plays. Ayeesha entered this man's classroom for her final year of school, looking forward to, perhaps, a nice grade on a test (she was clever, after all) and later, who can say, a civil service post.

We already know Ayeesha's lowest parts were pretty. And as it happened, this dreamy man's soft head was so filled up with misted things he could not stand to look too closely on the world that glittered at the level of his head. He often looked down at the ground. On that ground, spectacular and firm, Ayeesha's feet were sugar roses and the wings of pretty birds. Ayeesha's feet, permit me, sang. Shaken from his reveries by an accidental, first-time notice of her feet, the teacher thought he'd never seen appendages so fine. As though he'd never known a heel before, or sole. After teacher's second look, the shake became a quake. The vision of those feet kicked right into his heart. Quite oddly, at Ayeesha's able feet, this man who had never once been tripped up by a passion, or treated any girl with less than great respect, or felt with any shivers the fragility of elbows, wrists, or knees, was suddenly a shipwreck. He began to minister his classes never looking up, eyes along her ankles.

He scrawled notes across the board without seeing what he wrote, without once turning his own spine or bottom to the room. He tapped his fingers on the desk without ascertaining first what things he finger-tapped: a frightened piece of paper, for example, or a rare and lonely pencil, leery of the floor. Perhaps the other girls he taught, Ayeesha's chums, her less lovely and less clever, but not quite jealous, twins, lacked imagination. It did not occur to them he might have been habitually vulnerable to feet (which he was not) or to their friend Ayeesha's in particular (which he was) or that anything exciting, toes tensed and light-fingered, was waiting in the wings. They thought, with shrugs, floor-love. A handicap, a tic, who knows? *Our teacher's strange,* they thought, at the beginning, *but we are only students here, and we must never, never mind.*

The teacher's ogling of young Ayeesha's feet brought him (he would spell out through a poem, later, in old age) a refreshment that—as the poem was to prove—could not be described. Forgive me: he had never felt so grounded. He was able to write quatrains about feet. Toes splayed like shiny leaves of date palms, soles like desert slopes, bones like ribs on sated cows, ankles like the billowed sails of dhows. He saw her footprints in his books, heard Ayeesha's steps in dreams.

Ayeesha's feet both focused and disturbed him. He knew he must look odd. Now and then, exhausted by his passion, he tried, when teaching, to seek out other toes. Most girls, after all, do have a full collection. But what did this man find? Salma's feet, long and fleshless, ten prongs beneath her chair. Khadija? Flatter than the plains, big toe aswoop far forward, ungainly hillock dwarfing all the rest. Naima?

Sweet, but seven on each side. Always, always, in the midst of talk about an epic, or bridges built in China, to Ayeesha's feet he would helplessly return.

If the teacher asked a question, he did not look up to choose a timid girl whose hand was finally raised. Eyes on dear Ayeesha's feet, he simply stood until a brave one coughed and lobbed the answer to him like a homemade rubber ball to thunk him on the head. If he wrote a poem on the board, he wrote it eyes still fastened to the ground. How his chalky letters looped, betraying their own words, how *plums* were *prims* and *goats* were *gowns* without his even knowing! By and by, Ayeesha's girlfriends did catch on, though not quite sure to what. They could not help themselves. They passed notes to one another, made wild signs in the air. Eventually, they laughed. And once they'd started laughing, as you can imagine, it was hard for them to stop.

After one too many giggles, he thought Ayeesha's pals perhaps were smarter than their tests showed. He sensed them getting free, that they took advantage of his gazing to do things they should not. Doodling designs for henna, for example, which they were not allowed, or planning tricks on him. Helpless, he feared humiliation. He tried to shake himself. *Too much,* the teacher finally thought. *There are other girls to think of, girls who need my help. I must, I must,* he told himself, *reduce my looking at the girl Ayeesha's feet!* There were state exams to shoot for, after all, and lessons to be made. He struggled. And because there was some strength in him, some vision in the mist, before the girls could say to anyone—their brothers, parents, village leaders, for example—that surely he was mad, the teacher took a turn.

Tugging on the blanket sharply like a mother snapping at a sleeve
to get a brutish boy's attention, Shama interrupts. "Listen, what
does *she* think?" she asks me. Who? I say, frowning so she'll
know I am annoyed. "Ayeesha, the girl? This teacher man of
yours, okay, I see. But what about Ayeesha?" Shama's leaning
forward so her chin is not far from my bed. In the light from
the high window, her cheeks have a gray glow. "This *is* about
Ayeesha, have you been listening at all?" But half of Shama's
pleasure lies in contradicting me. She lets the blanket go, and,
watching, blows hard air through her nose. She won't speak
unless I do. "Well, what *about* the girl?" I ask. Shama shakes
her head. She says, "*I* would not stand for such behavior."

Shama, I believe, has visions of herself firmly in control,
issuing refusals, and pointing out injustice. She would like
Ayeesha to be ferreting her feet under the hem of her long
gown, or drawing, inappropriately, her feet up from the floor to
hide them at her bottom, between her flesh and chair. Think?
I say. She isn't thinking, Shama, this thing is *happening* to her.
Shama raises her eyes sadly to the window and nods her head
just once, as though motioning to someone I can't see, to say,
Just listen to this talk. She looks at me and shakes her head some
more.

I say, She doesn't think, Shama, she's just sixteen and she isn't
very bright. "Bright?" Shama has an ear for double-talk. "Just
wait, you, this is how you started." She makes her voice sharp
in her nose, set to mimic me: "'Such a head for numbers, isn't
it? Such a clever, shapely girl.' Oh, 'Will get an office job!' But
can't see teacher's eyeballs suckle as if toes could give out milk?

What a story." Come on, Shama, I say, the foot thing's almost done. "All right, all right," she says. She covers up her own toes with her hand and smoothes the blanket down. "Go on."

Now then, I will say, too good to be upset by a minor interruption. To free himself of thoughts of feet, the teacher moved his eyes. "Well, finally," says Shama. Yes, *Feet stay on the ground,* he told his sorry self. *Your eyes must leave them there.* The teacher man decided he should seek out higher things. But sensible will only go so far. So, I say, eywah, he looked up. But lucky? Or unlucky? When he saw Ayeesha's face, his mistiness and vagueness became something else entirely. A face is mightier than feet. He understood his destiny, or something. He approached her and he spoke. *I offer you tuition,* said the teacher. *When all the girls have gone. On Thursday afternoons.* His voice shook hard, but his courageous eyes did not. Ayeesha, if you're wondering, thought this was just fine. She did vaguely consider office work, and it was clear this teacher liked her. So why not? A girl with unformed aspirations, a girl exactly on the verge, you see, should take help where she can. *Tuition,* Ayeesha told her mother. *Free. So I will pass the state exams.*

Ayeesha's mother, a hard-worked woman whose proud head was ever-cradled by a bitter cloud of worry for the future, in the end, agreed. First, a smarter child is all you can depend on when the men you had have died or otherwise escaped. And second, if the teacher had designs on this fine girl, Ayeesha's mother might have something she could trade (a teacher, don't you know, must keep a reputation). Ayeesha, for her part, focused only on the nearest of the future, was delighted. Her own family—a mother, sister, little boys, no dad, and no one old—had none, really, to speak of. And we shall not speak of them. But weren't men the ones who did things, could find long roads in the world? The teacher man was strange, she knew, but still, he was a man. She piped up, he listened. She could see he would be gentle.

So. Cool room, cool desks, blue shadows from the yard, Ayeesha's fingers wrapped around a pen. A little bit of work. Tender teacher asking questions, probing at her mind. Bidding her recite all manner of wise things—GDP and GNP, for Peru and for Korea, verses, a sura here and there. At first he was quite proper. Then? You know. He couldn't help it, in the end, though it did occur in steps.

With Ayeesha, after the other girls had gone, the teacher liked to sit down at his desk. No need to pace the room with only one sweet girl to talk to. Moreover, if he sat, and she sat, too, he couldn't see her feet. He could focus on her face. How bright and handsome this girl was! One day, he asked Ayeesha to come closer, which she did. She brought a chair across the tiles, not lifting it but dragging it so that with the sound of wood on floor there slid a heavenly thick stroke all up the teacher's spine. He must have known what he was doing—for closeness, we agree, gives rise only to itself.

On another afternoon, as she scrawled the word *gratuity* in English on a sheet he had prepared, he touched Ayeesha's hand. Ayeesha, surprised but not surprised, let out a comely gasp, curled her hand into a ball, unfurled it, and touched his. Something in him melted. Ayeesha put her pencil down and rose. She had seen this looming, after all, why not get up to meet it? Teacher also rose. Next he draped his arms around her and gave a mighty squeeze. "I've never done a thing like this!" exclaimed this tenderest of teachers, chin hairs all aquiver, concealing with his shoulders and his back the verses he had written on the chalkboard earlier that day for his students to absorb. Nor had our Ayeesha, but, splendid feet still firmly on the ground, certain without having ever tried them of her very special skills, she wiped the board with him. They shook, they shivered, Ayeesha gave out dainty giggles now and then and the teacher man a moan. Just kisses and some pressing, mind you, nothing too dramatic. But still! When the thrilled and shaken twosome finally left the room, the poetry was gone, embedded now among the folds and pockets of their astounded clothes.

Just as I expect, Shama takes a moment to talk back. "This I don't believe," she says. "He didn't do the thing?" There's a shudder and a roundness in the way my Shama's mouth offers up the three words *do the thing*. I smile. I wait while Shama waits for me. But her whole face has gone sour and she won't wait very long. "He kissed her, that was all? Listen, I will hear a thousand lies before I die and for some I may be a fool. But this? A girl wrapped right around his neck and letting him *embed* things in her clothes, and he stops at just a kiss?" I say, What, you want them hot-hot in the classroom? I wonder, as I often have, what Shama's own man did when she was straight and slim. He's useless now, but surely in his youth he had a fetching move or two.

Don't you like romance? If I did not know better I would say

THEFT

Shama snarls at me. "Romance, he says." She's talking to that
unseen friend of hers, who sympathizes quietly with Shama's
every doubt. "It's all a trick," she says now. "He'll make her
think it's only kisses and one day he will lock the door behind
her and go fishing in his pants." When Shama is upset it's often
best not to respond. I wait. I pluck at the frayed edge of my
blanket. I raise my face up to the avenue of light that links my
window to the floor. There's a hint of frying in the air, and
something sour, too. I'll wait until she's begging me to talk.
Smell that? I ask. Wouldn't some jelebies do us good, Shama,
or some gulab jamun? Visheti, if you please? You know, I say,
as far as I'm concerned, there's nothing more to tell. And sugar
would be sweet.

But Shama comes around. "All right," she says. "But remember I have things to do upstairs. Cleaning, cooking, looking at
the television. Fruit juices to make. So if there's something
good here, you ought to hurry up." Something good, she says.
As though I am not the good thing that she needs, adoring
tales aside.

At first the kisses and the clutching were enough for this girl's
teacher. But one day, he had a catchy thought. As Ayeesha
struggled to describe, in writing, the geography of Spain, the
teacher (misinformed as to the precise relation between local
theater and cash, and the economy of film) declared, "I'll make
you a star." She squinted at him in the dimness of the room. "A
star?" He rose up from the desk and looked, for once, away from
her into the courtyard. Being in some sense an artist, he deci-
phered in the dust motions and potentials that Ayeesha could

not fathom. "Oh yes," he said. He took a great, loud breath that swelled his concave chest and gave him, for a moment, the look of a proud bird. "I am a playwright, don't you know?" The teacher's fate was sealed by sight, ten toes, good feet, and eventually a face, but Ayeesha's domino was the sound of an idea. "Don't you want to act, Ayeesha? To speak my words, perform fantastic feeling? Make an audience cry?" Acting. Yes. Why not? Maybe she'd been waiting just for this her whole, entire life. Shama likes this moment, too. She's quiet. I go on.

Ayeesha's first: she played an educating mother, touting modern methods to keep one's children clean. Next, she made a moving, socialistic speech while boys acting the part of Britishmen were sheepish to the left. Ayeesha's mother said she couldn't see what playacting in the courtyard had to do with state exams, but it was certain the most modern villagers approved. Ayeesha's teacher sent word to her mother that Ayeesha was the most capable girl he'd ever had the pleasure to— And Ayeesha's mother thought, *Teachers know their business,* and turned her eyes away. In Ayeesha, who found unexpected satisfaction in the accolades, and in declaring noble feelings, the acting seed was sown. For almost a full year Ayeesha studied, acted, stroked his glowing face when no one saw, and all in all thought her trembling teacher fine. He himself had longer visions of the two of them, well married, putting plays on with a parading, endless stream of students, for years and years, until their own plump kids were writing plays for blooming actors in new courtyards, and it was time for him to die.

But girls as bright and gifted as Ayeesha often feel that something sharp in them will perish if they simply settle down. One Friday, after a successful piece that centered on the benefits of state-supported inputs for the growth of river wheat, Ayeesha's eyes got bigger. Her slender lover's city friends, with whom the teacher had attended university, had come down for the show. Precocious and demure, good-humored, well proportioned, and apparently naive, she charmed them. The teacher let her sit among them in the modern city style and allowed his friends to tease her. They had, they said, enjoyed her soundly in the play. These young men from the city seemed, and were, wise and quite artistic. Nothing like her playwright, who, she saw now very clearly, had come down in the world. Ayeesha saw a future vista, gleaming.

One of the sophisticated visitors—whose heart contained not simply enervated blood but also a real vision (and who knew, besides, a professional director and someone else in casting)—must have seen it too. He whispered to her when he left, and slipped into Ayeesha's sweaty hand a scrap of folded paper. What was written there? His own sister's address. And this other little bundle? Bus fare, too, quick thinker. Ayeesha kissed her teacher man that night, expressly making promises she knew she could not keep. Later on she kissed her sleeping mother. The bus fare was exact; the address was neither false nor dangerously shabby. The teacher's city friend was true. He did put her in films.

Because Shama interrupts me, pulling at the sheet and saying "Psst," I am lifted out of Egypt, no longer on my way to Cairo in an early morning bus, and find myself in bed. "So?" she says. "What about the boy, this Khaled?" Shama is, as usual, a step ahead of where I want her. First it was Ayeesha before she came into her own, and now she wants the boy. What about Ayeesha, I ask her, what about her, first? "That's his mother, hanh?" Shama, light of my dim life she is, finds it hard to sit and wait. I remind myself that if she didn't love me she would not come every day and ask me for some talk. I remind myself that Shama took me in and that without her I might be somewhere else indeed. I remind myself as well of other, painful things.

But, I want to know, was Ayeesha too ungrateful? Should she have told her mother? Kept the money for herself? Used it on a sewing machine to set up her own shop? What would you have done? And, what I am always thinking, Shama, what about your sister? Shama doesn't pay attention in the way I want her to, but today I will insist. Ayeesha. Did you like her? Shama lets go of the sheet and she reclines again. She sometimes likes her own voice, too. "Like her? You want me to listen close, then you ask me to stop and think now did you like her? I should do two things at once? And life's not about like, old man," she says. Shama's closed one eye, and she curls her nose at me. She wears a tiny stud there made of glass. It twinkles. "This is all for what's-his-name, this Khaled, is it not? Or did I hear you wrong?"

I know why she's focused on the boy. Shama knows my tricks, you see, that I have girls beneath my pillow and think one of them's for her. She wants and does not want Ayeesha. Both eyes open now, she's saying something serious. "I know what you are thinking," Shama says. "But she's nothing like my sister." The glass shard flashes like a signal. "My sister, for example," Shama says, "did not know what boys were for. And if you think"—she's stretching now, pushing with her hands down on the floor to lift her bottom up and get right on her feet—"that girl could spell a single word in English, well, I'm Jomo Kenyatta."

Shama is not Jomo Kenyatta. Heroine, perhaps, but on a one-man, dim-room scale. Though faith in her I have, she could neither sway a crowd nor bring the British to their knees. Plus Mr. Kenyatta was as straight and slender as an arrow, al-most—well, almost—to the end. Okay, I say. But what about the bus ride? She couldn't have met a nice young man who put some shillings in her fingers and told her where to go? Been led away somewhere? Shama doesn't think so. "Too scared to walk to school without me by her side," she says without a bit of doubt, as if she's thought about this question for some years, though she often says I think about her absent sibling far more than she does. She's bending over now, picking up the bowl my soup came in, and reaching for the tray. Her back makes giant shadows on the wall. "You said this was about a boy, old man." She thinks my sister-medicine is just a fool idea. "You don't treat what doesn't hurt." Of course I think she's lying. That vanished little sister has been sliding gummy hands along her Shama's shoulder blades and neck now for some years, don't think I don't know.

"Wait a little, Shama. Wait, okay? The boy's not far away." Shama looks down at the empty bowl and senti platter. "The boy," she says, although her voice is not quite right. She is not ready to look up. This all began exuberantly, with us avoiding sisters, but now we've hit a sharp thing in the air. It was foolish work, perhaps, to start this story with a boy. We both remember now why I am not allowed upstairs.

Before I moved into Shama's downstairs room, I slept in her uncle Akberali's shop. I made no secret of the fact that he was only being kind and that I gave him nothing, but Akberali liked to tell his friends that I was his night watchman. A Samburu man had been employed for years, to watch the shop from the outside. That man, with his violet gown and spear and glorious braided hair, checkerboard beside him, was wide awake all night, a professional, an expert. But when I met him, Akberali felt a sudden need for someone with the goods, you see, someone else for the inside. Night watchman! I slept among the sugar sacks and boxes, turning in my sleep and slapping at the walls whenever I awoke to the nasty sounds of mice. I'm not a guard, I'd joke with Akberali in the morning, I'm a cat, which made Akberali smile. When the shop was open I boiled coffee for the customers, who sometimes came to sit. Now and then Akberali stroked me as he passed when no one saw, just here along my chin, or there, along my arm, as though I were a girl. He sometimes spent an evening with me. Things were fine with us until Akberali died. His wife—a skinny thing, nothing round to speak of, hard skull full of missing teeth—sold the shop and shoved off to Nairobi. She had no use for any cat. And so Shama took me in, because, just like Akberali's, Shama's heart is soft for wicked things like me.

I used to visit all the time, up there, before my feet became too heavy to be taken up the stairs. This is what we say.

"You can't manage without help," says Shama. "If you went up the stairs, with your fallen-asleep feet, you'd need three of us to hold you. And what if the steps broke underfoot?" This is Shama wanting to forget the truth about my exile, what Shama's husband's mother maintains happened with the boy. I don't complain as I once did. It is easier to leave things as they stand, sometimes. As Shama also says, when she is not insisting that truth is all we need and lies are serpents in the wrinkles of our clothes, "Better to have people think exciting things, or what? Never mind that they're not true." Perhaps she says this to be kind. In any case, at present, Shama wants the boy, and now that we've paused awkwardly and both re-membered what we have contracted not to mention, I am ready to proceed. Do you have time for this? I ask. That boy is really on his way.

Shama's face looks vaguely like her uncle's in the dissipating light. Her compact forehead is a smooth, familiar dome. She sits herself back down, but keeps her hands flat on the floor be-side her to imply she's in a hurry. "All right," she says, opting for some courage. "But boy there'd better be." I think, How unafraid we are. Sisters, boys, lost girls, escapes, and little loves, all looking very separate, I see, but very much the same. Now then, Shama, I tell her. Girls don't make a baby by themselves. First we need a man.

In films, Ayeesha tried on varied loves like gowns and paint and shoes. She liked to take up new emotions and to feel them very deeply. She meant every word she said the moment that she said it. *How sweet to be a sister!* Ayeesha told herself—never minding she had left some small, dear siblings weeping in the country. *How dear to be abandoned by a brutal, brooding man!* Yet she, and no one else, just yet, had always done the leaving. *How sad and dark to be bereft of one's own pious, loving ma.* Ayeesha's mother, ruthless in her piety, let *us* not forget to say, had quite forgotten *her.*

Because her interest in love was democratic, now this kind and now that, each as worthy as the other with no difference between them, Ayeesha would not be a super, superstar. But because she was charming and determined, rise she did, respectably, reliably, to make her way in small-scale, medium-scale, and sometimes in successful films. She acquired a loyal, modest following of teenaged boys and grandpas. She wore pretty gowns with style and she could do her handsome face in any way at all: now a sweet girl, now a fury, now a wounded sis.

After acting for some years, living ably on her own—in a third-floor flat not far from the first, the written-down, address—all but disavowed for shamelessness by the family that bore her but buoyed by the true affections of those who loved her on the screen, Ayeesha was transformed into a wife. The suitor? A sickly whiskered man far older than her grandpa. This fine, upstanding babu caught sight of her through cataracted eyes on television once while visiting a friend, and when the teenaged boys explained to him exactly who she was, the grandpa fell in love. Onscreen, especially with shadows taking hold of babu's ailing eyes, Ayeesha glowed and glowed. And so he sent his nephew with a message to the studios, and later to her house, and later—not much later—Ayeesha caved right in.

Ayeesha let this grandpa make a home for her because she thought young men were too foolish: the teacher, all hot dreams and talk, had never left the school; the dark-eyed, talented director who had also tried his hands already had a wife. The babu never spoke of her especially nice feet. He never mooned about her face. He simply said he'd like her near, please, in the night, to soften his old age. Ayeesha found some pleasure in his means. *A house, with no more rent to pay!* She also thought, *Nearly blind, and old!* A man who couldn't see too well, and what's more who was weak, would not, she thought, restrain her.

Ayeesha's husband did not, in fact, prevent his wife from acting on the screen. He thought, *She's an orphan, the film folk are her family.* So Ayeesha kept on acting, and she also made some money. A good thing, this, since the babu was not extremely manly. He was very good at sleeping, for example, and at yawning, and at rubbing his soft belly with a frown, and at dragging one gaunt hand from jaw to cheek as though to bring the skin back to where it had been in his youth, then grunting and then napping once again, almost unaware. Nor was he a husband, understand, who can pet, and kiss, and stroke. He did his duty only once, with everything he had, then didn't anymore. But nine months after that one time, thank God, Ayeesha lay right down and set her pretty teeth and pushed and pushed and out popped and soon began to bellow a real live tiny child. Lucky man, Ayeesha made a boy. This is Khaled, now, remember. Ayeesha, apart from feedings and some wipings, didn't pay the baby too much motherly attention. But when she did peek down at Khaled, now and then Ayeesha felt her son as sweet as Turkish chocolates, yes, or the plumpest, pinkest pomegranate on a windy little tree.

"That's enough," says Shama. "I have seen the boy, and now I have to go." It's late, it's true. She's collected all the plates and leavings, and has been squatting for a while, not flat-bottomed on the floor. No longer in her ordinary place, she's not far from the door. How quickly time goes by with Shama. It seems to me she has hardly even entered and laid the soup beside me. She says, quite serious now and no longer playing games, "The children will be coming back." We pause in a round silence. Our aging ears grow large. There, yes. As though she's conjured them herself, I can hear them in the alley, kicking-growling at the sand, yelping at each other, and descending like a storm. Does Shama want to be upstairs before the children come? Because as I've been leading her towards little Khaled, outside coming back from soccer practice there's another boy named Jussa who has no idea what once happened in his name.

Upstairs on the landing, Shama's husband's mother has rolled over to the steps, which is as far as she can go, and so precarious for her it is probably quite thrilling. "Shama!" She calls Shama's name three times—and Shama, with whom I am ensnared, does smile over at me. "Call three times and no more," she whispers, because that's anybody's due. Call four times, however, we both know, you don't deserve an answer. But Shama's got no right of refusal, which no doubt happens when you marry. The bibi shouts Shama's name again, and says, in a voice like brakes on a big bus, to me, "What, you think she has no family?" My turn now to seek sympathy in Shama's unseen friend. "All right, old man, I'm going up the stairs now." She's standing in the doorway, and the dusty light from my small window catches at her face. There's something green about her skin this time of day—green but fresh, not dying.

"All right," I say. "But you'll come back tonight." If one of Shama's children has given her a gift (Tasleem, who works so well at Walvis Travel she now owns two pairs of glasses, or Kamila, who crochets coats for armchairs on the side), Shama will buy paraffin for me and we won't talk in the dark. I'll watch the light on Shama's face and think how beautiful we are. "Tonight you'll bring a lamp, or what?" I say.

Shama's skin goes slack. "Look here," Shama says, putting on a teacher voice—we all of us had British masters once, or some who liked to speak as though they were. "Look here." Shama's peering down now, as though made curious by her feet. "No?" I say. "No lamp?" Shama's collected up the tray and bowl, and she's also found a dank old shirt I'd long forgotten in the corner. She's tucked this rag between her elbow and her waist. "We'll see," she says, and I can tell there's something else. "What, no boy for you?" I ask. I'm smiling, though the ground is getting soft. Shama raises her small head again and frowns at me exactly as her uncle Akberali used to do if I asked him not to go. A frown with half the brow only but with a twisting of the nostrils. I tell myself with Shama just as I did with Akberali that this frown is full of love. Standing in the doorway, Shama says, "Old man." She shifts the tray from left to right in her thin arms, then left again, as though trying to deceive it. "It's Wednesday," Shama says, examining the tray. "You know there is a film on." There, she's said it. And while we always act as though we have forgotten, and though I tell myself it's nothing anymore, Shama's hurt my feelings.

I compete with the night shows for my Shama's attention, which is why I've put unlikely country girl Ayeesha so wildly on the screen. "There'll be films in my little story too, Shama, for you. I put it there for no one else but you." I've planned, in fact, a screen career for Khaled. But Shama's already stepped into the hallway. She doesn't look into my eyes or promise anything. She points her heavy back at me and if she speaks again she will be speaking to the stairwell. "Oh," I say. "A film." Shama says, I think, "That's right."

I look down at my feet—such mounds under the blanket! I look away from them. Usually as she goes up, Shama's steps are slow, but today they have a quickness, as though something very bright upstairs were much better than me. When I first moved in below—before I was cast out by that enormous bibi, *after* I'd put wheels on her, mind you—I'd go up and watch the films. Don't think I don't remember, like a smoker near a cigarette or drinker by the coffeepot I was, no film I could miss. Though Shama cannot hear me, I go on: "A film, is it? A film?" So be it. I'll wait. In the meantime I will fashion second sisters.

It was because I told Shama I had seen a hundred films that she started coming down to see me after I was banished. As I've said, Shama likes the pictures. Everybody does, and though Shama's husband's mother is a crazy woman now, when they first installed the set—courtesy of Tasleem and Kamila, with their mad inflows of cash—the films had quite an audience.

Children from the neighborhood would tumble up the stairs with screams and slaps and giggles, especially the dark ones, whose parents don't have funds for modern sets, or any sets at all, and sometimes the big bibi'd even call the coffee sales-man, whom she wanted to impress. Already she was far too large to leave the house, and it was something grand for her to bring folk up to see that she was still alive, and well in touch with the big world. I haven't yet asked Shama, but will soon, if the bibi came into her marriage slender, went upstairs a light and shapely thing, and then began to eat so much she couldn't get back down. I also wonder what her long-dead husband thought, if he fed her sweets and did not fix the stairs with foresight, because he feared that she might leave. Of course while I complain about the bibi, and make much of her great weight, I'm not one to talk. I became a tenant here with feet I could still manage, ankles barely thick, and very full of feeling. I could, at first, still identify my toes, but the more I stayed, the more massive they became. Now, after five years, I trip on them, they're only frills like lace above a soft and rounded mass. Bibi can't come down, and I'm not welcome up.

Before I moved into the house—because Akberali took me if the toothless wife was gone—I had already been upstairs. When he died I had seen five films there already, and of course the thuggish newscasts. When I arrived with my old clothes in a basket and a chit to say that I was born once in a hospital, I already knew that Shama's sister was an absence, and the bibi was a force. Tasleem and Kamila were, in those days, fun to be with, young and clever women (loving sisters both, and still today a busy pair). Tasleem had been deserted by her husband,

and Kamila, to keep up, thought she might be soon, though it hadn't happened yet. She came with kids in tow. When I first got the downstairs room, I thought, How wonderful, I'll watch television daily. I will sit among the girls and children, and witness Akberali's smile on that hunchbacked Shama's face. And for a while, I did.

Tasleem and Kamila, who still spoke with me then, would sometimes come to fetch me, calling me their uncle. "Come up, Uncle! Tonight *Sangam!* Air Force love and suicide! Nothing you can miss!" or "Tonight an oldie, *Alam Ara!* Gypsy queens and princes, Uncle. You had better come." And the three of us would make our way up the chipped blue stairs. Shama would have cut up some bananas, or made simsim bars to eat. The boys, still young, not yet enamored of kung fu, would sprawl below the soft brown sofa, legs and hands entangled, eyes agoggle at the screen. All of us together rapt with love and singing in the mountains, bloodshed, tears, and fate. Shivering at stab wounds, nodding at the gunshots, feeling not for just the lovers or the parents or the beggars, or the lost souls of the villains, but for all of them at once. Sometimes, too, pretending tears and laughing all the while. I am good at both, and they were glad to have me.

Even Bibi, already crawling in those days, not able to stand, managed giggles here and there. After so many years of being stuck upstairs and only guessing at what saunters in the world, Bibi found a novelty in me. A man no longer on the move, a stranger, someone Akberali praised, not related to them, someone who had traveled, amenable to talk. A very tray of treats, I was. And at first I loved her, too. For example, when faced with but a single sweetmeat remaining on a plate and all the awkwardness of shall-I-take-or-not, I would slide the saucer towards her so the fit girls couldn't see. Quietly, without a word about her seeping flesh or heart or "pressure" or her bursting too-tight clothes or how the fat was squeezing all the hair out of her head, I thought, Let her get the things she loves, or what. I did like it up there with the family. I wanted if I could to please each one in turn.

After watching one nice film in which a legless baba rolls all over India on a wooden board with wheels, looking for his son, I had my idea. I'd make a board like that for Bibi. So I did. I went out in the morning and I traded things for wheels. I watched Yusuf's Hardware Shop for him while he went out for something secret, for example, and I cleaned out Hamed's storeroom. I gave Omar what he wanted. Came home with four wheels and screws and tools Yusuf had lent me.

I gave the roller board to Bibi just before we watched *Deewar,* where mother-love turns ugly, as it will, and mama makes a choice between her children. She blinked at me until she understood, and then she squeezed my arm. How could I have known that putting Bibi on the rollers would let her sneak around and come upon things in the stillness that she wouldn't understand? Boys, I tell you. Trouble.

I can hear them finish eating up there. Glass on glass, and metal-water sounds. The children talking nonsense, and Tasleem and Kamila—not so fine as they once were—make a din that more and more resembles Bibi's. Age will change a voice, of course, and tone. Complain-complaining now, they are. Sounds that say nothing's good enough, *Can you believe that*

Walvis, chasing after boys, and *Don't you know I made four jackets for the sofa set and they've paid me just for three saying too-too much yes miss we cannot afford, as though afford-afford I can,* and more, and other things I cannot really hear. Shama's quiet, though, and I tell myself perhaps the sister tale is working. Perhaps she will come back with more than waterbread and tea. I wait. It's very dark downstairs, though the upper rooms are bright with electricity, the TV and some bulbs. Outside I know the vendors have come out with tiny oil lamps and that people see what they are eating. Upstairs, it's also eating time. In my own room, ink black. Darkness is the best for thinking of cold things. Let's try to tell the truth.

To look at little Jussa now, you wouldn't know that when he was a child his parents (Tasleem and a man whose name cannot be spoken in the house) thought he would not live. Too thin, he was, nothing like that Khaled we are working with, who is plump and rich and fine. Jussa's limbs had no flesh on them to pinch or even speak of, no matter what he ate. It took three years for him to try his feet, and even then, he wobbled like an eel. Then he would fall down in a heap like twigs made out of string, and down he'd stay until a person picked him up. When I moved in, the boy was four and hopeless still. Tasleem had maalims tramping in and out, with bowls and pens and water, incense, leaves to burn, and everything, a new trick every day. She brought a Maasai woman once, a wrinkled one who smelled so strongly of things Tasleem announced she could not bear or name she washed the steps with rose marashi after. Nothing doing, Jussa couldn't walk. My own feet were showing signs, back then, swelling, losing memory. Hard for me to make it up the stairs, what with one foot and another. The day our bibi rolled into the parlor and attacked me with a spoon, I was sitting on the sofa with the tired, broken boy. Bear down, shall we? I will tell it as it was.

Shama was asleep. Her husband, long-bald by this time, but not yet so astounded by the world or by his mother that he couldn't rise from bed, had gone out to buy a prayer cap or something. Tasleem was at work. Kamila, not yet free of her own man, still prospered on the waterfront with hopes for love and joy. Jussa's older brothers, boys who'd run and jumped from birth, were still at school and not expected back. I had gone upstairs because, as I have said, I was still welcome in those days, and downstairs it was lonely.

It was legs, you see, not—as Bibi later said, when she announced to Shama in case Shama didn't know that since the house belonged to Bibi she could banish whom she chose—it was legs, and not *salaciousness,* or anything like that. I do know how to work with flesh. It's true, it's true I worked the beaches in my time, massage-massage-and-cash. Now a stroke and now a squeeze. I can bring relief. A hand feels good on bones that want some softness. I was sitting on the sofa, thinking how wonderful to have a fan awhirring on the ceiling, and how brave it was of Shama to have hung a painted picture of naked-Adam-naked-Eve in that green garden by the tree, right above the cabinets where the lightbulb showed it off. I heard Jussa make a sound in the dark room behind the television set, and I went in to look.

Just five years old, he was, but his square head looked large as a small man's, because the rest of him was sticks. "Come on," I said. "It's cool in the front room." Always burning with a fever, that boy was, a red-coal child from all the danger in the world. I lifted him from his hot bed and brought him out onto the sofa. It will be better by the fan, I thought, and also, if those doctors and the Maasai ladies have all but given up on you, little bwana Jussa, I promise *I* will not. When you move into a house and don't know everything there is, you think you'll turn things upside down, just as I had thought when I put Bibi on the rollers. Jussa was looking at the ceiling, limp, breath scratching at the air. In the kitchen, Bibi clinked the cups and bowls together, out of anger, maybe, not related to the cooking or the cleaning, just a clattering to register complaints.

I told Jussa a story about a shipwreck and the children of a sailor whose first wife had been a djinn, and how, when the human children found his body and staged a burial for their dad, the djinn kids had to watch it from the high crest of a palm tree since they weren't wanted down below. Jussa said he'd like to sail a ship and wondered what it was to go swimming in the water. "You'll go swimming yet," I said. He slipped his legs onto my lap, and I thought, completely innocent, you see, I will rub his ankles.

It was my own ankles smarting, too, and my feeling-nothing feet. I know what sorry limbs are like, I thought. He seemed to fall asleep and then wake up, and sigh, and shiver now and then, and I thought, Oh, it helps. His skin was very hot, and fine, like onions. And the eyelashes around his too-big eyes got damp and very dark. In my big hand his knees were tinier than dwarf limes. His poor thin thighs weren't like thighs at all. I thought, if I do this enough the Jussa boy will walk! Such faith, you think! Such determination. The fan spun on and on, and Bibi's clatter faded, and Jussa's round eyes closed, and so did my own eyes, you see, I slept right there, too. And next.

And next the bibi rolled into the television room and threw the spoon at me. It was me she meant to hurt, but as I woke up I saw that she'd hit Jussa on the head. And next the boy was crying and when boys are crying in that way, well, what are you to think? Enormous Bibi got her voice together in a ball at the bottom of her throat and screamed at me like a komba in a tree. I won't say how much she batted at me from her round place on the floor with her fat hands, and how she growled and I was pelted down the stairs. I fell, too, at the bottom, hurt my ankle and my knee. Lay there like a pile of Jussa twigs myself. Bibi got settled on the rollers *I* had made and hurled things down at me. She must have gathered them along the way, top speed: a cup, a knife, a cooking book of Shama's, and Tasleem's makeup bag. Salacious. Don't come back, she said. You're an animal, she said. I'll have you thrown out of this house.

Enough. If Bibi hadn't been so threatened by the steps, she might have killed me, this I know. It's Shama I must thank for waking up and calming Bibi down, collecting all the shattered things and taking me to bed. What passed between us I won't say. Only that if I almost died because of Bibi, I did not because of Shama. She started bringing food because the bibi wouldn't let me up the stairs even to eat. She brought me Maasai ladies, too. Shama owed her uncle something, after all. At first she came because she felt ashamed of Bibi, and because of Akberali, and because she was so sorry. Especially when I could hear the films up there, and wanted more than anything to drag myself upstairs. And I did wonder all the time how that little boy was doing. But it's not easy to sustain things, even feelings of injustice, even indignation. And not long after that of course Jussa got fat just like his bibi and started walking on his own. So Shama, step by step, forgot. She had enough things to be sad for. And I forgot a little, too, what else can keep the days right? One afternoon, I said to Shama, Shama, you think the films are where the real things smash and blubber. She'd brought okra and a little piece of liver, a kindness I remember. But I have things to tell you, too. I've seen two thousand films, at least. You think it taught me nothing? By then I had another plan for making someone better.

Speaking of the films, I can hear all the sounds of *Baazigar* up there, a song I think I like, but it's hard to tell when you can't see the story on the screen. Bibi understands exactly what they're saying, but that's no use to me these days. I listen to the film and hear the girls and children talking, too, and arguing. But Shama, unless she's speaking very softly, which I've not known her to do, still hasn't said a word.

Last night, I thought, she's coming any moment now, just now. She's not interested in *Baazigar* or poverty and illness, she's thinking of Ayeesha and waiting for this actor-baby Khaled to take exciting wing. She wants Mother Two. But then I heard the anthem play, which closes the night's programs. I remembered how the nation's flag flaps and ripples in the wind, and then the colored bars. Now, I thought, she'll come. I tried to turn in bed, I thought, I'll face the wall to hurt her, but my big feet were heavy, got entangled in themselves. Shama sometimes does come very late, apologizing, having reheated the tea. But then I heard their now-it's-time-for-sleep sounds, Shama's baby-husband splashing fitful water, Shama, with her easy steps, locking up the storeroom, Tasleem and Kamila sighing, laughing like two women who are tired of everything there is, and also all the boys, the quietest at night, dissolving in the dark. I thought, Shama's coming now, she's waited until everyone's asleep. That bibi sleeps so lightly it's good to wait till you are sure. But look, it's morning now, and I can hear the sweepers in the street and all the Indian House crows, shrieking. With Akberali on a night like that I'd say, I've slept like a dog with fleas on. I have thought of her all night, and of Ayeesha and of Khaled, and of that second loving mother, whose future is now clear.

When Shama did come, my room was barely lightening. She was standing in the doorway. Not quite clearly Shama in the dark, but who else would it be? Upstairs, Tasleem and Kamila were only crawling out of bed and thinking about prayers, Shama's husband sleeping still, and Bibi just pretending but surely thinking up already all the sweet things she would eat. The boys hadn't started speaking. They're shuffling in their room, I thought, looking for the hair oil. Shama didn't walk right in, as she often does. In one hand she had a plate, and a cup of water in the other, and no doubt they were for me. But she waited on the threshold. "Osman?" Shama said, and there was something very sad in how she said it, which I noticed then especially because it isn't often Shama says my name. I thought at first that I would punish her a little. It was dark, but I think she could tell. The same look I'd give to the police at the Jazeera Jazz Club or Fairuz's tembo bar. My mouth closed. Eyes small.

"Osman?" Shama says again. She wants to come in. I want her near, too, but really, there's still some pride in me. I should grasp the feet of everyone I see and cry there like a monkey on a string? What is it? I ask her. Something you forgot? She does come in at last and sets the platter down. Her breath smells—like black salt and something old. She looks at me and sniffs, pauses, then lists a little on her hip. With the shifting of her weight, I can see she's changed from sorry-careful Shama to Shama-who-can-charm. My punishment won't work. She hunkers down beside me. "Don't be mean, Osman, please, don't be mean. I've brought you samosas."

She says she fell asleep. She had been planning to come down, she had. She had the plate prepared for me. But after the film's end, she'd lain just briefly on the bed—"just for a single moment, yah, I thought, I'll just close my eyes"—and found herself asleep. "I fell asleep because I was doing so much thinking," Shama says. "I was thinking about everything." Everything? What everything? I say. Everything like you forgot to bring me food, and downstairs there's an old man who wants to see you tall, and everything like what, exactly? Everything like Osman will have to come up by himself if he wants something to eat. But Osman's not allowed, that's right, oh, I'll just dream a little first? Mention of my exile isn't wise, I see. Shama-who-can-charm is fragile. All right, I say, while I counted up the ceiling beams you were thinking up a storm?

Shama holds the cup above a metal bowl and helps me wash my hands. "Are you hungry now, or what?" she says. And next I have samosas on my lap and though they're cold they're not so bad. Green mango and red pepper. Shama isn't staying long. She hasn't ever come this early and it will be time to make the tea for Tasleem and Kamila, who, in skirts and blouses now, are ready for the world of courier post and airfare. "I was thinking about Khaled's actress mama," Shama says, turning herself a little to the side to let me eat in peace. "I was thinking of Ayeesha." Well, that's enough for me, and I'm too smart to ask her what exactly. She wants to hear what happened next. She's even crossed her legs as though she'd like to stay, though it's not the right time yet. What, I say. The film was not enough? And when Shama turns to me again, she's smiling so much like her uncle it's difficult for me not to reach out for her hands. No problem, I go on. I'll tell you if you like. Shama looks as though she's won a raffle. She says, "The film was not so good, all right? Nothing much to miss. So give me just a little, make it quick."

I tell her: Khaled's mama was a little star, or what. I pause so Shama will desire my next move. Or what. Okay. But the boy was, are you ready now, the very blazing sun. I check. Shama's eyes are not quite open, which means she's listening hard, or trying to, to make up for last night, from which, though I am piling on the story, I have not yet recovered. "Go on, go on," she whispers. "Sun." And so. Almost right away, Khaled took to all the shiny things his mama liked, and even, later, more.

He liked to lie down on her gowns and jiggle there, holding his own feet and digging with his back into the glitter and the silk. They were, Ayeesha thought, very much alike. *This boy knows beauty when he sees it,* she would think, *and see how sure he is about what hands and feet can do.* A performer, this one was, just like his own mama. But this Khaled boy was born that way, with no teacher man intruding and no bus fare in his hands. Oh yes, at just eleven months, fat boy-hips awriggle, Khaled pumped his fingers to the beat of "Ya Habibi" and made charming, timely cries. Just a bit of blubber, really, just a pishi of a boy, but already he could dance. When she came home from work behind the camera, Khaled, one year old, would tumble from his sleeping papa's bed onto his tired mama's lap. *Good night, oumi,* he'd say. Then the boy would whisper, *When I get big I'll be an actor too.* "A healthy one," says Shama, thinking that she might get into form. It's not an interruption, so I tell her, Oh, yah, healthy like a bull.

But let's talk about his mama. Occasionally, Ayeesha thought she loved her little boy more than any of her fancy gowns, more, perhaps, than she even loved herself. Looking down at his round face, her very heart would hurt. She'd squeeze him hard and murmur prayers on his head. She'd make certain in the future that her son would be a star, she'd think, and then she'd pray some more, and next she'd go to work, where she'd forget about the husband and the little growing boy. Forget, oh yes, completely.

Perhaps Shama thinks an early morning visit, cold samosas and a glass of drinking water, are enough to stuff a crack. Despite her sorriness that she has wounded me and must make

up for it somehow, and regardless of her hurry and that upstairs
the bibi must by now be so awake, her eyes are popping from
her head, Shama now speaks up: "Forget? What's this, now,
she forgot? Mama makes a son, and next thing she forgets?
About this, you are certain?" I'm surprised at Shama's tone. If
she wanted everyone upstairs to wonder where she was, she's
told them now with her loud voice. Yes, she forgot, Shama,
she wasn't thinking about children when she let the babu in.
Formalities, that's all. You get a man, and he gets his. Just once,
too, remember, what's the likelihood of that? She *forgot*, I am
insisting, though I see now this forgetting thing is a sore topic
at the moment. Shama, too, forgot. Or not?

"Hmph," she says. "If I'd known this was about forgetting,
I'd have come down a little later." I love my Shama, yes, but my
love has little blades. That's what films are for, I say. Forgetting.
Shama's mouth shuts tight and pulls down at her cheeks so
much her chin shrinks back into her forward-swooping neck.
She's trying not to speak. Sit tight, I say. Let's think about the
babu. Look, I say, Ayeesha did forget, sometimes, but things
were not all bad. At home, Khaled's papa loved them both.
He'd call the halva seller in the road and buy fat lumps for
Khaled, and save some for his wife. He wasn't up to par in
many ways, but he loved his own Ayeesha, and he never once
forgot his little baby son. Shama looks a little brighter with
this news, someone who's unable to forget his tiny dear boy.
But there's a rascal in me, and I cut the nice thing short. Alas,
I say, since all things come to tearful ends, Khaled's papa died.
Shama blinks, surprised, but for the moment quiet. Oh yes, I
say. Poor Ayeesha, widowed.

Just think! Baby Khaled looks all right, mama's making films, baba buying sweets, and everyone feels good. Then, imagine, papa tires of age and sickness and—successful man—expires on his first try! And, worse, this husband's even older family—sisters with hands full, brothers too respectable for words, and children from an early bride who would not greet the upstart—didn't care for starlets. They let Ayeesha keep the house, but otherwise (no visits, no tears, and no love) they left Ayeesha cold. Life's not fair to women.

Shama hasn't interrupted. I see she's shocked about the ancient husband's death. She thinks I'm being cruel. Upstairs the boys are racing in the bedroom. Thumping at the floor. Shama's husband's racking his old throat and spitting in the toilet. It's time for her to go.

When Shama comes back after lunch, she's got a loaded tray. Octopus and stew, some okra on the side, and a lovely plate of rice. Bananas. A feast, I say. And she's got other things to give me. "I know what she did," she says. Who? After our early morning awkward gloom-and-charm, Shama looks transformed. She's looking happy with herself. Her step is lighter than it ever is, as though having left me by myself when she was supposed at least to feed me had released a catch in her. She's fairly floating in the room, sets the heavy tray with food down by the bed as though it weighed no more than a seed. She turns to that secret spectator of hers, who must be hungry, too. "This Ayeesha girl, of course. I know exactly what she did."

I don't know what to say. I look at her as though I'd never seen her once before, not even on the street. She's so glad, she's

almost leering. "Oh, yah, Osman! And I know who she met."
What does she mean by it, exactly, telling me what my plump-
toed, graceful girl did once her husband died?

"Old man, you're going to listen, aren't you? Let Shama tell
a story? I told you I was thinking." The look on Shama's face
is one I've never seen on her, but I have seen it elsewhere, and
I know what it is. It's the look a lover has when he's about to
say that there's been someone else for months now, those very
months you felt the keenest and the best. It's kind, of course.
It has that but-no-one's-quite-like-you glow, and a nervous,
ardent force. The look of someone who has won a prize you
thought belonged to you. "Eat up, Osman. I made the okra
soft for you, that's right." She is going to sit down, but for the
first time I have ever seen her do it Shama clears the floor first,
plucking at my papers and my bottles, moving them aside, and
she smoothes her trousers down before she sits, so she will look
a lady. Again, she says, "For no one else but you." Something
in the air tells me it's my turn to be quiet, though I have second
sisters swarming in my throat. Another something in my stomach has turned upon itself and slowly starts to chew.

"From India, dear Osman," says Shama, "Cairo is a long, long
journey to the West." She pauses now, as though uncertain that
that rising voice is hers. I close my eyes and open them again.
I'm listening. I would like her to be brave. "Journeys to the
West, we think, no, don't deny it, hold extraordinary promise, am I right?" She's like a child, looking for a nod. And so
I nod. She winks. While my stomach twists and turns, I am, I
have to say, entranced by Shama's lips. She has me. "Now lis-

ten," Shama says, taking a big breath, "in Abu Dhabi, U.A.E.,
I swear Salalah, Aden, and, yes, even, even Cairo, you'll see
five thousand Indian boys, and girls and women, too, drown-
ing in their work to save and make a life and see what they can
see. It's true, now, isn't it?" She tucks a strand of hair behind
her ear and then examines her own finger as if the whiteness
would rub off. Looking up, she says, "Or not?" Oh yes, I say,
for sure.

I see now Shama thinks I really have traveled to Cairo and
that the sailor tales were not quite made up on the spot. It's not
my place to fix Shama's geography, or question her logistics.
Shama's trying out this role, and for now I see she likes it. "It's
like that Amit from the pawnshop, no? Went off to Dubai and
came back draped in gold and whatnot. Compact Discs and
Bread Machines in every pocket of his pants." I can't think
what to say. I'm watching Shama's glass stone shimmer in the
light and am forgetting to eat okra. "Amit, you know. Clever.
Tall. Black sunglasses. Pretends he's limping all the time." As
it happens, I know Amit well, and when I could still manage
we would sometimes meet behind his father's shop. But that's
nothing for my Shama's newly daring mind. In fact, let's get
past Amit if we can. Go on, go on, I say. "Well, like I said,"
says Shama, mouth so nice around that *like I said* I feel a wind
rise in my chest. "Like I said, there's all these Indians there.
So it won't surprise you, will it, that Ayeesha found a girl they
called Sayida. No. No wonder in the least.

"You know, Osman, it was hard to be a mama. This Ayeesha
was an actress! She was to stop now, suddenly? Change her life
and everything, sell dumplings in the street so she could be at

home? No way. But now her sugar man was dead, and a dead man can't be counted on to watch a little son while an actress goes to work, or what, or can he? And her neighbors didn't love her, either, don't you see? Too good-looking and successful, this Ayeesha, plus what kind of respect did she really give the babu, going out and coming late without an explanation? Do you know what she did? I know. You wanted two mamas for this boy, Osman, am I correct in this? Two mothers for the mother-love, or so. Well, here is Mother Two. Ayeesha found the boy an ayah. Past her twenties, if you know what I am saying, hardworking and clever. But she had been uncared for: losing teeth already, and lots of stories on her back, far from her own family and lost, and, oh, thinner than a switch. This is our Sayida, now, remember. In a moment she'll be happy."

I'm shocked. Our Sayida, Shama says! She's planned the second mother and has made a sister for herself without any sign from me. Okay. Not what I had planned, but still. And what about poor Khaled, whose whole life I have imagined? That wind in me has shifted something, and I would like, if possible, to set my feet upon the floor. I pull the blankets off and try. For such a shortened woman, it seems to me that Shama has sat up quite tall. That glinting stone is higher than it should be. Is her head protruding less, her neck a little longer?

"I'll tell you where this Sayida started, yah. Not born just in Cairo, if you please. But elsewhere, far away. Sayida, like your friend Nitin at the paper shop, grew up in Bombay." At this point I could prick her. Shama's odd new height aside (and perhaps I see her taller only since I myself am now unused to sitting brightly up), I could say, India, what? Have you even been? And Shama, attached or so she says to truthfulness some-times, could not reply that yes she has and won't I please be quiet. But I'll let that be, for now. I'm a little curious. What's she going to do? Who's this upstart sister? But Shama, smarter than can be, has also seen it coming. "Well, no, Osman, I *haven't* been to India. But my own mother did, and you know how people talk." Oh, talk, I do. Oh yes. For a moment I can sense the gory mass of my own feet on the cold floor, damp and soft like pillows. Shama looks precisely at me now. Her small eyes are in focus. I'm going to close my own. "Let's put two and two together," Shama says. "Or shall we?" She taps me on the leg, and I can nearly feel it. " I know very well. Yes. I know exactly how it was."

❧ *Setting Up Shop*

When Zulfa told Masoud Hamad that she would only be his wife if he divorced the three he had already and gave up all his children, she didn't think he'd do it. Crouched behind the counter of Our Price Is Your Price Fancy Store, she rocked backwards on her heels and crossed her arms over her chest. Her lips a rosy mound, she bent towards Masoud. When Zulfa spoke, her voice was soft. "If you can do that for me, bwana, then I'll know you really love me." The look on Masoud's face—a young look, younger than he was, mouth pulled back, eyes turned down and glossing up with tears—meant, thought Zulfa, that she had finally crossed a line beyond which his I-want-to-marry-you insistences would stop.

When Masoud regained his voice, he spoke in a ferocious whisper that was no whisper at all. "How can you ask me such a thing?" With a scowl and a clicking of her teeth, Zulfa raised a hand up to her mouth. She warned Masoud to keep his voice down: just outside the shop, Babu Issa's coffee cups were not clinking in the basin. The drinkers' voices had gone still.

More quietly, sadly, Masoud said, "No decent woman, no good woman at all, would have me treat my wives so poorly." Zulfa, tugging at her earlobe with a forefinger and thumb, turned her eyes away. She was no longer listening. "If I leave my wives for you," Masoud said to the air, "how can you be sure your turn won't come one day?" Pumping softly at her ear, Zulfa stared right past him at a holographic image of the Kaaba in a frame.

"I love my children, bibiye," Masoud whimpered. "That's exactly right," she said, voice cold and nearly glad. Wiping at his eyes, Masoud crawled to the far wall below the row of hanging dresses they had ordered from Malaysia. Zulfa spread her legs before her on the floor and set to plucking misprints from a new pile of kanga cloths. Zulfa and Masoud stayed quiet in the shadows of the Fancy Store until the muadhin called out at one. Babu Issa and his customers left the coffee stand to pray. Masoud snuck out so stealthily, so glumly, that Zulfa, soothed by all that silence, didn't see him go.

Alone, she shrugged and put the kanga cloths away. *I'm not as I was,* she thought. *I have things I want to do.* She counted out the profits she would hand over to Masoud. She unlocked her private cash box and confirmed she'd taken what was hers.

As Zulfa closed the wooden doors, old Mafunda, who sold uji up the road, ambled past with bowls and ladles in her hands. Mafunda would have liked to hear from Zulfa how things were going with Masoud. Everyone was curious. But Zulfa only nodded, gave a silent smile, and crossed the road into her mother's house.

Habiba, Zulfa's mother, had finished doing dishes, and in her front room was watching an Egyptian film on the shining, squat TV. She turned the volume down to ask how things were going at the shop. "Oh, just fine," said Zulfa, as she washed her hands for lunch. But to herself she thought, *Masoud Hamad has finally understood that I won't play his game.* Her flat refusals hadn't worked. She had won now, hadn't she?

Masoud Hamad, thirty-seven, handsome, clever, had gone away from Usilie when he was still a boy. Four years before begging Zulfa one last time to be his wife, Masoud had come home to the modest town of Usilie after a long stay in Saudi Arabia and the Emirates, where he'd learned everything to do with oil and electronics. He spoke Arabic and English. His beard was neat and mostly dark. Making everybody proud, he had come back to Usilie because the Arab girls he had encountered in his travels were nothing next to the ones he had grown up with. Or so he said to wizened, too-smart-for-anybody's-good Mafunda, who knew what was worth knowing. He was done, Masoud told old Mafunda, with the bachelor's life abroad, with going here and there and only passing through. Home for good, to settle down, he was looking for a wife.

The first bride he tried to stick to was his uncle's daughter Husna, a pious girl with eyes like zaitun fruit, and—underneath the billowing black buibui coats her father's friends imported from Dubai—what everyone suspected was a very pleasing figure. Things were as they should be; the families were proud. Women old enough to voice their views in public praised Masoud's virile look for everyone to hear. Younger ones, who couldn't speak so baldly, whispered: *Masoud's knees are good, his lower back is strong, just look at how he walks!* They saw vitality ahead. Energetic afternoons to whip up healthy babies just as manly as their dad.

Masoud did right by his first wife. Just beyond the bakery, a pretty four-room house was built from pricey cement blocks, then caked in yellow plaster chipping, which (according to Mafunda) was the very latest style. Spending just over four lakhs, Masoud set a tin roof down and ordered electricity. As it should be when a man's knees are as hard and fine as Masoud's were, Masoud was at first only seen at prayers, and very briefly at the market in the afternoons, where he often left with fish just enough for two. If Masoud purchased beef, Mafunda, watching from her place before the hardware shop, nodded her old head up and down and said, almost to herself but loud enough so everyone could hear: "And it's not only that. Our Husna's also getting fatty meat from her husband's able tongue."

People in Usilie told Masoud that they were waiting for the babies, which, just so, they got, on schedule: a sturdy girl after nine months, twin howling boys soon after. Once the house beside the bakery had swollen up with healthy kids (and Husna with experience), Masoud went back to Saudi Arabia for a visit. He stayed away three months. People said, "What a good man Masoud is. He doesn't want the people who were kind to him to think that he's forgotten. Just as we care so much for him, he has been beloved abroad."

Masoud returned with a well-fed look and gifts. Nazir, who manned the Tailoring and Petrol Stand, got a belt with a big buckle. Masoud brought Babu Issa a new radio, which, set beside the coffee urn, plucked tinny taarab tunes from air. Masoud presented Husna with a freezer. He suggested she make fruit ice pops for money. It would be good for her, he told his uncle and his father, to feel a little independent. "See how much he loves her?" other women said.

Even old Mafunda got a gift, an outrageous, flirty gift, which it was all right to give because she was so shameless and so ancient: Masoud brought her a glittering pair of gold-embroidered trousers he had purchased in Oman. Though she swore when she accepted Masoud's pantaloons that she would only sport them plainly when there was no one there to see, Mafunda soon began appearing at the uji stand with skirts hiked slightly up, stylish leggings on display. It was a chance to demonstrate that she had been on Masoud's mind. "See?" people said. "He loves us so much here that he remembers the most abject of our elders."

Mafunda, who, because of the bright trousers, felt her tie to him was special, started making some suggestions. Pressing free bowls of steaming uji on Masoud, she'd say, "It's selfish keeping all your goodness to yourself. Your wife is tired from the freezer and the babies. She's a busy woman now. She can't take care for you alone." Masoud liked talking to Mafunda. She was quick and funny and always spoke her mind. Masoud liked giving people gifts. He liked making women happy, which was a duty, after all, if you could afford to do it. And women were so warm that falling hard for one of them was easy. He took Mafunda's words to heart.

The second girl he made a bride, a distant cousin on Masoud's father's side, lived several miles away in Hausemeki town. She was younger than the first, quick-footed, and darker. Masoud built a nice house for her, too, right beside her mother's—which was not usual exactly, but what could you do, when houses were springing up all over, and it was hard to find free land? This one got pink chipping. Mafunda said that it was smart of him to put some miles between the first wife and the second, so they wouldn't see each other all the time, and so the neighbors wouldn't tell exactly what soft noises coming from the other's house had kept them up when by all rights they should have been asleep.

At Hausemeki, where jackfruit grew in plenty and paths were edged in ylang-ylang trees, Masoud paid to have the town's first power line since 1970 put up. Everyone who could afford it mounted low-watt lightbulbs on their homes and hooked into his cables. While he didn't give the second wife a freezer, he opened up a shop for her on the road to Hausemeki town, where she sold multicolored thread, sturdy baskets from the north, and Chinese stones for knives. He spent the same amount on the new wife, it seemed, that he'd spent getting Husna—which was only right. In Hausemeki town, everyone agreed he was the best and brightest husband any of their girls had ever had the luck to find.

The men of Usilie thought Masoud was doing a good thing and that he did it well. Babu Issa at the coffee stand said there were more women in the world than husbands, and those who could should try to give them homes. But though it was a fine idea, a religious duty and all that, he said, it was very hard to do. "The man who keeps two households up without making someone jealous, or losing his own mind, is very, very rare."

The boys at the garage, who now and then had time to spare, and whose mouths were very clever, made jokes about Masoud. They feared his knees might give out at any moment, what with all that running from the yellow house down to the one he'd painted pink. Mafunda, who was loyal, thought Masoud could manage anything. "He's really something special," she declared. "What a man he is." She did like her new trousers. Babu Omari at the gristmill dozed against the doorjamb, filling up with dreams. He wondered: what would it be like to go from one wife to the other, get loving in two places?

While Masoud was setting up his second house, Zulfa, whom at this time Masoud did not know, was preparing for a marriage of her own to an old, unpleasant man. Kassim Majid had rented Zulfa's father, Mzee Abeid, thirty hybrid orange trees. The trees would be for keeps, he said, if he could marry Zulfa. Mzee Abeid was of the definite opinion that he could use the money. He himself had taken up a second wife several years before, and for things to be all right had had to buy Habiba the TV. Having two wives was expensive. It was time, Mzee Abeid told Habiba, their Zulfa made a home. Zulfa, busy feeling bitter about her own upcoming spouse, didn't pay the news of Masoud's nuptial plans a great deal of attention.

The younger girls of Usilie, who crowded round Habiba's big TV to watch love films from Bombay and soaps from Argentina, felt it was too bad about Zulfa's old man, but they didn't like to say so. Instead they talked about Masoud: the first marriage with Husna was for duty, they averred; the second tie must be for love. They petted one another's arms and screwed their lips up, kissing loudly at the air. Zulfa had no wish to hear of other people's happiness just then. It seemed to her that she had better things to do than get married to a man who traded orange trees for love.

Zulfa watched the romance tales like everybody else, but was not taken in. "All men want," she said, dropping tiny Indian almonds from her fingers to her mouth, "is to be taken care of, and to make a lot of babies." She wasn't looking forward to Mzee Kassim. When the girls said *they* surely wouldn't mind making babies with a young one like Masoud, Zulfa shrugged, and said, "All you want is getting stuck at home and fatty in the belly? Nothing else but that?" She finished all the almonds, and did not stay for that romantic film's finale.

These same girls took Zulfa to her new home on a hill, which overlooked a pair of cassia trees and a pretty coffee orchard. Clapping, they serenaded her with songs about kicking soccer balls between the goalposts, and bits of tasty meat that nobody could name. "You didn't get a young one," some of them said then, but they did try to console her: "This means he'll have experience."

Zulfa took in Kassim's half-blind, drooling face and his gnarled old bony hands, and could see right away that the thing was a mistake. She was proven right: too busy dodging Kassim's blows when the warped old man was hale, and healing his diseases when he wasn't, to notice when Masoud selected a third bride, Zulfa had her hands full. If she'd been able to visit with Habiba, or the girls, they would have told her she'd missed nothing. There had been no music and no luncheon at Masoud's latest wedding. In fact, the way third weddings can be that first and second wives don't care for, the union was cemented without fanfare, quickly, in the middle of the night.

Masoud took care of his third wife almost as he had of the first two, though there were some who wondered if he didn't spend a little less. This one got a sewing machine—a fine black Shanghai Stitcher with well-oiled pedals and a scarlet-emerald butterfly embossed on its round chest. Every month Masoud brought her cloth he'd purchased in Mombasa, where he often went to stock the shops he ran in Kudra's bigger towns. But after the third wedding, some in Usilie asked themselves if Masoud hadn't come home in the first place because he'd had troubled loves abroad. Robustness and virility, at decent intervals, with care, were one thing, but this, some people said, might be something else instead. Could he be disturbed?

Mafunda was among them. Maybe he had hoped, by coming back, to cure himself, she said, of an unfortunate propensity. Maybe our Masoud, she said, likes women more than a reliable man should. Babu Issa at the coffee stand was heard to say that if Masoud kept taking wives so quickly, one after another, he might make the men ashamed.

By the time Zulfa finally fled Kassim Majid's hill house and, with the help of a well-placed purple bruise and some needling from Habiba, convinced Mzee Abeid that she should be divorced, some in Usilie no longer praised Masoud so highly. Oh, they hadn't turned against him; in fact everyone still liked him. But it was clear by then that Masoud was not simply an able man with riches to bestow on the townsfolk who had raised him: no, Masoud Hamad, they started to agree, was a man who liked to marry. Young girls did still feel a thrill when Masoud passed, and Zulfa's father in particular remained very much impressed. Babu Omari with his notebook at the gristmill had not married even once, so it was ever awesome for him that a man could do it so relentlessly, with style. But, all in all, Masoud's reputation underwent a change.

Mafunda—who had given up on the idea that she had a special bond with him, though not yet on her trousers—said, her feelings just a little hurt, "Taking wives is the only work Masoud knows how to do. Some men know how to teach, and some men only farm. Masoud Hamad can marry." As she handed regulars their bowls of pepper porridge, Mafunda hitched her dress up. "He likes women, that boy does. Women of all kinds. Look, he even gave me these." She preened there on the stoop, showing off her ankles. Masoud, it was now fashionable to say, was a man enslaved by passions. It was nice that he could give his wives new clothes, and that all of his six children would be sent to school, even, yes, the girls. But how seriously could you regard a man who took three wives in under half a decade, and showed no signs of slowing?

"He's allowed to marry up to four, remember!" said Mafunda, thumb curled into her right hand, other fingers flailing while her wrist shook. "Four!" She was so vehement about it that she spilled a bowl of porridge to the ground. And so, instead of reveling in electricity, and in how Husna's sugar pops could ease a too-hot day, people began making bets on who was going to be next. Babu Issa, in particular, liked to make pronouncements. People went to drink and listen. Turning off the radio, Babu Issa would shake coins in his closed fist, to get everyone's attention. "If I know Masoud Hamad, he'll push it to the limit. He'll take the four wives he's allowed. And when that's not enough for him, he'll leave the first one to make room, and do it all again. Who's it going to be?"

In a way, the thing between Masoud Hamad and Zulfa was Zulfa's Aunt Khadija's fault. If not for Aunt Khadija, Zulfa might never have met Masoud Hamad at all. When Khadija came back well rested and plump from a season's holiday in Oman and the Emirates to her old house in Kiguu, she invited Zulfa to a party. Zulfa, who loved her Aunt Khadija because she was so pretty and had seen so much of the world, was desperate to go.

At Kiguu there was a cove that girls could swim in; there were mibura trees in fruit, and lots of berries in the bushes. There were also kindly people who felt that Zulfa had been wronged in her brief marriage to old Kassim Majid and should be treated gently.

Zulfa saw herself already stretched out on the floor of Khadija's airy house, rose and jasmine on the breeze. She would lay her head in her aunt's lap while Khadija combed and twisted at her hair, telling her how pure the air was on the garden slopes of Sharjah. She might meet clever ladies who, swigging cups of bitter coffee, would discuss the weddings they had been to: who was wearing what, who was eyeing whom, and who hadn't been invited. Oh, she would have a time! Khadija's girls would refuse to let her help out in the kitchen. They would make her lie down with a pillow and give her cups of mango juice to drink while they did all the work. Little boys, impressed by Zulfa's looks—she exuded city style, although she'd never lived in one—would collect pink pomelos and lemons for her and leave them gently by her mattress while she slept. But Kiguu was a full day's walk away. Zulfa didn't want to walk. She would have to find a ride.

First, Zulfa begged Habiba's help in sweetening her father: "Please, won't you talk to Ba, ask him to make Salum find a driver and a car?" Salum, Zulfa's cousin, hardworking and young, usually did his utmost to give Zulfa some pleasure. But Salum was upstanding: he often wished to know if Zulfa's plans had Mzee Abeid's approval. And Mzee Abeid, for his part, thought it was high time his youngest daughter stopped behaving as though she'd never had a husband and still had lots of time to play. Zulfa couldn't tell her father to his face why she wanted to leave town—not to Kiguu for a party!

Habiba was not keen on Zulfa taking off for several days, not when Zulfa's sister Warda had come home from the mainland with three small children and a baby and the house was full of stomachs. Habiba, who had unfulfilled desires of her own, didn't look at Zulfa when she said, "Ask your father by yourself." She kept on with her washing. Zulfa went over to her mother's side, wrung three dresses for her and hung them on the line. She wrapped her arms around Habiba's ample middle and laid her head beneath her mother's breasts. "Please?" She pressed Habiba's belly. Habiba shook her daughter off and sniffed. She squeezed the dress she'd taken from the basin hard, making sure the water ran right down her daughter's toes. Zulfa waited in the courtyard, hoping that Habiba might grow soft and say that she would help her, but Habiba kept hanging up the washing and she didn't speak again.

Finally, Zulfa went out the back way and walked through

the cassava plots to her father's father's place, *her* Babu, to ask him to say something to his son, or, even better, call Salum to his house and speak with him directly. Babu liked Zulfa's Aunt Khadija. He felt warmly towards her. He'd be glad if Zulfa made a journey to Kiguu. Babu, Zulfa thought, was kind, and he would surely help her. But when she found him spread out like a spider on his bed, he was in no mood for easy talk. He had the shortwave pressed up to his ear as though it were a telephone, as though the *Deutsche Welle* people had called him up especially. "Just listen to this," he said, having sensed Zulfa's arrival without opening his eyes: "Children in the U.S.A. are shooting schoolteachers with guns."

Zulfa sighed. She sat with him on the bed, snapping with her fingers now and then at the skinny chicks that scurried in and out. *When I get to America,* thought Zulfa, *I'm not going to be a teacher.* She knew that once the program ended, Babu would fall right to sleep. Zulfa tried the words out in the room: "If I make it to America, Babu, I'll make sure not to be a teacher." Babu frowned, and pointed at the radio. "I'm listening to the news," he said. Zulfa rose, picked up a small banana from his table, ate it, and left her granddad on the bed.

On the way to the main road from Babu's, Zulfa kicked at the mimosa on the edges of the trail to make the leaves furl back. She took a back path up the hill towards the gristmill, where Babu Omari sat sleeping on the threshold, spectacles high up on his brow, Lion notebook on his lap. Zulfa paused to look at him and made a face to test how deep his dreams were flowing. Then, moving past him down a gully that was plugged up with dead tires, she emerged behind the workshop of Usilie town. She would ask Salum herself if he could take her to Kiguu.

At the shop, Salum was banging at the underside of a bright blue Morris taxi. Zulfa didn't want Salum's coworkers to see her. The fat, thick-bearded one was her ex-husband's youngest brother, and the others, fox-faced, muscled, had roving eyes and mouths. Zulfa leaned against the light blue wall of Bi Faida's house, facing the garage. From inside, she could hear Bi Faida's chatty girls making ice pops from sweet juice. Below the open window, Zulfa squatted, balancing herself on two flat, white coral stones. "Psst. Salum."

Salum started at the sound and hit his head on something hard under the car. Zulfa bit her lips to keep from laughing. Pressing with a hip against Bi Faida's house, she hunkered even lower. She called her cousin's name again. Salum eased out from below and rose, tugging at his coveralls. He looked around a little and he frowned when he spotted Zulfa squatting.

"Wallahi, Zulfa, can't you announce yourself politely?" Zulfa made her mouth sweet. She liked how Salum's eyebrows met sharply in a vee at the center of his nose and that he was easy with a smile. Sometimes she could get him to do exactly what she wished. But when she looked at him demurely and raised the question of a car, Salum interrupted. "None of these will run," he said. "The first car I get working goes straight back to its owner."

Salum wasn't smiling. Perhaps he was coming to suspect that Zulfa was fetching mostly when she needed things from him. That it didn't matter how much he thought of sending news to Mzee Abeid that even if Zulfa was a divorcée, Salum would be glad to have her, cherish her and treat her well. Maybe Salum could see that she would always be like this, looking to escape, begging rides from those who loved her. "No," he said. He frowned so that the outer edges of his eyebrows leapt almost up into his hair. "I'm not in the mood." Even when she rose and placed a soft hand on his forearm, never-minding it was black with engine grease, Salum pulled away and said he had to get to work.

Looking sadly at her feet, Zulfa shuffled back the way she came. At the gristmill, Babu Omari, now awake, adjusted his thick glasses. Seeing Zulfa could make a man alert. He tried to have her stop with him a little, but she stood only long enough to ask if he'd got lemons growing on his land, and when he said no, he hadn't, Zulfa kept on moving.

She was just stepping onto the main road again when she saw a tall man in a well-pressed kanzu gown stop at Nazir's Tailoring and Petrol Stand to fill up a big red and orange Honda. The bike glowed brightly in the sunlight, much more nicely, sleekly, than a taxi. *That's Masoud Hamad,* she thought. Now *there* was a generous, well-rounded man with a means of transportation.

When Masoud saw Zulfa at the bottom of the path across from Nazir's Tailoring and Petrol Stand, he couldn't think, at first, exactly who she was. But while Nazir put away the shirt he was resizing to fit a brand-new owner and got the gasoline for the new Honda from a plastic gallon jug, Masoud watched her carefully, and Zulfa, pleased, could feel his eyes right on her. She knew just what she'd do. First, she looked

away from Nazir's Petrol Stand and down the road that led
to Hausemeki town. Then, as though she'd dropped a small
thing in the leaves, she looked down at the ground. Finally, she
pulled her scarf around her face a little tighter to be modest and
stood still for a long moment, frowning slightly, as if consider-
ing something personal and secret. When Masoud called out
a greeting, Zulfa pretended that she was not sure to whom it
was addressed. After one full minute, she bowed her head in
answer. *Oh! Me?*

While Nazir bent over the Honda, Masoud took a step towards Zulfa. "Whose child are you?" he asked. Zulfa saw a
dainty tuft of gray at the edge of Masoud's beard, just below his
mouth, and noticed his soft lips. She hadn't heard his voice so
clearly before this. It had a winning tone, she thought, a voice
that would be heartening at dawn, calling from the mosque
while you were still in bed.

Nazir looked up from the gallon jug, glad Zulfa had come.
He, for one, had not been pleased when Mzee Abeid's last
daughter went to live in a hill house far away from town with
a rich, bad-tempered husband. Not that Nazir could have got
her for himself. Zulfa's family (on Habiba's side) was pious, and
Nazir was not ardent about praying. On Mzee Abeid's side,
they had once been rich and still behaved as though they were.
And all Nazir knew how to do was stitch and pour out gasoline. But he'd been thrilled when Zulfa finally escaped from
old Kassim Majid. A man can always dream.

Zulfa told Masoud that her father was Mzee Abeid, and that
when Masoud took on his latest wife, she had been away. "I was
sad to miss your wedding," Zulfa said, though she hadn't been

invited, and she knew there hadn't been a party. Her manner subtly suggesting that she knew what wedding nights were like, Zulfa cocked her head. "It was a long time ago, but still."

Nazir, who could tell how Zulfa looked from the honeyed sound of her high voice, screwed the lid back on the jug and called, "Hey, Zulfa! Itching to be number four?" She looked down at him and laughed, and Nazir's legs went soft. Zulfa was a pleasure, really. She took teasing very well. She never made it cheap. It wasn't disrespect or looseness that made her such a joy. It came from having been a wife and being free now, free to name things if she wished, having looked them in the eye.

"No," she said, tilting her head up so that Masoud (who was taller than she was) could contemplate her face, "I won't share *my* husbands." Zulfa stepped up to the Honda and hoisted herself sidesaddle up onto the seat. Turning to Masoud, she said, "This bike is very beautiful." Then she asked if it was his. She stroked the burly handles with the fat part of her palm. "Did you buy it? Is it new?"

Nazir answered for Masoud, because he liked to speak to Zulfa and it wasn't often she came down his way. "Brand-new! Sixteen fifty. Take you all the way to Mkumbuu," he said, as proudly as if he'd bought the thing himself. "And you won't have to get off once to walk it through the mud. This bike will plow through on its own."

Zulfa didn't need too many details about how well the Honda ran. Still looking at Masoud, she said frankly, "I don't want to be a wife just yet. But I would like a lift out to Kiguu." Masoud couldn't help himself. He smiled at her. "Kiguu, eh?" Nazir understood that everything that happened now would

be between Zulfa and Masoud. He sat back down at his own
old Shanghai Stitcher and started pedaling again. "Tomorrow
afternoon," said Zulfa. "Tomorrow afternoon at two." She
slipped lightly from the Honda and bent to tug the bottom
of her cotton dress to cover up her ankles. Masoud, open-
mouthed, looked on. Then, very quickly, she was gone, moving towards her mother's house. She looked straight ahead of
her, so Masoud wouldn't think it mattered much, and Nazir
wouldn't see how very much it did.

At almost two o'clock, with three minutes to spare, Masoud
stopped the Honda at Habiba's house. When she heard the
Honda's rumble on the road and saw her man about to knock
and call out at the door, Zulfa gestured through the window
for Masoud to be still.

Mzee Abeid had come from Babu Issa's coffee stand for
lunch. Zulfa went to find him in the kitchen. "Ba," she said.
Mzee Abeid looked up at his daughter. Though he did think
Zulfa shouldn't be so free, he could not begrudge her little joys.
He regretted how things had gone with Kassim. He set his
plate of stewed greens down beside him on the mat and asked
her what she wanted. Zulfa apologized for asking at short notice. "Ba," she said, "Masoud Hamad has business in Kiguu."

Abeid nodded. "So?" He plucked a piece of white-fish
from the bowl beside him with a spoon. *He doesn't know about
Khadija's party,* Zulfa thought. "Poor old Aunt Khadija's asked
to see me. You know how we neglect her." Zulfa could already
see it: her dad was going to agree. It was better if it looked like
Masoud's accidental doing. "He's outside," she said, picturing

the place where she had, in preparation, left her newest shoes. "He says we have to leave right now." Aunt Khadija was Mzee Abeid's own sister, so how could he refuse? He didn't think about the work Habiba had just then, with Warda and her babies home to stay; no, he didn't see a reason to object.

Zulfa hadn't known for sure that Masoud Hamad would come, but she'd got her things together just in case. Outside, she handed him her nylon bag and let him strap it to the plank behind the seat. Once Zulfa settled sideways on the leather cushion, her feet crossed neatly at the ankles, Masoud bore her away. The people who were not asleep or in their houses saw, and each of them took note. When Habiba woke up from her nap and found her daughter gone, she was riled, but said nothing to her husband. She knew Masoud Hamad had no business in Kiguu except to do their daughter's bidding. Indeed, Habiba could imagine just how Zulfa had convinced him. At Zulfa's age, Habiba, too, had known how such things were done.

To ensure that nothing shameful will occur when assisting a strange woman—no loose talk and no flirtatious questions, and certainly no looking in the eye—some men will keep quiet. And many women, too, when taking kindness from a man they don't know well, will refuse to answer questions, ask none, and keep their eyes turned down. Nonetheless, no matter who the man and woman are, or how quiet they will keep, on the long seat of a motorbike subtle intimacies bloom.

For example, Zulfa's shoulder and the length of her soft upper arm were necessarily pressed close to Masoud's spine. One of Zulfa's hands, which when the road was smooth stayed properly behind her on the belt across the seat, crept up to hold the loose cloth of his shirt when the road turned full of pot-holes. Zulfa found that if she turned her head towards Masoud, she could eye her own reflection in the rearview mirror's circle. Masoud quickly found, once they were heading for the hills, that he could see it, too.

Just as Nazir had promised, the Honda plowed through sand and mud and up and down sharp slopes without their having to step down. But it also bucked and shivered, and the bucking made Zulfa, who was brave but not accustomed, really, to riding on a Honda, press more tightly up against her driver. They talked (or shouted, rather, since the engine roared and rumbled), and Masoud learned that Zulfa was, in an important way, a woman after his own heart. Zulfa liked, she said, to travel. Moreover, she announced, "I want to see the world before I die."

Her next words must have got lost in the wind, or maybe Masoud just didn't pay enough attention. When Zulfa said, "I'll see the world before anybody marries me again," Masoud was thinking of his wives. They all liked to travel, too. Husna had once spent three months in Abu Dhabi with an older cousin who had married there: she had seen the inner walls of a dozen well-appointed houses, reveled in the air-conditioning, and gotten beautifully fat from drink-ing lots of water. His Hausemeki wife had as a girl spent sev-eral Ramadhans on the mainland, where she had shopped and watched a great deal of TV. Masoud's third wife had never left the island, but she had stayed with relatives up north, where the yams, she swore, were sweeter than any she had tasted. All of them, he knew, would have liked to go on visits to their families abroad, assess the growth of children they had seen in photographs or known only as infants, and enter shops filled up with goods they could not get at home. The third one in particular, he thought, would have liked to visit fabric markets in a city, for the dresses that she made.

But none of them would have formulated their desire quite as Zulfa did: "Traveling," she shouted in his ear, "is a means of education! I want to see how people live." She was not looking at him in the mirror when she said this. She was frowning at a pair of houses on the edge of Kiguu road, painted in pink earth, embellished with a black design of leaves. This neighborhood was poor, with people who only dreamed of motorbikes and didn't have Toshibas. To Zulfa and Masoud, their dialect was strange. "For example," Zulfa said, "what's it like out here?" Gazing at her face in the bright disc of the mirror, Masoud thought briefly that had she been a wealthy woman contemplating novelties in a sophisticated shop, her expression would have been the same.

When she spoke again, Masoud felt an exquisite mist of spittle settle on his neck. He shivered. "You, Masoud. You've been around the world." With Zulfa's glassy twin looking so divine, Masoud forgot to watch the road. The Honda bounded towards a tree root that was poking from the ground; at the ensuing jerk and rear, one of Zulfa's beaded sandals escaped the clutches of her toes. She yelled at him to stop. He did, ashamed, and Zulfa got down from the bike. As Masoud watched her scurry off to find the single shoe, desires he thought he had conquered came welling in his chest. Zulfa was so small, so strong! Luckily, Khadija's was not far. Otherwise, Masoud might have made pronouncements whose time had not yet come: *I too still have new things to discover.* Or, *I'll build you a house, get two stand fans and a freezer. We'll be happy, you and me.*

At Kiguu, Masoud didn't stay. He greeted Aunt Khadija properly, and got back onto the Honda much more modest, all in all, than Zulfa had expected. Two days later he returned, and Khadija, with a wise look in her eye, congratulated Zulfa for securing the generosity and kindness of such a fine, respectful man. As Zulfa got onto the Honda and Masoud bent to hook two baskets full of fruit around the handles, Khadija handed her a gift: a ninja-niqab face-veil she had gotten in Dubai. "It's the latest thing," she said. "You'd be surprised how nice they are." The veil made Zulfa feel very up to date. She giggled, then kissed the air beside Khadija's cheeks, one-two, saying, "We are parting Arab-style." Khadija pinched her arm, and said, "Look pretty, now. You might be number four."

After the visit to Kiguu, Masoud took Zulfa everywhere. He took her north to buy adesi beans and carrots. Sometimes he would take Zulfa along when he went south to pick up shipments—in Baharini town, she would visit her old school friends and toss their babies high into the air. If she learned that rose apples were ripe in Shibayako, she left a letter for Masoud at Nazir's petrol stand. Nazir would deliver Zulfa's notice, and in the morning Masoud would show up with his own basket for the harvest, so Zulfa wouldn't soil hers.

Habiba was displeased. Necessarily suspicious when it came to men with many wives, Habiba thought Masoud Hamad had scandalous intentions. But Zulfa was a headstrong divorcée.

And Mzee Abeid approved. He did worry that his youngest daughter was too free, that if she did not marry soon, shameful things might happen. One night, as he lay bare-chested on his belly and Habiba rubbed his calves with oil, he said, "She will be the fourth. He's only had young girls, yet. He's surely ready now for someone who's mature."

More anxious than she knew, Habiba pressed her lips together and squeezed her husband's leg so tightly that Abeid winced and turned around. Habiba didn't want any of her girls to be a fourth, or third, or second. She knew how much a first wife can be wounded: Habiba hadn't made her peace with Abeid's second wife at all. Abeid tore his leg out of her hand. "Mtume! In the prophet's name, habibti, are you crazy?"

Mouth slightly ajar, surprised, Habiba examined the dark grooves her nails had made along her husband's naked calf. Abeid rose up on his elbow and turned to face his wife. He softened. "How have I offended you?" Abeid's eyes had gone all round. "If she wants him," his wife said, biting fiercely at her lip. "If Zulfa wants him. If he asks. We'll talk about it then." She reached over for the vial of oil and pressed a heavy hand on Abeid's tired back. "Now turn around, old man, and let me rub your sorry legs."

Zulfa's feelings had a pattern. When Masoud went away on short trips to the mainland or farther north to Kenya to buy cloths and radios for his shops, Zulfa felt relieved. At first, she would revel in his absence. She would talk nicely with her sister Warda, sometimes playing with her girls. Sitting with Habiba, she ground coconuts for rice. She took a modest pleasure in the uneventfulness of things. If a mood came to her in the afternoons, she might listen to the news from London or from Washington, D.C., in Babu's ancient house. She would walk the little paths and alleyways of Usilie town, and with a thrilled and painful sadness think how she would miss it all when she was finally abroad. She'd wonder why she spent so much of her time talking with Masoud when all he wanted was a wife. She would say aloud to Warda, "Thank goodness he's left town so finally I can breathe! He sticks like a leech!" Warda would give her little sister a long and knowing look, keeping, for the moment, her own experienced counsel.

If, however, Masoud stayed away longer than three weeks, although Zulfa swore she didn't want him, she would wish for his return. She wasn't always sure if she missed Masoud or the motorcycle most, but, whichever one it was, her feelings would take a sudden turn: there would come a tangy churning in her stomach; a bulky weight would house itself between her chest and throat. If she felt like that, breathless, with an appetite for foods she couldn't name, she sometimes used a cell phone that belonged to Masoud's cousin (a businessman in his own right) to send Masoud a written message: *I think of U. Buy me something nice.* Masoud (fearing that any message he might send—*have bought mattress covered blue cloth 4 U pls can we get married?*—would meet his cousin's eyes) never sent her a reply. His silences made Zulfa's complex longings announce themselves more sharply.

When Masoud came back to Usilie with a gift (a watch, perfume, a pair of platform shoes), Zulfa would feel right again. Forgetting all about America, she would sit out on the stoop, slipping groundnuts into plastic tubes for the neighbor boy to sell, right there for all to see so that if Masoud passed by on foot or on his Honda he would notice her and stop. For some days after his return, Zulfa would be thrilled, and do her best to please him. Masoud made her feel pretty. His Honda, she thought, made her free.

The day Masoud asked Zulfa to be his partner in a shop he planned to start by Babu Issa's coffee stand, he'd been back three weeks, and Zulfa, tired of being so delightful, had started hoping he would leave. On the stoop, Zulfa had been plucking petals from a batch of soft, pink roses that she wanted to set out to dry. Masoud sat down beside her. Before the mosque across the road, passengers laboring with bags stepped in and out of trucks. Drivers called out destinations.

Something in Masoud's voice made Zulfa set down the flower she'd just lifted up. In Zulfa's eyes, Masoud came sharply into focus. She slid just a little closer to him on the stoop. "Ebu, what's that you just said?"

"The shop. I'll need someone to mind it. You will be in charge." Masoud tossed the rosebud up into the air and made a net out of his palm to catch it when it fell.

"The shop," said Zulfa. Then, "I will?"

"Oh yes! No doubt! And . . ." Feet firmly planted on the ground, Masoud, thinking of how desperately he loved her, nodded gravely at his friend. "You'll keep a full third of the profits."

Zulfa made her eyes go needle-sharp. "You're not asking this so that I will marry you? Put me in a shop so you can buy me, too? So I will owe you something?"

Masoud made his face look shocked. He pressed the rosebud to his chest. "Me? What? No. I won't ask anything from you."

But Zulfa wasn't playing. She yanked the flower from his hand. "I'm very serious now, Masoud. You promise me? No games?" When Masoud said he promised, yes, and, utmost, absolutely, Zulfa opted to believe him, for it is expedient now and then to take a person at his word.

Three weeks later, Masoud and Zulfa's Our Price Is Your Price Fancy Store was born. A cargo container was brought up to Babu Issa's from the harbor and set down on its side. Masoud hired Nazir's little brothers to repaint it. Once the room-sized box had dried to a brilliant shade of red, the shop was filled with novelties: wall clocks from Japan, bright embroidered gowns from Thailand and Malaysia, Chinese pots and pans enameled with blue flowers, fine perfumes brought from Mombasa and the Emirates, and incense, jellies, of all kinds.

Masoud hadn't lied. Zulfa daily opened up the shop. She sold things, figured the accounts in a notebook just like Babu Omari's, and closed up shop at night. Masoud kept track of what had to be replenished and ordered special trinkets if he thought that they might sell. Zulfa got so used to everything, to chatting with the customers, to making jokes with Babu Issa, and to catching glimpses of herself in the flat faces of the clocks, that she sometimes felt she had been keeping shop for years, that she had never been anything but this: a charming, able woman, brooking no dissent, and only handing back the most correct of change. It was true about the profits. Zulfa kept a third.

Habiba could plainly see her youngest child excelled at keeping shop and that she did it without the ambling rancor that accompanied her movements when at home. *Masoud's behavior is not conventional,* Habiba thought, *but it is always—just—correct.* It was clear Masoud Hamad liked women, but, Habiba reluctantly admitted (though it made her set her teeth), at least he'd married them, so far.

At first Mzee Abeid was disconcerted to see his daughter at the heart of such activity, but Zulfa was always decently attired. And he could tell, even if Zulfa pretended not to know, that Masoud was thinking of the future. Moreover, Zulfa always gave a portion of her profits to Habiba, which made things easier for Mzee Abeid, with two households to run. What neither of her parents knew was that, one day when Masoud wasn't there, Zulfa bought herself a separate cash box, a Chinese lock and key, and started making plans.

During her first few months at home, Zulfa's older sister Warda stayed inside with Habiba, remembering her youth. *There* was the old, enormous tree with its sakua mango fruits, which people on the mainland claimed never to have seen. *There* was the floor's familiar slope, just beside the bathroom. *There* was Babu, looking just as wiry as he had when Warda was a girl. She ate Usilie treats and gained a lot of weight. She listened to the nightly thump and wail of bush babies askitter on the roof and took naps beside her mother. Her in-laws brought her letters for their son and told her she looked just as fat and modest as a bride. They pinched and kissed the children. But after several months of rest, and of remembering so closely how she had been raised that she didn't think she could forget again, Warda wished to make some special visits of her own. And wanted Zulfa to go with her.

"I've grown up," Warda said to Zulfa in the bedroom after both of them had bathed. "I can't go strolling by myself." Warda, Zulfa knew, was shy. And also there was something slightly shameful, or too proud, about walking out in daylight with her children, round and handsome as she was. Everyone would call her over, asking why she'd been invisible for so many, many years: where had she been hiding? They'd ask her if she'd brought them gifts, and if she hadn't, why. Warda knew they would be cataloguing everything: her size, the design and quality of her city shoes and cloak, if her little girls were far too thin or fat enough, or unbecomingly so fat that Warda must be showing off, if their frilly gowns were store-bought or hand-made. Going out would be a chore, a battle. But go out Warda would, with Zulfa at her side.

"I want to visit Husna," Warda said, her tight curls shooting up and out from her full face while she rubbed her hands with oil. "Husna who?" asked Zulfa, idly plucking hairs out from the comb and rolling them into a springy ball between her fingers and her thumb. Masoud was in Mombasa buying cloth, and Zulfa was distracted.

Warda took the comb from Zulfa and bullied down her spongy hair. "Husna," she said, motioning to Zulfa for the tiny mirror that they kept beside the bed. "You know. I went to school with all her sisters. So did you." Warda moved the glass around her head, to one side, then the other, then high up in the air, closing this eye and then that so as to see all her parts completely. "She's married to Masoud."

Warda didn't intend Zulfa any harm by pointing this thing out. Like their father, Warda thought Zulfa had been cosseted enough after splitting from Kassim Majid, that it was time she had a man again. Like everybody else—because although she herself did not go out, news comes creeping through the walls—she knew that this Masoud Hamad was getting set to make her little sister number four. Warda thought it would be good for Zulfa to know Husna, and to see how well she lived. And, as she'd mentioned to Habiba (who had winced, who didn't want to hear another word), if Zulfa did end up marrying Masoud, it would be best if she could befriend Husna now, so the transition would be smooth. But most of all, Warda, eager to see Husna for herself, didn't want to go alone.

Zulfa felt two ways about her sister's plan. She didn't want to go; she wanted very much to go. This doubled feeling matched the double feelings she had about Masoud when he was there and Masoud when he was gone. Sometimes she thought nothing was as nice as being free with someone and going your own way when you had other things to do. And she was sure that she had lots of things to do. But occasionally she wondered what Masoud's life was really like inside those proper households. While she believed that she herself was more exciting than any of the wives could be, and told herself she didn't want Masoud that way, once or twice she'd wondered if his wives could do some things for him that she couldn't even dream.

When Zulfa felt unease, she teased him: "If you talk-talk-talk to me so long, Masoud, they will start to grumble. They'll think you have forgotten them, or have you?" Or "What are *those* eyes for, Masoud, when your wives will let you stare them up and down?" Zulfa often thought Masoud was handsome, but now and then, when his face glowed bright with too much love, she'd think his beard was dirty, or see a weakness in his eyes. That was when she'd say, "Go home, go home! *I* haven't made you dinner!"

Masoud didn't like to talk about his wives with Zulfa. Only once, once when Zulfa had been closing up the shop, and everyone in town was cleaning up for prayers, or already at the mosque, Masoud had pressed himself against her as she unhooked the dresses from the doorframe, and she had let him do it. She had squeezed his forearms and she'd sighed. Despite everything he knew, Masoud had whispered, "Oh, Zulfa, they're not anything like you." And Zulfa, aware that, while what she held felt hard, it was also soft and fragile, closed her eyes and heard him. But when he moved away from her she had looked right into his face and said, her mouth a little swollen, "What? What is that you're saying?" The next time she teased him, Masoud closed himself against her and told her not to speak their names. "It's disrespectful, Zulfa," he had said. Then he had looked at her quite squarely. "Sometimes you go overboard." In the bedroom, Zulfa snatched the mirror from her sister, took a hard, deep breath, and thought, *Overboard I'll go.*

On the way to Husna's house, Warda gave out little nods and raised her hands in greeting to those who hollered after her. At the last mango tree before the turn, Zulfa bent to readjust her shoes, and Warda, who was thinking of this visit as the unofficial start of satisfactory proceedings, said, "If Husna's jealous, she'll be too well bred to show it." Warda tucked a stray curl back into her scarf. "You just be polite."

Zulfa had an awkward thought. *What if Husna likes me?* She tried to picture herself sitting next to Husna on a warm brown night beside a heap of cloves during the harvest, plucking stems from buds, or squatting at the well with laundry, but she couldn't really see it. How could a woman like you if her husband was a fool?

When Husna came to welcome them, Zulfa, doubled once again, felt at once very, very small and extraordinarily superior. The two boys and the girl who stood shyly in the hall behind their mother looked, thought Zulfa, exactly like Masoud. The three were sleek and long. Six slightly pointed ears poked up and out from either side of three pointed little faces. Six great brown eyes grew round beneath six matching inky brows. The youngest boy, the shyest, took to Zulfa right away. He beamed so hard his eyes crossed.

Husna was as beautiful as everyone had said, but bigger, older, now. She had a rich, slow look to her, as though she were not thoroughly awake. Her eyes were shaped like zaitun fruit, narrow at both ends, high, and widening in the middle. Zulfa, spiteful, found Husna's pupils very black and large. *As if she'd gotten drunk on nutmeg,* Zulfa thought and did not say. Husna took hold of Warda's hands with hers. The soft sounds coming from her throat made Zulfa think of Babu's doves, restive in their cage.

The two sisters were shown into what Zulfa couldn't help but call "Masoud Hamad's Front Room." While Husna went into the kitchen, Warda beamed, and said, "Isn't Husna fine?"

Something about Warda's fat, round face, and the way her teeth looked small inside her mouth, irritated Zulfa. *Husna isn't fine,* thought Zulfa. *I'm more beautiful than she is.* Warda curled her legs beneath her on the painted purple mat. She leaned against the wall and thought how comfortable it was to have left her children home, to be something like a girl. "If my husband takes another wife," said Warda, "I hope she will be as gentle and as well brought up as Husna. How warmly we would manage!"

Zulfa scowled. The small boy toddled towards her and collapsed in a hot heap at her side. He peeked at Zulfa through his hands. Zulfa edged away from him and catalogued the items on display: a wall clock like the ones on offer at the Fancy Store (bright ladybug ashiver on the slender minute arm), a vinyl carpet (blue design of roses), a picture in a frame (Buraku, the prophet's woman-horse), four big cushions (fringed in gold). Everything was nicer than anything Mzee Abeid had ever given to Habiba, except perhaps that big TV: Husna didn't have one.

When Husna came in with the tray, Zulfa saw that Husna's kanga cloths were even softer than those she sorted at the Fancy Store. With a businesswoman's eyes, she thought, *Her cloths come from China.* Zulfa drank three cups of coffee while the married women laughed and slapped their thighs. They reached out now and then and clapped their fingers heavily in one another's palms, smiling while they talked about their boys and—Zulfa unhappily suspected but could not quite be sure because she didn't want to hear—when they talked about their husbands. Husna looked at Zulfa now and then and encouraged her to drink. She pushed a bowl of mango pieces towards her, but Zulfa couldn't eat. She squinted at the open window and wondered why the light outside seemed bright, although the day was overcast.

But when she heard Warda asking Husna, "Do you see them? Do you see the other two?" Zulfa couldn't help but pay attention. Husna closed her fruity eyes and smiled for what seemed to Zulfa a long time before she spoke. "Oh, yes," she said. "I do." With a great show of nonchalance, Husna eased her kanga off her head and shoulders and revealed to her two guests a fiery pink gown aglitter with bright sequins. A beaded peacock sparkled on her chest. "The third one," she said, peering down at her own bodice, "often makes me dresses." The fine pink gown was more elaborate than old Mafunda's pantaloons. Warda's top teeth snuck over her lower lip like children peeking at the grown-ups. Her eyes went very wide. When she looked over at Zulfa, Warda's envious face was saying, *Well now, Husna's life's not bad!*

Zulfa, for her part, found herself wondering if Husna was as stupid as she looked, or if maybe she was clever. Husna brought her Chinese kanga back over her head with an apologetic sniff, as though she knew but could not help that Warda wished to bore her eyes into that dress until she'd memorized the pattern. "The second one sends me the best of her big baskets." The walls of Zulfa's mouth felt thick, as though she'd eaten something that had turned. She darted her tight tongue along the grooves behind her teeth. *How nice for them,* she thought, imagining Masoud's three wives ariot, laughing on a spacious double bed. *How nice that they all get along so well.* She spread her legs out on the mat and dropped her elbows to her knees, not caring she looked bored.

Although Warda knew full well that Masoud was in Mombasa, she nonetheless asked Husna, "Your husband is away?" Warda, Zulfa thought, was setting up a little demonstration to which she would refer at night, once they'd gone to bed. She had something to prove. Husna slid a mango square into her mouth, and, softly chewing, smiled. "Yes," she said. "Masoud is still away." She very delicately dipped her forefinger and thumb into the water bowl. "But," she added, taking up a quilted towel, "he's bought me a cell phone, and he calls me every day."

Warda said, "Ahh," and raised her eyebrows at her sister as if to say, *A cell phone! See how wonderful it is to be a decent wife?* Zulfa felt a wrenching at the very bottom of her stomach that continued down her legs. She wondered why Masoud had never thought of getting her a phone. She thought, *How nice for dear Husna that she is number one.*

It was almost six when Warda tugged at Zulfa's gown and said, "All right, dear Husna, it's been a pleasure seeing you, but we *really* have to go." When Husna said, "So soon? You've barely stayed at all," she was looking straight at Zulfa. Husna made as if to get her sandals on to walk them home a little way, but Warda whispered something, and both Husna and Warda gave Zulfa a look. "Husna, you stay here," said Warda, slipping into her own shoes and holding on to Zulfa for support. "The two of you together would just make people talk." Both the women laughed. When Husna took Zulfa's hand in hers to say good-bye, Zulfa thought she felt—briefly, so she wasn't sure—a harshness in her squeeze.

Back on the main road, Zulfa stayed three steps ahead of

Warda so she wouldn't have to see the satisfied expression on her older sister's face. It wasn't until after dinner that she spoke to her again. From beyond a mountain of soiled dishes, Zulfa said, "Don't think I'll be a wife with *her*." Warda gave her little sister a mild, beatific smile. She didn't comment until later, when they were close and warm in bed, with her baby tucked between them: "Chickens," Warda said, "can be lied to every day, but Masoud Hamad's a man."

Perhaps if Zulfa hadn't gone to visit Husna, if she hadn't seen how plump and sleek, how self-satisfied she was, if she hadn't seen the children, who looked just like their father, and who had gazed at her in the same soft way that Masoud gazed at Zulfa, too, Zulfa might have responded differently when Masoud broke down the first time. But the visit niggled at her. Zulfa saw the clock in dreams, felt suffocated in her sleep by heavy, tasseled cushions. She slipped on vinyl roses and landed on her back, waking up to find herself spread out on her bed as though she had fallen from a height, her fingers clutching at the frame.

It was not that Zulfa wished to be in Husna's place. She'd been married. She had cooked and cleaned and swept and sliced the throats of chickens for Kassim Majid's guests. She'd burned medicines for him and hosted all his visitors: healers, who hobbled up the hill with plain baskets dangling on their arms, denying (coyly so, because really, they were hungry) that they wished to stay for meals; Kassim Majid's relatives, who asked for money (which he never once released); and neighbor women, who came to take a close-up look at the poor thing who'd granted their own young girls reprieve. She'd rubbed herself with scented oils the way she had been taught; she had suffered all her husband's doings. She knew what being married was, she thought.

What she liked about being with Masoud Hamad was feeling free: that he took her places *she* wanted to go; that he wanted to please *her*; that he so wanted to please her that he had opened up the Fancy Store and let her make some money of her own, which *she* could choose to spend. If he ever married her, she thought, pleasing her would no longer be so vital. And besides, she told herself, she had other things to do.

But seeing Husna made Zulfa feel afraid. Husna did look happy. Despite the other wives, perhaps even due to them, Husna lived in pleasure. Perhaps the other wives were happy, too. If Zulfa asked herself, *Why aren't I happy as they are,* she sometimes blamed Masoud. But she also felt a trembling at her feet and remembered more frequently than ever that she really did want to seek and see the world. *My freedoms here are temporary,* Zulfa thought. So, after seeing Husna, not knowing what else she should do, Zulfa took her tiny Chinese key with her everywhere she went.

When she saw Masoud next, Zulfa's feelings burst, and she crossed a crucial line. They had been standing on the highest hill in town, among Masoud's father's clove trees, looking out across the rice fields and the many miles of dusty boughs at a sliver of blue sea. Assured of his good taste, Masoud said, "From Kenya," and handed her a tiny packet wrapped in pink translucent paper. Zulfa eyed his fingers for a moment, as though they were an interesting gadget, and then, without quite knowing why, as though they were a mousetrap. She looked up at Masoud and felt her eyes go narrow. Oh, there *was* something soft about his face, she thought, but could that be enough? She sighed. She didn't wait to be alone. Inside the packet was a slender russet vial of thick halud, topped with a gold cap the size of a small marble. She looked back at Masoud and saw him hold his breath. But instead of thinking what a gift it was, of how sweet the oil would smell, a question came to her: *Did he bring Husna the same thing?* She held the vial between her first finger and thumb. *Did he give her nineteen bottles, and I'm getting number twenty?* In an unexpected dissolution that Zulfa at first did not understand, the skin around her mouth and nose suddenly went loose, her legs beneath her burned.

Masoud quickly brought his hands towards her, to catch her if she fell. "What's wrong, mpenzi wangu?" In the clove trees, his voice echoed. A cluster of wild pigeons panicked in the leaves. "Star of my sky, my love," he said. "How have I upset you?" He knelt beside her and tugged her free hand down so that she would join him on the ground. He found a desiccated palm frond and slipped it just beneath her buttocks before they touched the earth.

Zulfa wept from fury. She knew the reasons for her anger. Specifically, she was angry at Masoud for bringing her a gift that she desired. More generally, she was angry that he took such good care of his wives. She was also angry that he had given her the Fancy Store, pretending he was doing it for free.

How merrily he could pretend! So merrily that she relaxed, sometimes, and thought, *Masoud and I will be a pair of man and woman friends, like this, forever.* Yes, she liked him, sometimes she really did. And then she would remember that everything

THEFT

he gave her had a secret string attached, a hopeful little noose. *When he says how nice it is that I am free, he only means he likes it now. When he says he'll let me travel, he means he'll let me visit Warda in the city, call me every day, send his cousins after me, and fetch me in a week.* Zulfa knew what marriage was. She would have to find another girl to mind the store six months into the thing—or worse, Masoud would find one on his own. When he sat down beside her and laid his knuckles lightly on her face, Zulfa didn't say these things. If you didn't keep some things very quiet, Zulfa told herself, you'd drown.

"What is it, dear?" Masoud asked, in his smooth and round, fine, best loudspeaker voice. Zulfa scowled at him through her tears, thinking, *I'm going to see America, do you understand me?* If she had spoken out then, in the black shade of the clove trees, if she'd laid it on the line, things might have gone differently between them. But her tongue was cold and fat, and she didn't think he'd understand. All she felt was mad.

Masoud thought she couldn't speak because she was too full of love, and so of course he sympathized. "Basi, basi," he said softly, stroking Zulfa's shoulder. "Stop. I'm going to send someone on my behalf to tell your father that I'm ready." He slipped his arm around her. "We'll tell him right away." Masoud thought Zulfa was finally admitting that a pretty house, a television, and a freezer might be all it took for joy. It was just the right thing to have said. Zulfa's weeping had made her feel confused, but when Masoud said, "We'll tell him right away," she felt her tears go dry. Her world came into focus.

She felt newly like a beast with thick strong legs and wicked teeth. When Masoud moved to squeeze her towards

~ *248* ~

him, Zulfa pulled his hand down from her shoulder to her mouth. She opened wide and clamped down on his forearm. She bit him near the elbow, where his warm flesh was the softest. She drew blood. Masoud, for his part, looked as though she had, before his very eyes, transformed herself into a dog. Shocked, really. Terrified. He fell and she rose. He twisted on the ground. His face was horrible. He looked as though he might start crying, too.

Zulfa's tongue felt loose again. Looking down at him from a long height, she said, "You won't, Masoud Hamad. You won't. You won't, and don't you dare." She was thinking, *Don't you ever listen?*

They had gotten up the hill on Masoud's Honda, and though it sometimes seemed to Zulfa that she'd forgotten all the footpaths she'd once known, she made it back to Usilie through the brush. It seemed to her for once that, just as she insisted to Masoud but couldn't ever prove, she could indeed find her own way.

After the proposal in the clove trees, Zulfa's private cash box acquired a pleasing shine. "You keep a third of everything," Masoud had said. "No tricks." Zulfa had kept track from the beginning. She'd been storing savings all along. But when she got home the day she bit Masoud, she opened the blue notebook to make doubly, triply, sure that she'd been taking what was hers. She opened her own box and the next, the box in which she kept the profits due Masoud. She counted out the stuff four times, in different ways: first the small notes, then the big ones; then the other way around; then the coins before the cash; then the coins from small to big—the silver tens and fifties to the hundreds; then again, reversed.

Biting now and then at the slender cap of her pin-striped Speedo pen, she made careful calculations. Bit by bit, avid, angry, wounded, Zulfa sensed a new economy on the open pages, its parameters now injury and love. Feeling justified and true, possessed, she determined a significant additional percentage. Her eyes drilled through the blue notebook and at the numbers written there and down into her lap until her eyes swam and her legs and fingers hurt. Then, with all of that—the cash, the coins, the records, more—underneath her pillow, she slept through dinner and past the prayer call at dawn. In the morning, Warda told Habiba she thought Zulfa was sick, and Habiba brought a bowl of lemon-chile-pepper-plantain-broth, to make her daughter better.

The doors of Our Price Is Your Price Fancy Store did not open for a week. Masoud's arm was healing nicely. The shock was what had hurt the most. His boiling love for Zulfa had not cooled. As he moved between Usilie, Hausemeki, and the third wife's little village, he stopped eight times at Habiba's, pretending to be passing by on business. But the messages he gave Habiba for her daughter were like this: *Please, is she very ill? Will she see me now? When will she forgive?*

At first Habiba was protective ("No, she isn't well" or "She's not seeing anyone"), and then she grew ashamed. ("Please, Masoud, don't come for a few days. I'll see what I can do.") Habiba wanted Zulfa to get up and be as well as she had been. But she knew that Zulfa had been living in a dream. Habiba was approaching Abeid's view of things. *Masoud takes good care of his wives,* Habiba thought, *maybe better than my husband does of his.* How could Zulfa back out now, after all he'd done for her? Clearly, Masoud hadn't given up, and, no matter what he'd said to Zulfa, or what Zulfa said to everyone, about the Fancy Store being nothing but a business, the shop had been a ruse. Habiba thought, *I know how men are.*

The seventh time, Masoud told Zulfa's father, "We're in business together, Mzee Abeid. What am I to think?" Mzee Abeid, on his way to Babu Issa's and wishing he had not run into Masoud, grunted sadly at the ground. Masoud wouldn't leave him be. "If you're a businessman, Mzee, you can't let a rope go slack." Mzee Abeid was not a businessman, but he admired businessmen and felt at least in theory that if a person made a promise, he should really carry through. He also felt that if he could, he'd like to make Masoud feel welcome. Who would take poor Zulfa off their hands if this man changed his mind? Pointing with his head in the direction of his second household, as if in explanation, Zulfa's father said, "You know how women are."

The last message Masoud brought, the one that finally pulled Zulfa out of bed, was "Your moods are bad for business." But before she went back to the Fancy Store, she invited Masoud into Habiba's house and stated her position. "I won't be married to you yet," she said, after a soft pause adding "dear." How much he had missed her! How tired and delicate she was. In the gentle morning light, arranging cups and opening the thermos, she looked almost wifely, Masoud thought. "First, as I have told you many times, I am going to travel." She poured two tiny cups of coffee. After so many parched and desperate days, Masoud was happy just to be beside her. The coffee tasted good.

"I'll work with you until I get the money to take myself a trip. I have a cousin in the U.S.A.," Zulfa continued. "And others are in London. I'm going to visit them to say I've been, that I have seen it with my eyes." Zulfa's chin was set, but she wasn't angry anymore. She felt that the divorce from old Kassim Majid had been granted her precisely so she could do something important. Looking at the plain, flat face of the Toshiba, Zulfa said, "When I come back, I'll marry you." Her dim reflection added, "If you'll let me go, I'll love you. Then we'll make some babies."

Masoud heard *I'll marry you,* and *babies.* He thought any baby Zulfa had would be more lovely than the moon. His cup shook in his hands. When he set it on the mat, he spilled some of the dark stuff in the weave. Zulfa looked down at his fingers, then at the mouth-shaped emblem on her business partner's arm. "But I'm not marrying you just yet." She dribbled water on the coffee stain and wiped it with a cloth. She didn't mention traveling again. Masoud left Habiba's with a bouncing in his knees

Zulfa took up her old place at the counter the next day. In her notebook, she made lists of things to do. When Masoud's cousin passed, she offered him some bills, and he gave up the cell phone for an hour. She called a school friend of her brothers' on the big island of Mjimkuu and asked him to please find her a fare. ("Maybe for my mother," Zulfa said. "I am planning a surprise.") She telephoned Habiba's younger sister, who also lived there with her husband. She dropped hints about how she might make a visit, vaguely, sometime soon. She gently fished, as though she didn't need it, for important information. And everything she learned she wrote in the blue book, in a special, secret code.

When Masoud came to see her, she was kind and reassuring. She didn't mention London or the U.S.A. Masoud thought Zulfa was finally getting used to how things were. Whenever he reminded her, just to feel his heart balloon, that they were going to be married, Zulfa smiled at him the way she had when they'd first spoken at Nazir's. "Be patient, now," she'd say. The more her notebook filled with information, the more her cash box swelled, the easier it was to smile up at Masoud and not remind him of the condition she had set. Sometimes she forgot she'd ever mentioned babies.

Babu Issa at the coffee stand was glad things at the Fancy Store were back to normal. He was as good at math as Zulfa was. When the Fancy Store was open, Babu Issa sold more sweets. From his hilltop threshold at the gristmill, Babu Omari looked down to where Babu Issa's men were drinking and over to the Fancy Store. Now and then Zulfa's high voice carried on the breeze, and, head spinning, Babu Omari would think how nice it would be when Masoud married Zulfa.

Mafunda said, "Maybe that Kassim Majid was just a one-time fluke." Maybe Mzee Abeid's unlucky girl was having a sea change. Mafunda's pantaloons were frayed by then, but her faith in marriage wasn't. She didn't know exactly when the final wedding would take place, but she believed it was already in the works. Hadn't she seen Warda and her sister walk right into Husna's yellow house?

Warda, for her part, had had enough of being home. Suddenly the city with its traffic jams and ice cream cones seemed very good again. She called her husband from a friend's in Baharini town and arranged for him to meet her when she got off the boat. "I can leave without a worry," Warda told Habiba, "now that Zulfa's taken care of." Warda, feeling personally responsible for Zulfa's transformation—how obediently she sat behind the counter now, how carefully, how obsessively, she kept the books—was proud. On her last day, this time by herself, she went to visit Husna, and they had a lovely talk.

Masoud had for the moment seen the wisdom of letting Zulfa do things on her own. He had her do inventories all alone and asked her to write up lists for orders. He cut down on his visits. He wanted Zulfa to relax. *If she gets comfortable enough,* he thought, *she will understand that I cannot live without her.* It wasn't that he wished to marry Zulfa and then lock her up and never let her go outside. She could keep her post behind the counter, for at least a little while. And he did have languid dreams about traveling with Zulfa. He just didn't think she meant it when she said she'd rather travel on her own. What would Zulfa do all by herself, without anyone for company? Without a person to take care of her? What would people think? Zulfa, Masoud told himself, was feisty and confused.

Mafunda, watching from her place before the hardware store, thought Masoud was doing the right thing. *Zulfa has no discipline, no sense,* she thought. *She needs a man to set her straight.* Mafunda felt admiration for Masoud Hamad's approach. He was waiting for Zulfa to come out with it herself:

When will you send someone to discuss me with my dad? At least
that was how it seemed. One morning, gathering her bowls
and buckets and making ready to go home, Mafunda said,
"Masoud Hamad has finally learned his lesson." She got up
and shook her dusty skirts. "No noisy lion eats."

Certainly that was how it looked. But finally, after two
months of only passing by, of inquiring politely, of smiling
carelessly at Zulfa, Masoud's resolve collapsed. He started up
again. "Zulfa, let's get married." "Zulfa, let me go talk to your
father." "Zulfa, let's make our plans now." "Zulfa, Zulfa."
And Zulfa, who had sworn that she would never weep again
if Masoud Hamad were present, and who could keep a promise better than most people she knew, felt her heart go cold.
She was becoming so adept at calculations that she could make
them in her head.

When Masoud, exhausted, heart in tatters, came to Zulfa
in the noontime and told her he was tired of her freely fooling
with his love, Zulfa felt like a cold kipupwe rain. "You want
me to marry you before I've seen the world? Is that what you
are saying? Is that really what you want? Is that what you are
telling me?" She plopped a glossy stewpot on the counter with
a clang. To Masoud, her jaw and chin together seemed enormous as a truck.

He sat down on the glittering silver sofa Zulfa'd ordered him
to get. He made his voice as gentle as he could and clutched
his hands between his knees. "We'll go traveling together,
dear, I promise." Zulfa raised her chin at him, not feeling any
warmer. "We'll go to London, you and me. And then we'll
visit Texas. But let's get married first, okay?" Zulfa pulled a

sheaf of kanga cloths from a shiny plastic sack and sat down on the floor. Masoud leaned towards her, holding out his hands. "This waiting for you for so long is eating up my liver, Zulfa. It's killing me," he said.

Zulfa knew all about things eating up one's liver, how painful unfulfilled desire was, and how you could feel that you were dying. She turned her face away from him and gave attention to the colored cloths that she was sorting from the sack. She scoured them for misprints. The first one said, in a black design of rice grains, *Forgive me, Ma, but living in the world is hard.* The next one, red- and yellow-checked: *I promise I know nothing, so why look at me that way?* Another, purple like a plum: *Light teeth, dark soul.* No, no errors there. Zulfa made a stack.

"Zulfa, darling. Answer me." Masoud's voice was all atremble, not what it had been that day at Nazir's Tailoring and Petrol Stand. "All right," she said. "All right. I'll tell you what, Masoud." Zulfa put the kangas down and looked right into his eyes. "If you leave all your wives, you can marry me before I travel." Masoud made a sound, at first, that was something like a laugh. Zulfa continued, very steely. "And don't think I want any kids to raise from you. You give up on them, too. Cut off, split up, *bye-bye*. And *then* come back to me, and we'll see what we will see." Zulfa was feeling strong, as if someone else were speaking through her. Oh, the way the words slipped out! Very, very easy. Her teeth in her soft mouth were razor blades, or knives. *If he can ask me to give up what I want,* she thought, *then I can do the same.* She wished to teach Masoud a lesson. If he were worth anything at all, as good a catch as he insisted that he was, he would surely turn her down.

"Don't play with me, my love," he whispered. He reached out to stroke her ear. She flinched. "Do you see a game here? Do you?" That's when Masoud began to cry. Then, not whispering any longer, said, "How can you ask me such a thing? No decent woman, no good woman at all, could make me treat my wives so poorly." *Regret will be your grandchild,* Zulfa thought. *I'm asking you no more than you are asking me.* The next cloth, aburst with onions and square windows, said: *Don't stink up the street with what you're cooking in your kitchen.*

Masoud stayed away for several days, and Zulfa thought she'd won. In the mornings after breakfast, when she'd done the dishes for Habiba and walked into the sun and windy air, the Fancy Store looked lovely to her. *My shop,* she thought. *He can't take it away. We had a business proposition. Now he'll leave me be.* She thought perhaps that after all her travels, if she ever did come back, she might feel generous about Masoud. She might even, she thought kindly, take him as a lover.

Zulfa was so happy with herself that she organized a sale. She tore a cardboard flap from the lid of an old box that had held men's plain shirts and trousers, and wrote, in Speedo ink: "Sale! Bei poa! Half-price kanga cloths! 25% off enameled pots and pans. 10% off talcum! Sandalwood! or Rose!" Then she settled down to wait.

Mafunda couldn't read, but she knew a sale sign when she saw one; she sent Zulfa travelers from the bus stand. "There's a sale at Zulfa's shop!" she'd say, with every bowl of uji that went out. "Kangas! Teacups! Cheap!" Zulfa could hear her all the way inside the Fancy Store, and she felt warmly towards her.

For all the work Mafunda does, she thought, *someone ought to pay her.* She might give Mafunda a commission, when the accounts were nicely done.

Women from the neighborhood arrived. Nazir's mother bought two kangas and a cooking pot. Bi Faida came and purchased powder. Women from nearby villages came into town to look—they couldn't have afforded uji, even, but they liked to know exactly who in town possessed more money than she showed, and to see things changing hands. Babu Issa joked: he hoped his wife was far off in the rice fields so she wouldn't learn about it. When Mafunda had sold off all her porridge, she came down to take a look. Zulfa made Mafunda such a price on a new bucket that she went away with two. The buzz around the Fancy Store was so substantial that Babu Issa moved his bench and kettle far across the road, so his customers could watch in comfort. He confidently sent a boy to get him more kashata.

When Habiba came out of the house and finally made it to the counter, Zulfa thought her mother was going to buy a set of plates. She even said, "Here, Ma, don't worry, you just tell me what you want," and made as if to nudge a stack of china dishes to the side so no one else would stake a claim.

But Habiba hadn't come for shopping. She was there on serious business. "Zulfa. I have words to say to you." She said this through her teeth, and Zulfa could see her mother was afraid. Throat tight, Zulfa smiled bravely at the crowd and told the customers she would return. "But don't get tired, don't give up," she said. "We'll work something out!" Then she slipped out of the shop and met her mother behind the Fancy Store container. "What's wrong?" she asked Habiba, thinking Mzee Abeid was ill, or that somebody had died. "Ma, just tell me."

"Your babu came to see me," said Habiba, shivering in the breeze. *Your* babu, Zulfa thought. She didn't like the sound of that. In front of the container, the sun had made things white and warm, but back here, in the shadows, Zulfa, too, felt cold. Babu never went to see Habiba. He never went to visit anyone. Babu's house was like his palace. People went to him, not the other way around. "He did?"

"Babu came to see me, and he couldn't wait until your dad got home. He says that if you have anything to do with this he'll be very, very mad." Habiba pressed a hand on Zulfa's forearm and squeezed it softly, though her voice was hard. Zulfa couldn't look at her. Her stomach's pliant walls fell in; her chest's high roof gave way. She thought she knew already exactly what it was. *It can't be,* she thought. *Tell me it's not true.* It was.

Masoud had left two wives. In the farthest village, he'd left the same amount of money he had spent when he'd taken the third wife (more like two lakhs, it turned out, just as people had suspected) and told her that he wouldn't claim the kids, though he would pay for them to go to school. The Shanghai Stitcher stopped its humming for how sad its owner was. Next the red and orange Honda took him down to Hausemeki town. The neighbors had heard all the hard, unhappy sounds that come with unforeseen disaster. The little shop with its sharpening stones and baskets hadn't opened in two days.

"Where is Masoud now?" asked Zulfa, clutching at Habiba's hands. He was, Habiba said, hiding out not far from Usilie.

Not far, either, Zulfa thought, from Kassim Majid's house. Was this the old man's way of getting back at her? Racing to tell Babu so that she would get in trouble? "Listen. More than this," Habiba said. She told Zulfa the worst. Masoud, Babu's messenger had said, was gathering the strength to march right up to the original, to Husna, number one, and tell her he was through. "It's a disgrace," Habiba said, looming over Zulfa in the shade. A thick, cold heat seemed to emanate from her. Her mouth shook. She couldn't look her daughter in the eye. "If Masoud is doing this for you," she said, "if what Babu heard was true, I can't even think how shameful it will be."

Zulfa thought she'd faint or vomit, right there in the shade, but Habiba's handle on her daughter's arm was strong. "You're coming home with me." Gracefully, so that nobody who saw them could have known how tightened all their muscles were, Habiba ferried Zulfa down the road and disappeared inside Mzee Abeid's first house. Zulfa was so upset, and Habiba was in such a hurry, that they forgot the people at the counter, and Zulfa didn't think to close the Fancy Store. There were other things to plan.

For a long time they didn't speak. Zulfa couldn't eat. Habiba thanked the Lord out loud that Abeid was at the second wife's, and that he was still so thrilled with her that nothing could dislodge him from her side. Habiba wished that she could smack her daughter hard across the face, but Zulfa hadn't offered explanations, not a yes and not a no. She had only curled up on the bed and whimpered like a dog. Habiba closed the shutters on the windows that looked out into the street and bolted the front door.

တ

Zulfa watched Habiba eat in silence. Afterwards, Habiba went out behind the house to watch the rice fields moving in the sunlight. Her face was still, but she was thinking very hard. She came back into the kitchen just as Zulfa put the last glass dish away. "You're going to pack a bag," Habiba said. "And you're going to go away." Then Habiba slipped into her bedroom. Zulfa heard the door lock.

In the front room, Zulfa opened up the shutters, just a crack, so she could see how things were going at the shop. Babu Issa's coffee stand was back in its old place. The customers were gone. The shop's doors were still ajar. She counted up the buckets that still hung from the awning and found that two were missing. Well, what could you expect? She thought about her cash box and tried hard to remember if she'd locked it before she'd gone out back with Habiba. And if it was still hidden in the empty crate beneath the gowns. She said a little prayer. She would have to wait till dark came to make certain. *I hope so,* she thought. *I hope my reflexes were good.*

In the evening, Zulfa made Habiba water pancakes and brought out the bottle of clove honey Mzee Abeid liked to save up for himself. She made the tea as sweet as she could bear. They ate. Habiba told her daughter to wrap up the pancakes that remained and to make another thermosful of tea. Zulfa did as she was asked, then she snuck onto the road. There were people out. She kept close to the shadows. Someone had locked up the doors for her, and when she opened them she found the cash box in its place. She took a last look at the Fancy Store and plucked four gowns from the back wall, the best ones, stitched with bright, amazing birds.

At home she found Habiba waiting. "Get ready, now," she said. While Zulfa packed, Habiba went into her room and slept. At midnight, Zulfa woke her up. When Habiba stepped into the kitchen, she was holding a decidedly unstylish, old, enormous buibui gown she hadn't worn in years. "Put this on," she said. "We don't want people knowing who you are." Zulfa nodded. She went to find Aunt Khadija's ninja veil, and wore it, so only her eyes showed. Habiba nodded. "Good. I'll get mine, too," she said. Zulfa was surprised. She wondered where Habiba had gotten such a modern thing, and why, but couldn't bring herself to ask. *My mother has her secrets, too,* she thought. When Habiba reappeared, Zulfa was for a moment not quite certain who she was.

They locked the house from the outside and took back roads all the way to Baharini, roads Zulfa hadn't known existed. Habiba's footsteps hummed and shuffled on ahead, steady, without doubt, even in the darkness. Not speaking, they walked and walked until Zulfa could no longer feel her legs. She thought Habiba's feet must be made of iron nails.

At dawn, finally at the seashore, the pair approached the harbor by the sandy paths. Habiba, tired now, let her big gown trail into the water; Zulfa hiked her own coat tight around her knees. At the boat, Habiba bought six sticks of skewered clams and two sacks of dried toss bread. She didn't argue with the vendor, as she would have if she'd been going on this trip herself. She didn't want to make a scene. "It isn't fresh," she said. "Just tell your aunt that there was nothing we could do." She pressed the skewers and the sacks into Zulfa's loaded arms. Then she put her daughter on the boat, heading for Mjimkuu.

"Don't talk to anyone," she whispered. "When you get to the city, tell your aunt that she is doing me a favor. If anybody asks you, say it's all right with your father."

Zulfa found a little corner on the lower deck, a corner full of wind. She lay down on her bag and kept her hands and feet concealed in the folds of her unstylish gown, so nobody could recognize her ankles, or her fingers curled in sleep. The air was soft and cold. She dozed.

In Usilie, everyone was up. Babu Omari took his seat high on the hill, and it occurred to him for the first time that, just as he could see straight to Issa's coffee stand, so Issa, if he squinted, could see him. He wondered why Zulfa wasn't there yet and hoped she would come soon.

Mafunda hadn't brought her new buckets to work. She wasn't sure, what with how suddenly the sale had stopped, whether it was smart to advertise that she had had a gift from Zulfa. And given her sharp ears, she'd already heard some rumbles rise from Hausemeki town. She left the pantaloons at home.

Mzee Abeid stepped out of his second wife's small house to get some water from the tank. Looking through the breadfruit trees up to the road, he saw Masoud Hamad getting off the Honda just in front of Husna's place. *That's Masoud Hamad,* he thought, *taking care of all his wives. And he's got his eye on Zulfa.* It made Mzee Abeid feel proud. Habiba, who made it back a little before noon, lay down on her bed and didn't know if she was going to laugh or cry when Abeid finally came home.

When Zulfa woke, she couldn't see Kudra Island anymore. She only saw a silver field of sea. If she turned her head the other way, she couldn't see Mjimkuu. The boat rocked. She'd woken on the deepest part of that long channel. She was glad she'd sat outside. Surely in the cabins, everyone was moaning, and the thickening air was giving off a stink. Stewards scurried up and down the stairs dispensing light blue plastic bags. A few strong women from the inner decks stumbled out into the air, holding one another, hoping all that wind would blow their stomachs into place. A small girl not too far from Zulfa grew demurely sick in the black folds of her mother's gown, and Zulfa smiled a little to herself because her own guts were so strong.

A shapely man came out and leaned against the railing, just to Zulfa's right. He was perhaps a little older than Masoud, but had the same neat look. His black beard was sharply trimmed. His long-sleeved shirt was pressed and buttoned tightly at the cuffs. A gold watch glittered at his wrist. *He's all right,* thought Zulfa. *The water doesn't trouble him.* The shapely man saw Zulfa, but only her eyes showed, and, as though her parts being hidden meant she would see less than other people, he didn't seem to mind that she was not so far away. He shrugged. He plucked a tiny lemon from his pocket, turned to face the water, and gave the fruit a squeeze. The citrus smell would steady him. The shapely man tightly shut his eyes and took a sharp, hard breath. He was swaying with the waves; his strong knuckles turned white. Zulfa watched. The sea *was* harming him, a little.

Zulfa felt the tang of that small lemon come to her on the wind. She decided that he was—almost—just as handsome as Masoud Hamad. And because she was at sea, it seemed safe to ask herself a soft thing: she wondered if Masoud Hamad was ever rendered sick by motion on his journeys to Mombasa. Yes. Perhaps when Masoud traveled, he took limes and lemons, too.

N. S. Köenings spends most of her time thinking about love, accidents, evil, money, and the concept of "the nation." Her writing is influenced by her work and childhood on three continents, the world's many languages, and music. In addition to writing novels that she hopes are joyfully defiant, she is a toymaker and collage artist. She lives in Massachusetts.

THEFT

stories

N. S. KÖENINGS

Reading Group Guide

A conversation with N. S. Köenings

You spent part of your childhood in East Africa, the setting of your novel, The Blue Taxi. *How did your experiences there inform your writing?*

I've spent a lot of my adult life in East Africa, too, and I do still go there. That area of the world is part of my contemporary experience—my actual, continued life. In the spring of 2008 I went to southern Tanzania for the first time, and I'm planning to go next to Mozambique. But Uganda, Kenya, and Tanzania, these countries and places in them are not at all weird or exotic to me. They're just places, like wherever a person has grown up or worked or lived is an ordinary place. I can't write, yet, about places I've never been or seen. And at the moment the fact is I've spent more of my life in East Africa than elsewhere, though at this point I've been in the United States for a rather long time, too. I'd love to go to Ireland, to Spain, Hungary, Japan. And I have a dream of spending time in Bangladesh and China. There's so much going on! So many people to meet and get to know.

What writers do you most admire?

I learn something from everybody. And I learn as much about how to tell a story from listening to music and watching TV as I do from reading literature. From television—HBO serials, especially, like *The Sopranos* or *Deadwood,* but also animated series like *South Park*—I learn what keeps me glued to my seat even though I have chores to do, what keeps me worrying about a character while I'm at work and can't tune in to see what they're going to do, or (in the case of *South Park* and *The Simpsons*) how to generate a total atmosphere, with color, shape, and line. How do you do that with the written word?

Music is also very, very important—I think sentences, paragraphs, chapters, ought to be like songs, with choruses and movement. Images that cycle back again and take you somewhere else. I listen to great storytelling musicians: Tom Waits, Randy Newman, Nick Cave, Harry Nilsson. Bob Dylan, of course. More recently Regina Spektor and Martha Wainwright, singers who know what to do with words and voice and really set a scene, take you somewhere with the sounds they make.

I do read when I can, but honestly I think too much literature can ruin a writer's mind. I heard that Neil Young never listens to other people's music. And that seems right to me. You can lose your voice by letting in too many others. I did hear Ngũgĩ wa Thiong'o speak not long ago. He's wonderful and I'm looking forward to sitting down with his new book. I always reread Ruth Prawer Jhabvala's work, and Janet Frame is a big influence. I read a lot of British mysteries, too, for their insights on politics, race, class, the dangers of domesticity. Maybe more than anyone, Jean Genet, that gorgeous thief, has shown me that shamelessness and daring bring an undeniable, terrible beauty. I'm working on that, very much.

You often write about people in vastly different social contexts. To what degree do you think those contexts shape your characters?

Well, we all struggle with societal expectations, no matter who we are or where we grow up. Everybody does, whether they conform to those expectations or not. I've spent a lot of time in my life (wasted, more like) trying to belong in one setting or another, trying to "make sense" to other people. Trying to fit in is what most people are doing most of the time—and for some people it works. It hasn't for me. And more recently I've started to think that social expectations actually prevent us from discovering who we might be if we were freer to explore. History and social norms! These give rise to prejudice and discrimination, too. You know, "women are like this," "men are like that," "people from this group are like this or like that." Those ideas have had murderous, horrible effects in human history, have caused a lot of wars. As far as I can see, they're poisonous, limiting. And even for people with a lot of imagination and courage it's hard to step away from those categories completely.

A lot of the characters in my stories don't conform to social norms. Petra and Thérèse have a sexual relationship. Thérèse has a child and gives it up, continues to seek pleasure. Osman is transgendered. Zulfa doesn't want to be a wife again. Habib likes to dress as a woman. Other characters really suffer because they do conform, or want to at all costs. Celeste wants the world "just so." Gustave thinks he can collect and label experiences and people. Shama's mother-in-law can't hear anything but the conclusions she's already jumped to. Ezra's uncle is the only one who comes through transformed, because he's forced to rely on someone he doesn't like.

I think a lot of people are committed to playing the social role they've been assigned. They're unable to take intellectual or personal risks because they feel they'll disappear if they try to learn something new. Learning changes you, turns you inside out. If more people challenged themselves to be who they'd like to be, or said "Who am I?" instead of accepting what they're told, they might indeed disappear completely! But they might become something much more particular and interesting. And smarter and kinder and less interested in upholding the categories that separate people from each other. And happier, I think.

You've now published a novel, The Blue Taxi, *as well as this collection. How is the process of writing stories for you different from writing a novel?*

Stories are far more painful to write, and, I think, more constricting than novels are. A novel lets you wander in one world for a long time, lets you discover it in all its corners and peculiarities. Stories require much more decisive strokes than that. You have to say: this world is like so. But if I look out my window I can already see that the street will look different if I'm actually on it, or just cross it or move down the road a little. Or you look at a person in profile, and they look nothing like they do from the other side or frontally. For me, nothing is stable, and I'm trying to see everything, all at the same time. In real life, everything shimmers and dissolves. In a novel you can show that instability can be part of complicated happenings that unfold spaciously. In a story it's much harder to do.

I also don't believe that any story belongs wholly to one

person, or that one situation is entirely separate from another. A lot of writers and artists recognize this today—think of the recent movie *Babel*. Artists in the West are at last coming to see global history in ways that artists in other places have already been doing for centuries, and it's showing in the contents of all kinds of artwork. We're struggling to depict interconnection, the relations between apparently disparate worlds, which it turns out aren't disparate at all. We're all in this together, or we're nowhere. Some people can gesture to these urgent realities in a single, short, short story. Salman Rushdie, for a trite and undeniable example. I can't do it in under thirty pages, as these stories show. I'm not sure I want to try.

What theme do you see as tying these stories together? Is there a particular significance to the title?

Theft is a big deal to me. People steal from each other all the time—not so much money or possessions, but dignity, safety, love. Fear steals hope from us.

The stories in this collection move from North to South on our globe—a lot's been stolen from the South, what people call "the developing world." Emmanuel Wallerstein was right—the North is what it is because the South has been exploited.

But governments everywhere steal from their people, too, not just by destroying homes, as happens to Ezra and his neighbors, but through weird tax regimes that reward certain kinds of conformist behavior, by enforcing stiff ideas about nationalism, stealing people's ability to know each other as human beings first.

Death and illness steal from us—Osman's legs are swelling up and he's in pain; the outside world, the upstairs, has been taken from him. Shama's sister has disappeared for unknown reasons; Shama's lost the possibility of knowing her. Masoud loses Zulfa—her desire for independence does rob him (and her?) of a certain kind of happiness. For Zulfa, freedom of mobility is something she has to take utterly without permission, and it's going to cost her and her family a lot. It costs Ayeesha, too, escaping.

But all this shouldn't be surprising. Theft is a fundamental part of human doings. It's also, to be honest, fundamental to the art of fiction writing. Writers are thieves of a terrible kind—watching the world around them and taking other people's pain and secret hopes and making something else with these, something that gives them, and maybe readers, pleasure. We're stuck with that. Until death steals us all away.

As you mentioned, the stories move in setting from Europe to Africa. Did you structure the book this way deliberately? What do you find interesting about the interaction of people from different continents?

One thing that's been true in my life is that the whole world is always present, no matter where you are. People in East Africa imagine the United States and Europe in all kinds of ways, just as people in Europe have their own fantasies about "natives" and "dark continents." In Zanzibar, people talk about Cat Stevens and Malcolm X and Monica Lewinsky with ease. Spirits, like Sheikh Abdul Aziz (whom I interviewed, by the way, he's a real Indian Ocean djinn, the only fictional character who's taken directly from life), come from all kinds of places. East Africans get possessed by spirits in the form of British officers in knee socks or Danish nurses with syringes. And why not? Don't American kids dress up as Indian chiefs and hula girls? And Europe is full of ex-colonials and of scholars whose careers have been built on their travels to the South. Living rooms all over Europe contain souvenirs from everywhere. And East Africans themselves are in constant motion all the time. The Middle East, the Emirates, especially, India, South Africa, the Comoros and Seychelles, Thailand, Singapore. Tanzanians work on Russian ships, live in Scandinavia, in New York, work on chicken farms in Iowa. There's a whole world of international travel that many Westerners know nothing about. The idea that one place has nothing to do with another is a real fiction, and a bad one at that.

As far as my stories taking place in different regions of the globe . . . my life has taken place that way, and I think writers for the most part are just stuck with what they've lived. In that respect it's not a choice at all. And sometimes I do wish I could know one place and one language so fully that I could write "that" novel. But that would make me belong to a single nation, wouldn't it? And serve some kind of ethnic or national purpose. And though I see the need for literature like that (Chimamanda Adichie's *Half of a Yellow Sun* is a gorgeous, urgent book), I'm necessarily, helplessly against that. In the movie *Hedwig and the Angry Inch,* Hedwig, who has crossed the world and lost and gained by it, finally says at her most naked, "I'm working with what I've got." That's really, really stayed with me. Aren't we all doing just that, whoever we might be?

Questions and topics for discussion

1. Although these stories are set in various disparate places, all of the characters are aware of the existence of other lands and people. How do you think the characters' backgrounds have shaped their expectations of distant places? How might Zulfa or Masoud respond to Sheikh Abdul Aziz if he appeared on Kudra Island? How might Celeste and Gustave's visions of North Africa differ from Osman's or Ayeesha's? In your own life, how do visions of faraway places figure in the choices you make or the dreams you have?

2. In "Pearls to Swine," Celeste sees herself in relation to others in a very particular way. How do you think Petra and Thérèse see Celeste? How might this story be different if it were written from Petra's or Thérèse's perspective?

3. Celeste forms quick judgments of Petra and Thérèse when they come to stay with her. How are the young women different from Celeste's expectations of them? What does Celeste's reaction to them tell us about her?

4. The story "Wondrous Strange" makes reference to many magical elements. If Eva Bright's vision is genuine, what do you think is Sheikh Abdul Aziz's purpose in helping restore George to health? Is there a particular symbolism to the objects required for the ritual? Why do you think

the author chose to end the story before we learned the outcome of the ceremony?

5. "Wondrous Strange" is told from a number of different perspectives. Which character(s) did you find most compelling, and which least? How does the Sheikh's message change the lives of each of the main characters: Eva, Flora, and Susan?

6. In "Theft," among the bus passengers, the locals' reaction to having been robbed is very different from that of the strangers. Why, even though "it was much worse for them all because their things were more precious" (page 129), do they not try to file a complaint or get their things back? Whose reaction makes more sense to you? If the same incident had taken place in the United States, what do you think the passengers would have done?

7. In "Sisters for Shama," what are Osman's feelings towards Shama? Why do you think Shama continues to care for him and let him live in her house? Do you believe his version of the story about why he was exiled from the upper floor?

8. What does Osman hope to accomplish by telling Shama the story of Ayeesha and her son? How does Shama's taking over the storytelling at the end surprise Osman? Has Osman achieved his goal?

9. On page 216 of "Setting Up Shop," we are told that "the men of Usilie thought Masoud was doing a good thing" by marrying multiple wives. Given the social and cultural context of the place where Masoud lives, do you agree with this assessment? Why or why not?

10. Whom do you sympathize with most in "Setting Up Shop": Zulfa, Masoud, Masoud's other wives, or another character? Did your answer change over the course of the story as you learned more about each of them?

Books N. S. Köenings Rereads

The Magic Toyshop by Angela Carter

Waiting for the Barbarians by J. M. Coetzee

The Wretched of the Earth by Frantz Fanon

Scented Gardens for the Blind by Janet Frame

The Thief's Journal by Jean Genet

The Third Man by Graham Greene

Dottie by Abdulrazak Gurnah

The Nature of Passion by Ruth Prawer Jhabvala

Blood Meridian by Cormac McCarthy

Sputnik Sweetheart by Haruki Murakami

Decolonising the Mind by Ngũgĩ wa Thiong'o

Also by N. S. Köenings

The Blue Taxi

A NOVEL

"The world Köenings has created in her accomplished debut is tragic and exhilarating, as is her portrayal of weary, left-behind colonialists, poverty-stricken natives, and the uneasy manner in which each regards the other." — *Publishers Weekly*

"Mesmerizing. . . . Köenings anchors her characters' near-constant internal monologues with elegant, concrete details about their everyday lives. . . . Readers who enjoy psychological fiction will be impressed by Köenings's ability to flesh out the inner landscapes of Vunjamguu's diverse citizenry, while those concerned with style will appreciate the clear, graceful sentences that simplify the navigation of these multiple realities." — Leigh Anne Vrabel, *Library Journal*

"Köenings's debut is lush and charismatic." — Emily Cook, *Booklist*

"A first-time visitor to any East African city needs an experienced guide. And a visitor to 1970s Vunjamguu, Köenings's imaginary town, needs something more: an omniscient narrator, attuned to both the streets and the small seismic dramas unfolding in upstairs rooms. . . . *The Blue Taxi* spins with the languor of a dusty ceiling fan: nobody in Vunjamguu is in a hurry to conduct their daily lives, much less to resolve their mounting tensions. Köenings examines the minutiae of her endearingly flawed characters in slow motion and at high, exacting resolution." — Todd Pruzan, *New York Times Book Review*

LITTLE, BROWN AND COMPANY
Available wherever books are sold